STRIPPED

The Watch - Book One

FINLEY BROWN

Published by Blushing Books
An Imprint of
ABCD Graphics and Design, Inc.
A Virginia Corporation
977 Seminole Trail #233
Charlottesville, VA 22901

©2021
All rights reserved.

No part of the book may be reproduced or transmitted in any form or by any means, electronic or mechanical, including photocopying, recording, or by any information storage and retrieval system, without permission in writing from the publisher. The trademark Blushing Books is pending in the US Patent and Trademark Office.

Finley Brown
Stripped

eBook ISBN: 978-1-64563-964-0
Print ISBN: 978-1-64563-965-7
v1

Cover Art by ABCD Graphics & Design
This book contains fantasy themes appropriate for mature readers only.
Nothing in this book should be interpreted as Blushing Books' or
the author's advocating any non-consensual sexual activity.

Prologue

It could have been vengeance, betrayal, sabotage, or even an accident. However, those weren't the first words that sprang to mind when one entered a ballet studio. Graceful dancers, beautiful costumes, and the elegance of classical music brought together in the telling of a story, that was the image ballet evoked. But she knew better.

The music began, and she put her hand on the wooden barre, smooth and worn, and closed her eyes briefly, taking a deep breath before the préparation and the start of pliés. The ritual was so ingrained in her, it went beyond all thought or control, becoming nothing more than a meditation as she warmed up her body and stretched her sore muscles.

She looked across at the other dancers, each in their own space, both physically and mentally. Some were friends, others were enemies, all of them her greatest competitors. She could not get distracted. The discipline it took to wake up every morning and start again was what kept her going. The constant, self-centered need to reach both outstanding body and emotional control. She had worked her whole life for this, sacrificed most everything, enduring strict diets, long and demanding rehearsal times, bloody feet, rejection, and it had finally paid off. This season, she had been named a soloist, a move up from the corps de ballet. It was not without controversy, though. Her grandfather was a major donor to the company. Whispers circulated through the dancers that her promotion had been bought. She was young at her age, to become a soloist in the Scottish National Ballet. She tried to let the rumors and nasty comments roll off her back; it was to be expected, jealousy ran rampant, and she needed to remain focused.

The ballet master walked around the room as he led class. "One, two three," he counted to the music. "Arm in fifth and relevé." He touched her shoulder, lowering it a millimeter. "Hold it. Hold it. Hold it. And relax. Other side."

The company was premiering the season with the debut of a new take on the classic Swan Lake, retold in a stripped down and contemporary way. With class over, she went to her assigned rehearsal room. She was understudying the dual role of Odette and Odile, the white and black swans. The principal dancers were already there speaking to the choreographer, along with the artistic director. She sat down to put on her pointe shoes, tying the ribbons around her ankles. The accompanist began to play Tchaikovsky's Second Act of the White Swan Pas de Deux, the melodic sounds of the piano contouring the light and shadow of the harmonies, evocative of the cursed swan and what was to come. The principals took their spots while she and her partner marked it at the back of the studio. The lead dancer, Irina, playing Odette, went to the corner to prepare for a complicated sequence of steps in which she ran and jumped into her partners arms as he lifted her high above his head. She did the same, but at the back, staying out of the way as she visualized the running pattern and hummed the steps to the music. Irina waited as the music built in intensity, then hitting the mark, she took off. Instead of a coupé, a step where the right foot cuts the left foot away and takes its place, she slipped, twisting her ankle. The prima ballerina landed with a thud and the sound of a loud pop was followed by an ear-piercing scream. Everyone gathered around as Irina writhed on the floor holding her leg.

Her partner called for help. "Her foot just went out from under her," he bellowed.

She froze, unable to move. The role was hers now. She would play the part of Odette and Odile. Rarely, did an alternate get the chance to take over a starring role. After years of hard work, sweat, and pain, now, in the blink of an eye, success.

The director went to the corner, wiping his fingers across the gray marley floor. "It's slick. Someone's put something greasy here. This was intentional."

In 1725, following the Jacobite rebellion of 1715, George 1 sanctioned General George Wade to form six watch companies to patrol the Highlands of Scotland. These companies were in charge of disarming the Highlanders, bringing justice to criminals and hindering rebels. The force was known in Gaelic as Am Freiceàdan Dubh, the dark or black watch. Their moto- Nemo Me Impune Lacessit. No one provokes me with impunity.

Chapter 1

Wraith drove the short distance to Eden Court Theater in Inverness, turning his black Mercedes GT into a tight parking spot. The blustery February wind skirted across the river Ness, cutting through him with frigid fatality and constricting his breath as he made his way from the car park to the entrance of the newly renovated building. He reached for the accursed inhaler in his pocket and took two puffs, opening up his scarred lung as he looked around at the modern building. Eden Court housed two theaters, two studios, two cinemas and three galleries, bringing the arts to the Scottish Highlands and the future.

He adjusted the bow tie on his tuxedo, making sure it was straight. It was opening night of the ballet, and anyone who was anyone in the influential Highland society would be here this evening. His grandmother used to take him to the ballet in Edinburgh every Christmas, to see the Nutcracker, but he wasn't here tonight as a spectator. He was here for work. He pushed his past down. It was no longer relevant in his life, and he rarely let himself think about it. In fact, it no longer existed. Funny, the memory would pop up now after eleven months. He gripped the trombone case he held tight, showing the usher at the door his Scottish Ballet Orchestra badge.

"Take the hall to the left and down the stairs," the older man said, pointing to the forestage.

Wraith gave the man a brief nod. "Thank you." He proceeded down the hall, stopping when he got to the stairs. Instead of going down, he went up to the third floor and veered off to the right, going through a set of double doors and into the auditorium. He looked down; the orchestra was already in the pit. The sound of string and wind instruments being tuned vibrated through the air. He made his way to box forty-one, located house left, and set the trombone case under one of the blue seats, taking the badge off. He looked out over the theatre. This box gave him a horrible view of the stage, but he wasn't here for the show. Again, he was here for work. A nervous energy tickled his spine, causing the hair on the back of his neck to stand up. This was his first assignment, so he couldn't afford to make a mistake. He already knew where all the exits were located. He had spent the greater part of yesterday scoping out the venue. He knew his exact path, running through it in his mind one more time.

Guests and patrons would be arriving. He exited the theater. People mingled at the bar and restaurant, dressed in their finest attire, a sea of black suits and designer ball gowns. Wraith used the lavatory, keeping his eyes peeled the entire time. He was careful to blend in with the gathering crowd. He returned to his box seat, shutting the door. Ten minutes, until the show started. He stood at the back, out of view, and pulled a pair of theater binoculars out of his pocket, scanning the audience. There was movement in box thirty-six, on the opposite side of the theater. He tightened in on the space, bringing Angus McNeil into focus. The older man was alone. That was an advantage. He had spent the past month in Glasgow, trailing the business tycoon as he learned his mannerisms and patterns. For a man in his seventies, he still managed to throw off a threatening presence with his blocky build and face like a cratered moon. McNeil unbuttoned his tuxedo coat as he sat down. His white hair was slicked back, and he ran his hand along his tightly manicured goatee, a gesture that only added to his menacing self-assurance. Few people crossed this man. The lights flickered, indicating the start of the ballet. Wraith laid out his gear and waited.

The theater went dark and the music began. He knew the musical score by heart. He knew exactly when to make his move and had it timed out to the music as he counted the beats. His own tormented dance with death wouldn't begin until right before intermission. His eyes drifted to the stage as Odette emerged, the white swan, ethereal and graceful. It was Angus' granddaughter, Primrose McNeil. When she was suddenly thrust into the starring role after the unfortunate and suspicious accident of the Russian principal dancer, Irina Beilkov, it opened up the perfect opportunity and place for Wraith to carry out his mission. Most of the time, his job was spent watching and waiting, as he collected the necessary data the tactical plan required, demanding extreme patience. But he had all the time in the world now, nothing but time. His life wasn't his own anymore. He waited, the music ticking down the minutes in his mind. At the start of the second act, he put on his night vision goggles, adjusting the chin strap as his attention was focused singularly on box thirty-six. He took his high-powered rifle from the trombone case. The .338 Lapua Magnum cartridge was already loaded; he had one shot. He knelt behind the seats and brought it into position, adjusting the scope. Angus sat watching the stage, entranced and unguarded. A bouquet of two dozen white roses sat next to him. He was infatuated as he watched Primrose float across the stage, fragile and beautiful, and it left him vulnerable. The music began to build as the story and dance unfolded, powerfully melodic in its synergy. Wraith closed his eyes briefly, letting the notes become his guide. He put his finger on the trigger as the coda climbed and the tension of the piece reached its climax. He and Angus were about to become one.

A shadow in the box made him blink. No more than a dark presence, he watched as the old man struggled, trying to stop the intruder but not before he was silently pushed over the edge. The curtain closed, and people began to scream as twenty-four white roses accompanied Angus down in a wicked and lethal pas de deux to where he lay face down on the cement floor. Act two was complete.

Chapter 2

Pim maneuvered her way off stage, stopping only long enough to accept the congratulations from fellow dancers. She gave them a fake smile. She had missed the double pirouette coming out of the grand jeté, only doing a single turn. Compliments aside, she would have to do better next time, or she would lose her role. She looked at the clock. She needed to hurry. She had exactly fifteen minutes to go visit her grandfather before the start of act three. When he'd found out the part of Odette and Odile had become hers, he had insisted on coming to Inverness to see her debut performance. She rushed to her dressing room, changing into a pair of warm-up dance pants and sweater, then she snuck toward the stairs, backstage. Light and stage crewmembers were gathered in huddles, talking in lowered voices. One of them called out to her. "Stay down here, Pim. Rumor has it someone fell from one of the balconies."

"Oh God, how gruesome," she said. "Are they all right?"
"No idea."
"I'm just going to pop up and say hello to my grandfather.

He needs to leave as soon as the performance is over, so I won't have time then."

"Be careful."

She opened the heavy emergency door, taking the concrete stairs to the third level. It was a back passage not intended for the general public. She stuck her head out the door on the top floor. A crowd had formed at the end of the hallway. She hurried toward it. Two ushers were telling people to keep moving as they directed them toward the main stairs and exit. Pim located the box her grandfather was supposed to be in. "I'm sorry, miss. You can't go in there," a woman said, blocking the entranceway.

"It's my grandfather's box," she said nervously. The sight of the growing crowd was unsettling.

"You're a dancer?" the woman asked.

"Yes.

"We need you to go back and be with the company."

"Is he all right? Was he the one who fell?" She felt herself starting to panic as dread washed over her. This couldn't be happening.

"Miss, it's best if you go back down."

A tall man approached, pulling her alongside him. "Let's go."

"What's going on?" She tried pulling out of his grip, but he held on to her arm tight. He kept his head down, the top of his brown hair all she could see of his face. "Let go of me."

"Hush and come with me." He punched the code into the keypad, unlocking the door to the backstage stairs.

"Was that my grandfather who fell?"

"I don't know who your grandfather is, but the man in the box is the one who fell."

"No. Fuck." She tried turning around, but he still held her by the shoulder. "Are you with security? I need to get to him." She tried looking at his badge.

"There's no point going back up there. They're locking the whole place down. The authorities will come to you if it's him." He raised his head, running his hand over the shadow of his beard before pushing his way through the door leading backstage.

Tears filled her eyes and she stopped to wipe them. "I don't understand how this could happen." Fear, from so many years ago, converged on her, the memories carrying their ominous dread across time. Overcome, she leaned into him, resting her head on his chest as the tears began to fall.

Wraith didn't plan on getting involved. He only took the girl as an excuse to go down the back stairwell and get away from the crowd. There was a killer on the loose and he needed to find out who had gotten to Angus before he did. His perfectly timed strategy now playing out in chaotic disarray, he wanted to get to the auditorium before they removed the body. The girl was crying in earnest now. He put his arms around her, uncertain what else to do.

"Pim," a man with long, curly gray hair called out, coming toward them. "Darling, I need you to come with me."

She pulled away from Wraith, her pale blue-green eyes gleaming. "I'm sorry. I'm not sure what came over me," she apologized. "Was it my grandfather?" she turned and asked the man. "The person who fell?"

There was a commotion coming their way from the side of the stage. "Excuse me," a familiar voice called out. "I need an exit the duke and duchess can get out of safely, away from the crowds."

Wraith turned quickly, putting his back to the oncoming group, and grabbed the young dancer again in an embrace.

His heart was pounding. *Damn it.* He should have known they would be here.

"What are you doing?" she asked, trying to pry his fingers from her arms. "I need to get to my grandfather."

"Wheesht," he commanded in a hushed whisper. He dipped his head and kissed her to keep her from speaking as she struggled to break free. She bit his lip, bringing her knee swiftly up toward his crotch but he managed to stop her in the nick of time, increasing the pressure of the kiss.

"You can use this exit," the man said. "Peter Brindy, artistic director of the Scottish National Ballet. My apologies for the unfortunate turn of events, Your Grace."

"Christ," the duke said. "He fell right in front of our box. It was horrible. I need to get the duchess home."

"Of course, of course." Peter led them to a door that would take them outside.

Wraith chanced the exposure and looked over his shoulder. The duchess looked back, and her green eyes grew wide as they stared at each other for no more than a second before she composed herself, looking back.

He was thrown off kilter for a moment, thinking of all the things he wanted to say to her. All the things he had said to her in his mind since the day everything went to hell with Al-Saad. But he couldn't. He died that day and that is how it must remain. The young woman continued to struggle and was now glaring at him as she pushed out of his arms. He let her go, realizing just how hard he gripped her.

"Who the fuck do you think you are?" she asked, looking at his badge. "I'll fucking report you."

The director was returning. He needed to get out of there. He turned and ran toward the stage, keeping to the left as he pushed aside the curtain and jumped the short distance to the house floor. His leg burned, the effort of moving so fast and the jar of the landing tearing at the scar tissue in his thigh.

The police were already arriving. He tore the badge off, stuffing it into his pocket as he tried to blend into the growing chaos. The ushers had cordoned off the area where the man lay, and yellow ropes blocked the path. Wraith moved closer. He stepped over the cords when no one was looking and snapped several photos with his phone, the tinny metallic smell of blood thick in his nose. Angus lay, lifeless, surrounded by the roses, their white petals stained red. His head was twisted at an awkward angle as blood seeped across the concrete floor. He studied the macabre tableau, putting everything to memory. Anger welled inside him. This was his kill and someone had taken it from him, stolen in a blink of the eye. He backed up, exiting the scene, and followed a group of panicked spectators out of the building. Without warning, he was forcefully knocked from behind and his damaged leg gave out, causing him to fall to the ground. A fiery burn ripped through his femur, the sensation making him feel nauseated. A man pushed past at full speed, rushing through the crowd. Wraith looked up to see the person wearing an ominous owl mask, not unlike the one the evil Von Rothbart wore in the second act of the ballet. The bird of prey moved silently, knocking down innocent victims as he ran from the building. A deadly assassin who had broken the neck of Wraith's soon-to-be victim with his killer talons, stealing Wraith's own target.

Chapter 3

The Tower, as it was called, was the compound Alexander McKay used as the headquarters for The Watch. It was named for the tower house that stood at the front of the property. Originally used for military purposes, now it housed offices, the Great Hall and the colonel's personal residence. Wraith drove through the wrought iron gates and down the winding road that took him past it, to the mansion where the agents stayed. The estate was set back in a sheltered glen and sat along a meandering river that fed into the loch. As for now, this was his home and had been for the past eleven months, while he recovered from the bomb blast that crushed his femur and punctured one of his lungs. It was here, he learned that to the rest of the world, Robert McFadden, his former self, had died in an explosion and he was given a new identity, Robert Wraith.

He pulled into the curved drive and parked the car. He was apprehensive to face McKay after the botched assassination attempt and he wasn't sure how his reception would be received. Alexander McKay, the colonel, was the first person he met when he woke up after the bombing which involved

Al-Saad, the notorious terrorist and leader of the IWP, Islamic World Power. Al-Saad had taken a personal dislike to the Duchess of Torridon, Ailsa McLennan, an American who married into British nobility, and used her as a rallying cry to gain supporters. The radical extremist had issued several death threats against her and even shot her in the arm during a roadside ambush in the Scottish Highlands. As his threats became more sinister, Robert knew, as her Personal Protection Officer, the only way to end the madness was to take him out. Little did he know then, it would cost him his life or at least the only life he knew. His friend and fellow soldier, Dougal Murray, whom he fought with in the SBS in Afghanistan had given him the phone number to The Watch, telling him to use it if he ever got himself into a situation he knew he wouldn't get out of alive. He had no idea whom he was calling when he dialed the number as he lay dying, crushed under a crumbling building. He had no idea of the implications.

He opened the door to the massive house and made his way to the eastern wing, where his small apartment was located. It was no more than a bedroom and sitting room, but he didn't require anything else. Alex would know he had returned as soon as he crossed through the gates. Wraith would be expected in his office to debrief, but he needed to shower first and collect his thoughts. He was still reeling from the adrenaline of the whole experience but, mostly, from seeing her. Ailsa. He never thought he would look into her dark green eyes again. The ramifications would be numerous if anyone found out he was still alive, but he knew she wouldn't say anything. She was probably as shaken up as he, at seeing him. The spray from the hot water in the shower scalded his skin. He relished the feeling. It was better than the empty numbness he usually felt. For the first time since the fatal attack, he actually felt alive. He turned the water off and dried himself with a towel, the sensation of his blood coursing through his veins, empowering. Tonight, might not have gone as planned but he was alive, and Ailsa was safe. That thought alone would carry him for a while. He put on a pair of navy-blue, wool trousers, tucking a white button-down shirt into the waist and pulled a gray cashmere sweater over his head. The mistake would come at a cost, he thought as he ran a brush through his short brown hair, of that he was certain.

The colonel had extremely high standards for his agents; they were with all due respect to McKay, one of the most elite organizations in the world. The Watch was a secret division of The Black Watch that continued after the regiment was amalgamated into the Royal Regiment of Scotland in 2006. To the rest of the world, the organization didn't exist. As McKay explained to him in the beginning, '*There are those in the world who think they are above punishment, the most powerful criminals, involved in the worst crimes. Sex trafficking, child pornography, drugs and embezzlement, to name a few. They get off with no punishment because they are rich and have connections to members in government and law enforcement. A fair trial would never happen, nor do they deserve one, so The Watch takes care of them. No one is above the exemption of punishment. Like the original Black Watch, we are just employed to rid the world of the most atrocious criminals.*'

Wraith closed the door to his suite. The mansion was empty, the halls dark and deserted. Most of the agents would be out on assignments and those who were in residence would have gone into Aberdeen for the night, to enjoy the clubs. He walked the short distance to the tower house. The chill in the air pulled at his lung, forcing him to pause and catch his breath. He took the inhaler he carried out of his pocket and looked at it before putting it away. It had become a crutch. He hated he still suffered from the bombing physically. It made him feel compromised. Broken. Normally, he wouldn't care, but something had changed tonight, and he needed to hold on to the small bit of renewed life he felt. He forced himself to take a deep breath, the scar tissue stretching as pain seared through his chest. It eventually subsided, and he slowly recovered. He entered the stone building and walked down the hall that led to McKay's office and sitting room. Gabriel, one of the other agents, was just coming out.

"You're back," he said. It was a redundant statement, they would know he returned and the assassination was mishandled. "He's waiting for you."

Wraith nodded.

"I was actually coming to get you."

"I needed to shower first," he said. "Gather my thoughts."

"That's understandable. Injured in the line of duty?" Gabriel asked, pointing to his lower lip.

Wraith ran his finger over the swollen spot where Primrose McNeil had bitten him. There was something fiery about the wee lass. He wondered how she was getting on. "Something like that."

Gabriel opened the door, ushering him into the dark office. Mahogany paneling lined the bottom half of the walls, the rest were covered with dark green wallpaper. The room was rich and masculine.

The colonel sat on a brown leather sofa before a fireplace. The smell of burning peat, earthy like ancient moss, filled the air. He stood. "There you are. I thought you might be avoiding me," he said. He was in his mid-sixties, with short gray hair styled in a pristine cut. He had an angular and fit body that was accentuated by the expensive tailored suit he wore. Expectancy laced the office; explanations would be judged as either excuses or failures. The Watch didn't tolerate mistakes. Alex adjusted his tie before sitting down and pointed to a leather side chair. "Have a seat."

Wraith sat down, uncertain how to begin.

"Gabriel, would you pour us some whiskey please?" McKay turned to Wraith. "So, Angus is dead."

"Yes, sir, but I didn't kill him."

"I know. I saw the news. I knew you wouldn't deviate from the plan. What happened?"

"Someone got to him first." He took the glass Gabriel handed him. "I was about to take the shot when someone entered his box and threw him over the rail."

Gabriel sat down beside the colonel, crossing his legs in an elegant fashion. "Did you see who it was?"

Wraith shook his head. "It was no more than a shadow." He went on to explain the events that followed, omitting the part about running into the duke and duchess. He pulled his phone out and brought up the photos he took of Angus on the screen, handing it to Alex. "His neck was broken before he fell."

"Aye," he said as he studied the pictures. "That will be left out of the autopsy report, I'm sure."

"And this man with the owl mask?" Gabriel asked, his voice as smooth as silk.

"I'm sure it's our killer or someone who was involved in the operation." He paused. "Look, I apologize if I messed up the mission—"

"On the contrary," McKay said, interrupting him. "There are a lot of people who would have liked to see McNeil dead. He had many enemies. This might open up an avenue into some of his other nefarious associates. You don't become the head of the opioid black market in western Scotland without ruffling some feathers. Whoever killed him had a reason. They knew his guard would be down." He took a sip of his whiskey, thinking. "You say you had contact with his granddaughter?"

"Yes, briefly. I used her to get down the back stairs of the theater to avoid the crowds. I wanted to get to his body before the police arrived."

"She might be a way in."

"A way in? She's a nineteen-year old lass," Wraith objected. "Spoiled at that, I'm sure."

"She's his only heir. His colleagues and solicitors run his various businesses. There will be a funeral. His killer might be there."

"You're right, Colonel," Gabriel agreed. "We've been trying to infiltrate his inner circle for years. It's been impossible to breach."

Alex set his empty glass down on a side table and stood. Walking over to the fireplace, he leaned against the mantle. "I want you to go to Glasgow tomorrow and meet up with the girl. Get involved with her."

Wraith looked at him like he was insane. "Get involved with her? I just told you she's a child."

"We'll think of a cover. She'll be vulnerable. She'll need someone to guide her. Better us than one of Angus' thugs," he said, challenging Wraith to disagree. "It will give you an inside track to McNeil's business dealings. You'll be able to find out who might have wanted him dead. We need to find out who killed him."

"I'm a sniper, not a spy," Wraith said.

Alex's eyes hardened into steel gray slits as his voice sliced through the room in a growl. "You're whatever I tell you to be."

Wraith's jaw clenched, the price of his mistake now obvious and being paid out in the form of a punishment. He was reminded instantly, this man was only a friend as long as he said so and not someone to be crossed. When he first woke up after spending a month in a medically induced coma from the bomb blast, McKay was the first person he saw, and he thought he was looking at the devil himself. "Yes, sir," he said through gritted teeth. The colonel had told him then if he didn't agree to join The Watch, they would kill him. And they would; he knew it. McKay had him by the balls. It was the price he paid for dialing the number.

"Good. I'm glad we see eye to eye." His expression eased. "Gabriel, take Wraith to the infirmary, so Dr. Forbes can give him a once over. Then make sure he is settled in Glasgow. He can use the same flat he stayed in before."

"Yes, Colonel," the blond-haired agent said.

"And, Wraith," he said pointedly, "I was wrong. By nature, you're not an assassin nor are you a spy. It's not that you can't carry out those skills, but it's not who you are. You're a protector. You'll do just fine with the girl."

The colonel's words stung his heart. Ailsa had called him her protector once. She had it engraved on the back of the Victoria Cross medal he had been awarded posthumously for his part in Al-Saad's death and she'd left it at the foot of his makeshift grave. If Wraith had been looking for any kind of atonement or redemption over the past year, tonight reminded him there would be no forgiveness for him. Like Dante, he had passed through the gate of Hell when he sold his soul to the devil and the inscription at the end was clear,

'Abandon all hope, ye who enter here.'

Chapter 4

Pim sat in her grandfather's Kingsborough Gardens townhouse in Glasgow, thankful the solicitor and his close business associates had gone home for the night. The company had given her a few days off, canceling Sunday's show in Inverness. She had called her mother in Canada to let her know the arrangements, but she told Pim she had no intention of flying out for her ex-father-in-law's funeral.

"I'm sorry, Pim," her mother explained over the phone, earlier in the day. Her voice simmered with resentment. "You know Angus and I never got along, even when your father was alive. Nothing's changed. I would rather come and see you dance next month in New York when the company tours if we're available, than attend his funeral." She and her mother were never really close. Pim was sent off to the prestigious Royal Ballet School in London at age ten to study dance, only coming home on school breaks. When her father was killed in a horrible mugging in Edinburgh, she was just fourteen, and her mother, no longer tied down by marital duties, left to start a new life in Canada.

"I understand," Pim said, frowning at the phone. She

Stripped

couldn't help feeling hurt. She could use her support right now, but her mother had a new husband and a new family to occupy her time. "I'll manage." To her mother, Pim was nothing more than a burden her father had left her with when he died. She knew her mother was glad to be free from a man she never loved and more than happy to leave a city whose contemporary culture she never appreciated.

"I'm sure the lawyers will handle everything," she said.

"I suppose." Pim hung up. After her mother basically abandoned her, she started staying with her grandfather when she had time off school, spending holidays and summer breaks with him. They became close, as he was her only source of family. That was what made this especially hard. Now she had no one. A tear slid down her face, the pain of his loss overwhelming.

Her phone pinged, and she looked down at the screen. It was a message from Peter, her artistic director. *I'm at your flat, but no one is answering. Just making sure you're all right.*

She wasn't up for company and was glad she wasn't home. *I'm at my grandfather's place. The solicitor just left.*

He texted back. *Let me know when you get back. You shouldn't be alone.*

Peter had a reputation for being a bit too friendly with his female dancers. Pim had been careful to avoid him at all costs, but with her having been given the role of principal dancer, he might expect certain things and she didn't have her grandfather here to protect her with his name or his pocketbook.

She sent one last text before turning her phone off. *I have some work to finish up.*

The solicitor had spent most of the afternoon in her grandfather's office, arranging the funeral. Her grandfather had been the CEO of many companies, ranging from offshore drilling to owning bars and restaurants. He was a central figure in Glasgow not only as a businessman, but also a philanthropist, and he had been known for generously supporting the arts and various charities as a celebrated patron. It was still hard to believe he fell over the rail. Despite his age, he was not a frail nor fragile man and he had always been steady on his feet. She wracked her brain trying to come up with an explanation that made sense, but none came to her. And the only possibility the police could offer was that it was a freak accident. She pulled the teabag from her cup and sat down at the large desk in his office. Now she was going to have to figure out how to go on without him. She knew death and she knew the pain and isolation that came with it. She pushed it down into the dark recess where her other grief dwelled. Right now, she needed to be strong. The funeral was in two days and she had to finish writing her eulogy. She wasn't sure what to say and the paper in front of her contained more doodles than words. For the moment, she decided to tackle the easy part first and started with a short biography of his life. It was the other part that eluded her. She wasn't sure how she could pay homage to the most important person in her life in a few paragraphs.

She put her pen down and stood up, stretching, as the joints in her hips and back cracked, relieving the pressure from sitting too long. The room was becoming dark as evening began to wrap the day in its velvety cloak. She needed to get back to her flat. She took her cup to the kitchen and put the few dishes that sat in the sink into the dishwasher, the emptiness of the large house only intensifying her loneliness. She turned off the kitchen light and set the alarm, shutting and locking the front door, then walked the short ten-minute stretch from Hyndland through Victoria Circus, to her flat on Belhaven Terrace. Her two-bedroom residence was located on the top floor of a Victorian townhouse, a gift from her grandfather when she signed with SNB. She took the stairs up to the third floor, glad of the exercise, but stopped short of her door. Peter was waiting in the hall for her, holding a bottle of wine.

"My darling girl," he said, coming over and hugging her. "I thought you might like a little distraction." He held up the bottle. "It's a very good vintage."

Her stomach dropped as she braced herself for the inevitable. "I thought I might go to the pub." She didn't want to be alone with him in her place. "Òran Mór has live music."

"Are you sure you're up for it?" he asked. She didn't miss the disappointment in his voice nor the bitter smile he plastered on his face as she derailed his plans.

"I've been inside all day. Honestly, I need a break from everything." She unlocked her door. "I just need to freshen up." He followed her in, his eyes browsing over the contemporary architecture and minimalist furniture, a combination of elegant simplicity and discreet luxury. He set the wine down on the kitchen counter. "Gift from Granddaddy?"

She stilled, looking over at him. The grief she felt came bubbling up. She pressed her lips together to hide the tremble. Of course, he knew she never would be able to afford it on her salary.

"Oh God. How insensitive of me," he said, running his hand down the side of her face. "I can hardly believe he's gone too, our dear benefactor."

She stepped back, trying to get ahold of her emotions. "I should change."

"Do you mind if I pour myself a glass?"

"No, please make yourself at home. There's a corkscrew in the drawer." She went into her bedroom and closed the door, taking a deep breath. Maybe getting out would do her some good. The reality of her grandfather's death, all at once, was crushing. She went to her closet and pulled out a black dress, changing into it. It was tight and short. She turned to look at the back in the mirror, pulling down the hem that hugged her thighs. The tattoo she'd gotten in her rebellious years when she wanted to quit dance stood out as it wove its way down her spine between her shoulder blades—three primroses intertwined, their stems turning into script that read, *Behind every beautiful thing, there's some kind of pain.* It was a Bob Dylan quote and it summed up what ballet had come to mean to her. She ran a brush through her long brown hair and applied some red lipstick. It would have to do; she didn't have it in her for anything else. She slipped on a pair of black high-heeled boots and grabbed her coat, steeling herself before she went out to the living room.

"There's my newest Étoile." He handed her a glass of the deep burgundy wine, kissing her cheek. "Here's to your grandfather."

Pim took a sip from her glass and set it down on the counter, frowning. Étoile, the highest form of French dancer. A star. It was a bittersweet compliment as it sat side by side with the end of a life. To reach the pinnacle in her career when no one she loved was there to celebrate it with her, left her empty. "We should get going before the pub gets too full."

Peter's eyebrow arched. "I doubt you would have any trouble getting in. You're Glasgow's prima ballerina now. And with how gorgeous you look, they would never turn you away. Finish your wine."

She felt her face grow warm but nevertheless picked up her glass and drained the contents. "There," she said. "Let's go." She picked up her keys, bolstered by the liquid courage. Maybe drowning her sorrows wouldn't be such a bad thing after all. She could numb the pain and dull her feelings. Old habits bubbled to the surface, reemerging along with the heartache.

Peter finished his glass. "I like this side of you, Pim. You should let it transcend into your dancing sometimes. Loosen up a little." He followed her out the door and down the stairs.

Òran Mór was a few blocks from her flat. It was one of the things that drew her to the area. The pub was originally a church before it was renovated into a thriving arts venue. It hosted two pubs, a nightclub, several restaurants and an auditorium. Its founding principle was *'Arts for All- All Year Round'* and became a place that brought together the visual arts, theater and literature with local artists, actors and writers.

The crisp cool air was a relief as they walked along the pavement. Peter put his arm casually around her waist as they passed several other people out for the night. She tried not to tense. He had touched her many times before, all over, when he partnered her during rehearsal while demonstrating various moves. This was different, though; they weren't at the studio. At least the wine had started to take effect. She was going to need several more drinks to make it through this night.

Chapter 5

Wraith sat in a dark corner at the back of the bar, watching as Primrose laughed with the man from the ballet. She was drunk. The bastard kept plying her with shots and she didn't have the sense to say no. She looked different, no longer the fragile and beautiful white swan from the ballet. This swan had transformed. This was a seductress playing a thrilling game. Every man in the pub had noticed her. Beauty aside, she was still nothing more than a spoiled lass. The stupid girl was going to get herself in trouble. She flipped her brown hair over her shoulder as she walked to the bathroom, her tight black dress just covering her rear end, and stopped when she saw him.

"It's you." Her eyes narrowed. "From the ballet last night."

"So," he said, bent over his drink.

"So?" She rubbed her middle finger along her thumb unconsciously, swaying slightly on her feet. "Why are you here? Are you following me?"

"I was here first. How could I be following you?" he asked, brushing her off.

"So, it's just a coincidence?" she challenged.

Wraith's attention was on the ballet director. He had ordered two more drinks, and he watched as the bastard dropped something in one of them.

"I asked you if it's just a coincidence, or are you trying to pick me up, creep?"

Wraith shook his head. "I don't pick up little girls. It's not my thing."

"But you kiss them," she said then added defensively, "and I'm not a little girl."

"You've had too much to drink. You should go home."

"Fucking cunt." She walked off toward the bathroom.

Damn. He was going to have to get involved. He picked up his drink. Walking over to where the ballet director stood at the counter, he finished the last of it and set his empty glass down. "I'll take another," he said to the bartender. The woman behind the counter nodded.

He looked at the director. "Did you see that piece of ass back there?" He motioned with his head to a pretty woman with red hair by the pool table. The ballet director looked over. Wraith switched the two glasses on the counter.

"Not my type," the middle-aged man said, running his hand through his long hair.

"Too old?" Wraith asked, not trying to hide the disgust in his voice.

The director laughed. "Too big. I like mine a bit more petite."

Arsehole. The bartender handed him his drink. Wraith laid a twenty-pound note on the counter and walked away, returning to his spot in the corner.

Primrose came back to the bar. She let her hand brush across the director's back before he handed her the shot. She glanced back to where Wraith sat, her eyes hardening before she lifted the glass to her lips and downed the contents. He shook his head. He was here to find out who killed McNeil, not to babysit his reckless granddaughter. The lassie was a fool. The clock on the wall read one. He finished his drink before he noticed any changes in the director's demeanor. The man began to stagger, and sitting down hard in a chair, he grabbed his head. Pim knelt before him and pulled out her phone, typing in several things as she talked to him in a hushed voice. Then she got up and helped him stand, walking him out. Wraith followed close behind. He stopped her before she got in an Uber with the man.

"Let him go," he said, grabbing her arm.

"He's drunk. I need to make sure he gets home safely." She tried pulling away from him but she, herself, was too drunk to struggle.

"He'll get home but not with you." He leaned in the front window and spoke with the driver then watched as he sped off with his pathetic cargo.

"Let go of me," she said.

"Look, he tried to drug you. I watched him put something in your drink."

"No, he didn't. He wouldn't do that."

"Well, he did."

The girl began to sway on her feet as the color drained from her face. Wraith caught her before she fell over. Her lithe body was nothing more than a limp weight in his arms. He picked her up and carried her to his car, putting her in the passenger seat and praying she wouldn't vomit on the Nappa leather seats. Then he drove the short distance to her flat. She was easier to deal with passed out, and at least he didn't need to listen to her smart mouth. It was Alex's intention to punish him and the bastard was doing a good job. He carried her up the three flights of stairs to her place, the muscles in his bad leg aching from the effort, and found her keys in her purse. He unlocked the door and entered. Flicking on a light, the room lit up, the white walls and furniture a haven after the chaotic club. Wraith found the bedroom and set her down on the king-sized bed, removing her boots. She curled up on her side in the fetal position, covering her head with her arm, and let out a low moan. He covered her up with a blanket and closed the door. If she thought she felt bad now, wait until morning. His stomach let out its own rumble as he had yet to eat dinner. The fridge was practically empty; a withered pack of blueberries and a lone cucumber was all it contained. He shut the door and picked up the bottle of wine on the counter, pouring himself a glass. As least, it would stave off his hunger. He took off his suit jacket and made himself comfortable on the white couch, and kicking his feet up on a plush ottoman, he rubbed his sore thigh. Well, he did what he was told to do. He was now involved with Primrose McNeil.

Pim looked at the clock with one eye. It was going on seven. She needed to get up and get moving but the pounding in her head said otherwise. She couldn't remember how she got home last night and was thankful to find that Peter was not in her bed. A faint image of him in a car, driving off, flitted through her mind. She sat up. She still wore her dress but had managed at least to get her shoes off. She hadn't been this hungover in a long time. Not since she was a teenager, when she would stay out all night partying. The sound of a car horn honked outside. It would be her neighbor's carpool ride, letting him know they'd arrived. Every day, like clockwork.

Pim chucked the blanket off and made her way to the bathroom. She turned the water on and stood under the lukewarm stream, hoping to wash off last night. It had been a mistake. While it had provided her with a reprieve from her grief, she was embarrassed with her actions. When she was sixteen and told her grandfather she was quitting ballet, she used alcohol and sex to numb the pain she was really feeling. At the time, she was still trying to grapple with her father's death and her mother's apparent abandonment. Ballet dominated her whole life and she felt like she had missed out on a normal childhood. Missed out on time she could have spent with her father. The resentment she felt toward dance consumed her and she blamed it for everything. Partying and one-night stands became her only reprieve.

    She turned the water off and dried herself with a towel. The cool morning air caused goosebumps to appear on her skin as she shivered, and her warm bed called out to her to lie back down. Enticing as it was, she couldn't. She put on a pair of baggy gray sweats and a black wrap-around ballet sweater and made her way to the other bedroom. It had been converted to a small studio where she could practice. Full length mirrors lined two of the walls and a marley floating floor had been installed. She sat down and grabbed a roll of tape and a pair of pointe shoes. Her feet were a mess. Swan Lake was a demanding ballet. The constant pirouettes, pas de bourrés, and the thirty-two fouetté turns had taken their toll. She tore off what remained of her big toenail, wrapping it in tape. The rest of her nails were black from repeated injury. Her other foot sported a huge blister across her metatarsals. It was still raw from the friction of her shoes. She covered it with a plaster then taped the whole thing up before putting both her shoes on and tying the ribbons. She stood up and pulled the barre away from the wall, then placing her hands on it for support, she began to warm up her feet. The pounding in her head hadn't subsided and she felt her stomach roll. She pushed it aside. It was going on seven-thirty and it would take her thirty minutes to warm up her feet before she had to leave for class. Something popped in her hip, relieving the pain, as she positioned her feet in a wide second position, and she slowly began to relevé, going up on her toes. Her ankles cracked in angry protest. She repeated the move, again and again, stretching the tight tendons and getting used to the pressure at her toes.

A thud from the other room made her look up. The man from the orchestra, who was at the bar last night, stood in the doorway. She froze. Her mouth opened, but nothing came out. She was rendered speechless, shock etched across her face.

"I thought you'd still be asleep." He looked at her nonchalantly.

"What the *fuck* are you doing here?" she said, finally finding her voice.

Chapter 6

Wraith was surprised to find her up. With the way she drank last night, she should still be passed out. "You don't remember me bringing you home last night?" He knew she wouldn't, but she didn't know that, and it would help with his story.

She put her hand to her forehead, trying to think. "No. Fuck." She shook her head. "You need to leave."

"I don't even get a thank you?" he teased.

"*Now!*" She picked up her phone. "Or I'll call the police."

"Look, I'm not the enemy," he said, holding his hands up in surrender. "Do you really not remember last night?"

"No, I don't fucking remember last night. I hope it was good for you." She looked him up and down, scowling. "Get out."

"It was nothing like that. I told you, I'm not into little girls." Her seafoam green eyes narrowed at his remark, cold as arctic ice. "But your director seems to be."

"You don't know my director. And who the fuck cares. You can go." She couldn't be more than ninety-five pounds, but she threw her weight around like she was his size. "*Now!*"

Stripped

"I watched him drug your drink while you were in the restroom."

"You're lying."

"Why would I lie? I switched them, so he would take it. I guarantee you he's not up yet and won't be for a while."

She rubbed her hands over her face, taking a deep breath. "Who the fuck are you?"

"Truth." He cocked his head, looking at her, hoping she would calm down. "I work for your grandfather."

"Work for my grandfather? And what, you thought it would be fun to see if you could sleep with his granddaughter?" She pushed past him, going into the kitchen. "In case you haven't heard, my grandfather is dead. It won't buy you any bonus points."

He watched as she filled up an insulated water bottle and shoved it into a large duffle bag by the couch. "I'm a private investigator," he said. "Your grandfather hired me because he thought someone within his company or inner circle was trying to undermine him."

She sat down on the couch, the expression on her face turning to stone as she began to take off her pointe shoes. "Why would I believe you?"

"I'm not lying to you, Primrose."

She put the shoes into the duffle. "Are you trying to tell me that someone killed my grandfather and he didn't fall?" He didn't miss the slight tremble in her voice as she tied the laces on her trainers.

"I'm trying to figure that out."

She stood up and grabbed her coat from the sofa, put it on, then picked up the duffle bag. "Well, you're not a very good investigator if you let someone murder my grandfather." She opened her front door and stood there waiting for him to leave.

He grabbed his suit jacket and followed her out.

"Where are you going?" he asked as she locked the door and started down the stairs.

"None of your bloody business, arsehole."

"Primrose, I want to help you. Your grandfather was worried about your safety too."

"Really, because he never mentioned that to me, and regardless, I can take care of myself."

"I thought you had a few days off work?"

She stopped walking and turned around. "How would you know that? Are you some kind of sick stalker? That's it, you're stalking me. First, the ballet, then the bar, now my flat."

Damn Alex to hell for putting him in this position. Stalker? "No, I told you what I do. I overheard your director talking about it last night."

She continued down the street.

"At least let me drive you," he said, following her.

"I don't get in cars with creepy men," she shouted back at him. "Leave me the fuck alone."

Pim picked up her pace until she got to Hillhead Station, where she caught the outer circle of 'Clockwork Orange', Glasgow's infamous subway line. It was named for its orange and white cars. She swiped her smartcard at the terminal gate before finding a seat in the underground train car. The subway doors slid shut and she slowly let out her breath. He hadn't followed her.

The cheery voice of the subway driver came over the intercom, announcing, "The next station is Kelvinbridge," with endless enthusiasm for a Monday morning. It usually made her smile, but not today.

She clasped her hands together to keep them from shaking. The thought of her grandfather being murdered brought up all the anxiety and dread of her own father's death. Two murders in one family? The sound of the policeman's voice telling her mother of her father's death echoed in her mind. He had been bludgeoned with a lead pipe and on his death certificate, under cause, it read fractured skull. They never caught the killer. She took a new pair of pointe shoes from her bag and quickly sewed elastic and ribbons on them, a skill she had become a pro at when she started going through a pair of shoes in a day. She ripped out the insoles and, taking a pair of industrial snippers, popped the shank up, removed the nail in the heel, and cut the thick, hardened cardboard in half, in essence, de-shanking three quarters of the shoe.

The accusations the man had spouted were disturbing. Peter wouldn't drug her and if her grandfather had been in danger, surely, he would have told her. She hurried to finish, cutting the satin off the outside tip of the toe. She sliced it several times with a box cutter to rough up the edge, then she squeezed the box until she felt it crack. Caught up in her own thoughts, she almost missed the witty announcer call out Bridge Street. That was her exit. She put her shoes away in her bag and walked the short distance to where she caught the bus that would take her the rest of the way.

Scottish National Ballet was housed in the Tramway Arts Center, on the Southside of Glasgow. Pim entered the modern, purpose-built ballet center, making her way up to the second floor toward the dressing rooms. Voices could be heard coming from the one assigned to the women. She entered and stopped short when she saw her locker. Someone had painted a black X across the outside of it. The other girls in the room went silent. Pim set her bag down and clenched her jaw to prevent the tears that threatened from coming.

"It was like that when we got here, Pim," one of the dancers said.

"It's fine," she said, changing into her tights and leotard.

"We didn't think you would be back today or we would have cleaned it up."

"I'm just back for class." She put on a pair of knit legwarmer pants. Actually, she wasn't surprised. Between being named a soloist and getting the starring role in Swan Lake, she was bound to piss someone off. The worst thing she could do was react; she needed to let it roll off her back. She closed the door to her locker and made her way upstairs to the studio. Windows lined the top of one of the white walls and the weak morning sun came through in shadowy streaks. She sat down to put on her pointe shoes.

Niall Leonard, the aging ballet master, came over to her. "I didn't expect to see you today, Rosy."

She smiled up at him. "I'm just here for class. I can't stay in my flat all day."

"How are you holding up?" He wiped his watery nose with a handkerchief. She knew he'd had a soft spot for her ever since she came to the company.

"I'll do," she said, biting her lip to fight off the tears that welled up in her eyes.

"Aye, well, take it easy today." He was her favorite teacher. In his younger years, he had danced for the Ballet Russe de Monte Carlo and if you caught him in the right mood, he would regale you with stories of famous dancers and old-world glamour.

When all of the company arrived, Pim found her place at the barre. "Are you okay?" her partner Paul mouthed to her from his spot.

She nodded. The pianist began to play and class officially started. This was what she needed, the comfort of this non-negotiable ritual. Ninety minutes, to calm her mind and block out the events from the weekend while she warmed up her body and prepared for the turmoil of the upcoming day. The slow movement of Beethoven wound down and the accompanist began to play an upbeat tune.

Mr. Leonard bellowed over the music, "Épaulment. Épaulment. Watch your shoulders, ladies." Their legs moved in and out with fast controlled movements as they finished with tendus.

The door to the studio crashed opened and Zoya Petrov, the ballet mistress, charged in angrily. "What's she doing in class?" she shrieked at Niall.

"Who?" the ballet master asked, looking around.

"Pim."

The pianist stopped playing.

"Pim, come here," Zoya continued to squeal in her thick Russian accent.

Pim looked around before making her way over to the woman.

"You're supposed to be on bereavement leave."

"I just came in to take class."

"You need to leave," the woman spat.

"Why?" she asked. "Peter said it would be all right."

"Well, Peter isn't here. He's out sick today and I'm in charge."

Pim paused. She knew he might be hungover, but he never missed work. He was too much of a control freak. *'I watched him put something in your drink, so I switched them.'* The first inkling of doubt wormed its way into her mind.

"I want you to leave," Zoya continued. "You can return on Thursday. Right now, you're a liability."

Pim felt the heat in her face rise. She grabbed her bag and started for the door.

Zoya stopped her. She spoke in a hushed whisper. "I know you and your grandfather had something to do with Irina slipping."

"No, we didn't."

"Don't you think it seems suspicious that she was hurt, and you were suddenly given the starring role?"

"Irina slipping was an accident."

"Someone tampered with the floor."

"You're wrong," Pim said.

"Am I? I'll make sure you pay for this." The woman turned to the class. "Catriona," Zoya said. "You'll take Pim's place in rehearsal today. Paul will partner you."

Niall stood at the door, looking abashed. "I'm sorry, Rosy."

She shook her head. "It's not your fault."

"I have tragic news," Zoya continued to speak to the company. "Irina was admitted to hospital this morning. She tried to take her own life. The doctors told her with the fracture to her ankle, she would never dance again, and it was all too much for her to handle."

Several dancers gasped, and a few burst into tears.

Pim shut the door behind herself, letting her own tears finally flow. There were certain company members who already suspected she had something to do with Irina's injury. She didn't, of course, but now with the attempted suicide, it explained the vandalism to her locker. Irina had always been chilly toward her. However, she still admired and respected the prima ballerina. Pim understood one didn't get Irina's title without hard work and sacrifice. She changed her shoes and pushed open the main door of the center. The sun was now covered by a thick layer of clouds. Its feeble attempt to show itself this morning, overrun by a steady current of sorrow. She pulled the hood up on her coat, covering her head to block out the light drizzle, and made her way home.

Chapter 7

Wraith caught up to Pim before she made it to the bus station. He had followed her into the studios, in hopes of trying to better understand the girl before throwing in the towel and walking away. No matter how much the colonel wanted him to get close to her, he refused to become the stalker she accused him of being. He was shocked to find out how poorly she had been treated and he was beginning to realize where the chip on her shoulder was coming from.

"Primrose, stop," he said behind her.

She whirled around. "For the love of God, what do you want?"

Her pale eyes, clear as spring water, glistened with tears and he resisted the urge to wipe them away. "Please, just hear me out."

She set her bag down on the wet concrete and crossed her arms. "What?"

"Not here. Let's go back to your place."

"I'm not getting in a fucking car with you. I don't even know your name."

"Fine. Then let me get you something to eat." He pointed to a French basserie down the block.

She picked up her bag, shaking her head. "Fine. But promise me, after this, you'll leave me alone." She walked ahead of him, crossing the street before she got to the actual marked pedestrian crossing. A driver in a car leaned on his horn, barely missing her. She held up two fingers, flipping him off. Wraith caught up to her. Christ, she was testing his patience. Not only was she completely reckless, it was like she was being negligent on purpose, calling out for trouble with a neon sign. He opened the door to the café, holding it for her as she entered.

"Table for two," he said to the hostess. She led them over to a place in the back. Wraith pulled Pim's chair out for her before sitting down himself.

"Can I get you something to drink?" the hostess asked.

"Coffee please."

Pim nodded in agreement, watching as she walked off. They sat in silence until a waiter brought them each steaming mugs, the deep nutty aroma filling the air, and took their orders.

"I'll have a poached egg with avocado on the side," Pim said, setting the menu down.

"And for you, sir?"

Wraith's stomach growled. He was thankful to be eating soon. "I'll have your full fry up."

The young man smiled at Pim, flirting, before leaving to put their order in. Wraith could understand why. Take away the foul language and bad attitude, and she had a natural, almost innocent beauty to her. Her dark brown hair was pulled back in a bun, accentuating her high cheekbones and full lips, but it was her eyes that really stood out. Large and clear, they reminded him of a spring rain, neither green nor blue. Surrounded by long dark lashes and so pale, they appeared almost incandescent.

"Perhaps we got off on the wrong foot," he said. "My name is Wraith. Robert Wraith, but people call me Wraith."

Pim rolled her eyes. "Wraith." She took the business card he handed her. *Robert Wraith, Private Investigator* was embossed on the front along with a telephone number. She handed it back to him.

"Keep it."

She laid it on the table and took a shaky breath, frowning. "What do you want with me?" she finally asked, taking a sip of her black coffee.

"I want to find out who killed your grandfather."

"Why are you so sure he was murdered? I've heard nothing about that and I was with his solicitor all of yesterday. Surely, the police would have notified him if something had changed."

"Primrose, I'm not going to go into details, but I saw his body."

She stiffened. It was the same response her mother gave her when she asked about her father's murder. She wouldn't have ever known about the fractured skull or bludgeoning if she hadn't snooped through her mother's and grandfather's files or listened in on conversations. The images of the police pictures flashed in her mind like the reel on an old film. The swollen, puffy fingers on his hand, the awkward angle of his upper arm, bruised and engorged where the blood pooled and the jagged edge of his humerus bone protruded and, finally, the side of his head, depressed, his skull fractured to the point it exposed brain matter, and fluid drained from it. "I'm an adult. I think I can handle it."

"Please just trust me on this."

She let out a sardonic laugh. "Trust you? I don't even know you. Why in bloody hell would I trust you when you can't even be truthful?" She started to get up.

"Wait." Wraith rubbed his forehead. "His neck was snapped and not from the landing. Someone broke it before he fell."

She looked away as she sat back down, trying to hide her face and the look of horror she knew must be on it. "Why should I believe you? If that were the case, the police would have been able to determine that also."

"I was right about your director."

"Just because he's out sick, doesn't mean he put something in my drink." She bit her lip as the doubt she felt grew. He'd never missed a day of work.

"I called around. He went to A&E last night. He wasn't released until this morning. They pumped his stomach."

She looked up at him, eyebrows raised. Appalled, was the simplest way to describe how she felt, add to that shocked, disgusted and shaken. Peter was more than her boss. The company was her family, especially now with the death of her grandfather. There was more than just her career on the line. She wasn't sure what to say. She used the silence to hide her growing unease as she studied the man before her for the first time. Had her grandfather really hired him, she wondered. His short brown hair was perfectly groomed along with his close-clipped beard, not much more than a shadow on his strong jaw. A straight nose and green eyes finished out a handsome face. It was obvious he worked out, and the tailored black suit he wore still managed to look crisp, even though he'd slept in it. He had money. The waiter came back with their food, setting their plates in front of them. She was glad for the reprieve, for she found Robert Wraith to be a tad intimidating.

She picked up her knife and fork, stabbing into the runny yolk of her egg as it burst forth onto her plate. It looked like a duck. It was a game she used to play with her father when she was young. He told her every egg contained its own pattern, you just had to look for it. She swirled it around on her plate, no longer hungry. Wraith, on the other hand, ate with vigor as he cut into a sausage, finishing it in two bites. She set down her cutlery. "How do you think I can help you?"

He wiped his mouth with his napkin. "Your grandfather thought the threat was coming from his inner circle, a business associate perhaps.

"So, I don't know any of them."

"Yes, but this would have been someone he knew personally, someone close. Someone who will be at his funeral or the reading of his will."

"What are you suggesting?"

"I need a way in."

"A way in? You fucking want to use me as your way in while I'm trying to deal with all of this?" She set her napkin down. "Hell no."

"Primrose, I don't want to use you. I want to work with you, and I want to protect you. It's what your grandfather wanted."

"It's Pim. No one calls me Primrose." She shook her head. "And I don't need your protection. My grandfather is dead, and as far as I'm concerned, your services are no longer needed. If it's money you're looking for, I'll make sure his solicitor compensates you for anything you're owed."

"This isn't about money," he said. "Let me go with you this afternoon to the viewing. If anyone asks, we can say we're dating, that we met through the ballet and orchestra."

Now she really laughed. "Fuck no." She didn't want to think of her dead grandfather anymore. What she wanted, was for this nightmare to be over. She wanted to be in rehearsal, where she could go numb and forget this weekend ever happened. She wanted a director who wouldn't drug her so he could sleep with her. She wanted to be dancing her role with her partner Paul, not Catriona. She wanted a mother who would fly out and help her. But she had none of those things. Instead, she was all alone. "What do I get out of all of this?"

"You seem like the type of girl who would want to know the truth."

"You don't know what type of girl I am."

"I know you're strong," he said, his green eyes unwavering.

Her bottom lip began to tremble. She wasn't strong. She'd just built her wall so high, few people ever saw over it. "I'll need more than an empty platitude."

He pushed his empty plate to the side and leaned forward. "I know you didn't cause Irina's accident."

She shook her head, drained. "There's no proof. People are going to believe what they want to believe. Anyway, what if it *was* my grandfather?"

"I was watching your grandfather the night before and the next day. He didn't go near the studios."

"Watching?" she questioned.

"Guarding. Protecting. Whatever you want to call it."

"He could have paid someone to do it?"

"He didn't. I've looked at the CCTV film. No one came or left the building except for company members."

"That doesn't clear my name."

"No, but you were late that day. You wouldn't have had time."

A small bit of relief washed over her, knowing her grandfather wasn't involved. It wasn't that she believed the rumors, but doubt had a way of sneaking in and festering. She knew her grandfather had a reputation and she had been careful not to listen to the negative biases of those who spoke against him, only focusing on the good. If he was murdered, then whoever did it deserved to be brought to justice. "Fine," she said quickly, not wanting to cry in front of him. She didn't need him chipping away at her fortress anymore.

"Good girl."

The waiter brought their check. Wraith pulled his American Express black card out of his wallet and handed it to the young man. "Let's come up with a plan."

Chapter 8

Pim pulled her hair back into a loose, low bun and adjusted the bow on the neck of the long-sleeved, black crepe dress she wore. She slipped her feet into her Louboutin black pumps and made her way to the kitchen. She shouldn't have agreed to Wraith's plan. What kind of name was Wraith, anyway? But if someone did murder her grandfather and if it was someone close to him, she needed to find out. She took a bottle of Sauvignon Blanc out of the wine refrigerator and opened it, pouring herself a small glass to bolster her nerves. She had no idea how she was going to make it through all the pleasantries this afternoon. Her grief was personal; it wasn't something she wanted to share with anyone. She was fine with keeping it locked away tight in her heart.

There was a knock on the door. She set her glass down and went to answer it. Wraith stood on the other side, dressed in a dark blue suit and tie with a starched white shirt.

"You shouldn't answer the door without checking who it is first," he said.

Stripped

She rolled her eyes and, picking up her glass, drained it. "I'll remember that," she said sarcastically.

"Do you think that's a good idea?" He pointed to the wine.

"Yes, I think it's a good idea or I wouldn't be having a glass." She shouldn't have agreed to this, she thought, taking her coat from the hall closet. *Fucking cocky wanker*. She didn't know a thing about this man. But the idea that her grandfather was murdered resonated within her and she couldn't stop thinking of it. She knew he wouldn't have just fallen.

"Can you help me?" She turned around so her back faced him. The dress had a gold zipper up the back that she couldn't manage on her own. His hand brushed her neck briefly, sending an unexpected shiver up her spine. He finished zipping it up the remainder of the way and fastened the tiny clasp at the top. She was used to being touched by men—she couldn't avoid it in ballet—but her body never reacted this way. She took a deep breath before turning around. "Thank you."

"You're welcome." He helped her with her coat and followed her out the door and down the stairs to where his car was parked, a black Mercedes-AMG GT. He definitely had money.

She smiled up at him, giving him a smug look as he opened the door for her and saw her safely seated. "Nice car."

"Fasten your seat belt, Primrose," he said, shutting her door.

It was the first time Wraith had seen her smile. He took his jacket off, laying it down in the back, and sat down in the driver's seat. It suited her, and he was glad to see her wall come down a bit. It would make his job easier.

"Can I drive it?" she asked, running her hand over the dashboard.

"No."

"But I'm helping you," she countered. "You owe me."

"Do you even know how to drive?" He doubted it since he had only seen her take the subway and bus.

"Technically, yes, but I don't have my license."

"Then that would be a definite no. It would be illegal." He turned down Great Western, shifting gears and flooring it as the car accelerated up to speed in a few seconds.

"I always thought private investigators were supposed to be fearless and daring. I didn't realize you were going to be such a goody-goody."

Now it was his turn to laugh. "Hardly. But I am into safety." He pulled into the car park at the funeral home. "What can we expect today?"

"I told you I wasn't involved in the planning. His solicitor, Graham Rankin, handled it. He did say he only invited close friends to the viewing, so it shouldn't be too crowded." Gone, was the smile, the prickly tone in her voice returned.

He turned the car off and got out to open her door, but she was already standing, smoothing the skirt of her dress. "You should have waited for me to get the door," he said, putting his jacket back on and fastening the button.

Her nose wrinkled in distaste. "Why?"

"Because I'm supposed to be your boyfriend."

"You've got to be fucking kidding me." She walked ahead of him toward the red brick building.

He caught up to her and held the door open. "People will be watching. We need this cover to work. And I'm warning you, Primrose, watch your language. Your grandfather wouldn't want to hear those words from your mouth."

"You're warning me?" She laughed. "Or what?" She

turned on him, putting her finger in his face. "Don't you tell me how to act or be, or I'll kick your arse out of here faster than you can count. And it's Pim, not Primrose."

Wraith clenched his jaw to prevent saying something he would regret. He softened his tone, remembering where they were. Of course, she would be upset; she was about to go to the viewing of her dead grandfather. He took her hand. "Come."

A bald man with a head so shiny, it looked like he polished it, stood at the entrance to the chapel, greeting guests as they arrived. He saw Pim and walked toward them. "Sweetheart," he said, giving her a kiss on her cheek. "I'm glad you're here. There are refreshments in the room to the right. Your grandfather is in the chapel."

"Thank you, Mr. Rankin. I couldn't have done this without you." The lawyer looked over at Wraith. "Uhm, this is my friend Robert."

The man didn't offer him his hand. Instead, he gave him the once over.

"Why don't I get us some tea?" Wraith said, giving her hand a squeeze and leaving. He walked slowly, listening to their conversation.

"Who's the lad?" Rankin asked Pim.

"He's from the Scottish Ballet Orchestra, uhm, we've been seeing each other."

"Did your grandfather meet him?"

"No. I was going to introduce them but, well…" her voice trailed off.

"Why don't we get you a seat?" He led her over to a chair in the hallway. Wraith watched out of the corner of his eye as Rankin motioned with his head to one of his cronies to watch him.

He went into the refreshment room, pouring tea into a

paper cup, and scanned the gathering crowd. The group reeked of the upper echelons of organized crime. Huddled in small groups and talking in hushed whispers, were the managers and CEOs of the various businesses Angus used to launder his dirty drug money. There were even a few government officials. Wraith added some milk and sugar to the cup, smiling guilelessly at the thug Rankin had watching him. He brought the cup over to Pim. "Here you go, darling."

She took it with a shaky hand, taking a small sip. "Thank you."

He gave her shoulder a small squeeze, hoping to calm her nerves. People came up to her, offering their condolences. She smiled sadly as she listened to them tell their stories of how they knew Angus and of what a great man he had been.

"He was the best," she agreed stoically.

Wraith's stomach clenched. She really had no idea how corrupt he was and that he was responsible for the exploitation of not only the mentally ill and disabled, but also children and youth. McNeil had used both groups to set up "drug nests" by commandeering the homes of the most vulnerable individuals and then grooming them to sell drugs and travel across counties, bringing his illegal trade to rural areas. So many lives had been ruined because of him.

The crowd had thinned. Wraith had seen no signs or similarities within the group that reminded him of the mysterious killer owl. He watched as a young woman no older than Pim came out of the chapel room, along with a small boy. Rankin stopped them. The girl was clearly upset and clutching the child by the hand protectively. He pulled them aside and seemed to be speaking harshly to the girl as he ushered them outside. By the time Rankin returned, he was red in the face. Wraith noticed, as he approached, he changed his expression to one of concern, adjusting his tie and straightening his jacket. "Things are beginning to wrap up, sweetheart. Would you like to go visit him in the chapel?"

Pim rubbed her neck reluctantly but nodded. Wraith took the undrunk cup of tea from her, throwing it into a trash bin. She stood up and walked over to the chapel door.

"I'll be here if you need me," he said behind her. No matter what he thought of Angus McNeil, she was innocent in all of this, and apparently, the old man had been her only family. No other family had shown up. She stood back from the coffin as if it might explode, stiff and rigid. Wraith was unsure if she was praying or saying good-bye to him as her head was lowered and her eyes were closed. Rankin came and stood beside him at the door.

"This will be tough on her," the lawyer said quietly. "I didn't think she would go in."

"Aye, but she's strong."

"When her father was murdered, she refused to believe he was gone. It was Angus who forced her to go to the viewing and look at him, so she would finally accept his death."

Murdered. That wasn't in any of the briefs Wraith read. In fact, he had never seen the police report. All he knew was that her father had passed away. He would have to have Gabriel send him the actual files. Pim suddenly turned and pushed past both of them, running out the front door. He found her standing by the car. "Come here," he said. Putting his arms around her, he pulled her to his chest, holding her.

"I'm sorry." She wiped her face on the sleeve of her dress.

"You don't need to be sorry. I know that was hard."

"I'm fine. It was just a moment." She stepped away from him, composing herself. "Would you mind taking me home?"

"Of course not." He opened the passenger door and helped her in, pulling the seatbelt tight across her.

She stopped him, taking the buckle, and gave him a strange look. "I can manage."

His jaw clenched. Never, had he met someone so willful. He shut her door and made his way around the car. The girl from the chapel stood outside a coffee shop across the street with the young boy, watching them. She drew back when she realized he saw her and grabbed the boy's hand, walking down the street.

Chapter 9

The sun glared through the windshield in blinding rays as it began its descent in the horizon. Pim shuffled through her purse for her sunglasses. The day had taken its toll. Seeing her grandfather dead in the coffin made it real. It was like she was reliving her father's death all over again. Her mother had been absent from that viewing also, feigning a migraine. It had been her grandfather who held her hand that day. Now, he too was gone.

"You okay?" Wraith asked, turning onto the main road.

"I told you I'm fine," she said sharply. Finding the glasses, she put them on.

"Can I ask you something? I don't want to upset you, but it might help with the case."

"You won't upset me." She hesitated, then added, "And I wouldn't quite call this a case. I'm still not convinced he was murdered. Graham said nothing to me about foul play and he was my grandfather's closest friend."

"Will you tell me about your father's death?"

She looked at him, taken aback. He kept glancing back in his review mirror. "There's nothing to tell. He was mugged."

"Is there anything else you remember?"

She stared out the window. Wasn't it enough she was helping him with her grandfather? She wasn't going to discuss her father with him. "I'm not talking about this right now. I need a drink." Wraith turned the car right on Great Western. "You've turned the wrong way," she said.

His eyes skimmed the mirror again. "We're being followed."

"Followed?" She started to turn around to look, but his hand came across her chest, stopping her.

"Don't. They'll see you." He sped up.

She looked in her side mirror. A silver BMW was closing in behind them. "How do you know they're following us?"

"I just do. They pulled out of a side street when we left the funeral home and have been on us ever since." He pushed a button on the steering wheel. "Call Gabriel." A number popped up on the touch screen on the dash.

"Calling Gabriel," a female voice said. The sound of a phone ringing filled the car.

"Wraith," a deep voice answered.

"Gabriel, I'm not alone." His eyes brushed past her before looking in the rearview mirror. "We're being followed right now. I need you to run a check on the number plate. SG68 FTH."

"Give me a minute."

Wraith veered across two lanes of traffic, making a sudden right turn.

"They're stolen plates," Gabriel said. "Let me pull you up on GPS. I'll help you lose him." He paused briefly. "You're coming up on a round-a-bout, take the second exit and then turn on your first left. I'll switch the signal to red right before you go through."

Wraith floored the accelerator, weaving in and out of traffic as they flew past other cars. The round-a-bout loomed ahead, and Pim held on for dear life as Wraith approached it at top speed. The tires squealed as he braked, and at the last second, he exited. The BMW kept up with him, matching his moves. He turned left. The light up ahead was already yellow and the car in front of them began to slow. Wraith swerved around it, barely making it as he blew through the now red light. The sound of screeching tires and the crunch of metal could be heard behind them. Pim turned around. The BMW sat in the middle of the intersection, demolished, after hitting a light pole. A stocky man exited the smoking car and fled down the street as they continued to speed away.

"We've lost him," Wraith said. "Thank you, Gabriel."

"Anytime, mate."

"Did you see the text I sent over regarding the report?"

"Aye, I'll have it to you as soon as I can."

"Roger that." Wraith ended the call. He put his hand on Pim's thigh. "Are you all right?"

"What in the hell was all that about? Why was someone following us?" She turned in her seat, facing him.

"I told you, your grandfather knew he was in danger. He was worried about you too."

"You think they were following me?"

"They wouldn't be following me, Primrose, no one knows who I am."

"Unless they found out you were working for my grandfather." She brushed his hand away.

"That's doubtful, since most of my investigation was done online."

"Who the fuck are you? I don't know many private investigators that wear designer Brioni suits and drive cars that cost four hundred thousand pounds. Not to mention, friends who can change the pattern of the traffic lights."

"I told you who I am and the fact I have money doesn't change anything. And Gabriel is an associate, not a friend."

He pulled up in front of a building. "Now, your grandfather paid me for my services, and I intend to finish the job."

"Whatever," she said, shaking her head. "I told you to take me home. Where are we?"

"My place. I need to pick up a few things." He got out of his car and walked around to her side, opening the door.

"I'll wait here."

"No, you won't," he said, reaching in and undoing her seatbelt. "I'm not leaving you alone. Especially with someone following us." He took her hand and helped her out. Not letting go, she was forced to walk with him into the residence. They took the elevator up to the fourth floor of his penthouse apartment. He unlocked the door, letting them in. "I'll just be a minute," he said, going upstairs.

Pim looked around. The place was beautifully decorated but sterile. There were no personal effects to give her a clue as to who he was or his past. She looked out the window. The last of the sun streaked the horizon in hues of bright orange and pink. Her place was only a few blocks from here.

He came back down the stairs, carrying a garment bag and a leather duffle. "What's that for?" she asked.

"I need clothes."

"What for?"

"You're not staying alone. We have no idea who was following us this afternoon, and they'll have no problem figuring out your address."

"Oh hell no." She started for the door. All she wanted was to be left alone. Between the turmoil at ballet, her grandfather's viewing, and now this person following them, she was exhausted.

He stopped her, taking her by the shoulders. "Primrose, listen to me. You're in danger. And whether you like it or not, I'm going to make sure you're safe."

Her heartbeat quickened. With his face just inches from

hers, he was no longer just intimidating. He was imposing. This man demanded compliance, something she rarely gave, but with the death and possible murder of her grandfather, she was considering. In truth, she was scared. "Do you really think I'm in danger?"

"I do."

She rubbed the bridge of her nose. "Fine, but only until we figure out who this person is."

Chapter 10

The blinds in Pim's flat came down automatically with the push of a button, shutting out the night sky. Wraith hung his garment bag in the hall closet and checked the rooms.

"I'm sorry. I don't have a guest bedroom," she said.

"No worries. The couch is fine."

"Would you like a glass of wine?" They had stopped and picked up dinner from a fish shop.

"Sure."

She kicked her high heels off and pulled down two glasses from the cabinet, pouring them each some as Wraith set the containers with their meals on the coffee table. Pim sat down next to him on the couch, tucking her feet up under her, and clicked the TV on with the remote.

The exaggerated lilt of the newscaster's voice filled the room. "Suspicion into business tycoon Angus McNeil's death continues to mount as reports of a masked interloper surface. A man wearing an owl disguise was seen running through the theater the night of the fatality. Was this a poorly timed stunt by the Scottish National Ballet or truly signs of foul play?"

Stripped

The reporter laughed at his own joke, leaving the audience with a vocal cliffhanger. "Coming up on the eight o'clock news."

Wraith turned it off, looking over at her.

She clenched her jaw and swallowed, tamping down the tears that threatened. "You didn't need to turn it off. I would rather know what people are saying."

"Facts are one thing. That's just sensationalism."

She picked at her fish, setting it down in exchange for her wine.

"Tell me about ballet?" he asked.

"What's there to tell?"

"I don't know. How did you get started?" He set his own empty container down, wiping his fingers on a napkin.

Her eyes narrowed. "You don't need to make small talk with me. We're not friends, and as far as I'm concerned, this is just business. You're no different than someone coming in to fix the electricity."

Wraith laughed. "Do you usually offer the electricity man a glass of wine?"

"Shut up," she said.

"Actually, the more I know about your life and your grandfather's, the better I'm able to connect the dots and hopefully, the sooner I'll figure this out." He leaned back comfortably, crossing his legs in a figure four. "Trust me, princess, I know we're not friends."

"Fuck off," she said, getting up to retrieve the wine bottle from the counter. She filled both their glasses back up before sitting down.

"Did you always know you wanted to dance?" His thumb stroked his glass casually, but Pim could see the control behind the subtle movement.

She took a deep drink of her wine. "I can't remember not dancing," she said, resigned, giving him a slight shrug. "My father wanted me to take ballet. I just happened to be good at it so when I was accepted into the Royal Ballet School, there was no discussion. I was sent away at age ten to London."

"But you do like it, or you still wouldn't be doing it."

She gave him a tight smile. "It's a love-hate relationship."

He uncrossed his legs and leaned forward, steepling his fingers. "You said your father was mugged?"

"Jesus Christ, this isn't a fucking therapy session." She picked up the food containers and empty wine bottle, taking them into the kitchen. Her heart hammered in her chest. She didn't know this man, yet he was stirring up something in her that had lain dormant, something she had forced deep into the shadows.

"I'm just trying to understand," he said, following her in and placing the wine glasses in the sink.

She turned and faced him, crossing her arms. "I don't talk about my father."

"Please, Primrose. I can't do this without you." His finger brushed her cheek, sending a shiver up her spine. Perhaps it was a warning. "I assume your father worked with your grandfather. There could be a connection."

She grabbed his arm, hard and rigid like steel, and looked him in the eyes. "Don't touch me," she snarled. She turned and opened a cupboard, and reaching up on tiptoes, she grabbed a bottle of scotch and two glasses.

"I don't think you need any more to drink," he said behind her.

"Let's get something straight." She pushed past him, heading into the living room. "I think we can both agree that we're *working* together. Well, if we are, then workmates don't tell each other what to do." She held up the bottle. The McCallum, twenty-five years cask. It was very good and very expensive. "Got it?"

His mouth quirked up at the corner and he arched his

brow. "If that's the case, then let me help you pour. *Workmate*." He pulled the cork off the top, smelling the contents before pouring them each a generous dram. Pim watched his eyes close in bliss as he savored the first sip. "At least we can agree on something."

She picked up her own glass and drained it, the smoky, chocolate orange hints biting at her throat.

"That's not how you drink scotch of that quality," he said disapprovingly.

She ignored him, pouring herself another glass. "You asked about my father. What do you want to know?"

"How old were you when he died?"

"Fourteen."

Wraith shook his head. "You said he was mugged."

"He was bludgeoned to death with a lead pipe that fractured his skull."

"Here in Glasgow?" he questioned.

She bit her bottom lip, focusing on the pain. The alcohol was taking effect and starting to dull her senses. She just hoped it would keep her emotions at bay. "No, Edinburgh. Well, actually, Leith. He was on a business trip, it was at night, and he was walking home from the docks."

He nodded, listening.

"I was sent home from school immediately. No one would tell me anything. Everyone spoke in whispers and if I came into the room, they stopped talking altogether. I only know so much because when the police came to speak to my mom, I listened in at the door, and then I found a file in my grandfather's house."

"A police report?" he questioned.

She nodded. "Along with his death certificate and photographs. Seeing the pictures, made it real. I looked up online how long he most likely suffered. I don't think it was long. He probably lost consciousness with the blow to the head, and after that, it was just a matter of bleeding out. I think that was the hardest part, the fact that no one would be truthful with me. I mean, I wasn't a child."

Wraith blanched. He didn't try to hide the look of horror on his face, and she hoped she had shocked him. "And they thought it was random, someone who robbed him, with that much violence."

"There was no other explanation."

"Did they ever catch who did it?"

"No." He had finished his whiskey and she poured him another glass. "I was sent back to school the next week, like nothing had happened. Four months later, my mother was remarried and moved to Canada. I've seen her five times since then."

"God, I'm sorry. It's hard to lose a parent." Normally, she hated that response but there was an empathy to his voice that led her to believe he might understand.

"Don't be. I'm lucky I had my grandfather." She put the stopper back on the whiskey. It had accomplished its goal, she was sufficiently numb. "I need to go to bed if I'm going to make it through tomorrow." She got up and went to the linen closet in the hallway, pulling out a sheet and blanket. When she returned, she froze. The hair on the back of her neck stood up and her whole body flushed with heat. Wraith had pulled a gun out of his duffle bag and was checking it. He could kill her right now if he wanted. He was nothing more than a stranger.

"It's not loaded," he said, without looking at her, and set it down on the table. "Do you have a security system."

"Yes." She swallowed hard, her throat dry, and showed him the panel on the wall, the situation now sobering.

He bent over, looking at the box. "What's the code?"

He was so close, she could smell his aftershave, warm and musky. As she leaned in, her hand brushed his while she entered in the number. She drew it back quickly, suddenly very aware that a handsome man stood inches from her as her initial fear and the rush of adrenaline that accompanied it turned into something more carnal.

She cleared her throat. "I'll show you where the bathroom is if you want to shower," she said. He followed her down the hall. "There are extra towels in the cabinet."

She looked up, and holding his gaze, she could read the same desire in his eyes that she knew was hiding in hers. This man was dangerous, the thought of having him, thrilling. She reached up and pulled his head down, kissing him.

He had her pushed up against the wall with her wrists pinned above her head in one of his large hands before she knew what was happening. She couldn't move, bound by his physical strength and at his mercy. He deepened the kiss, running his tongue over her full lips until she had no choice but to open for him, allowing him access. A moan escaped her as the intensity increased, the taste of spiced fruit on his breath an aphrodisiac, heightening the risk. He softened the kiss, the initial frenzied torment, now drawn out as he gently bit her lower lip. She was helpless and the rush she felt from it left her body throbbing.

"Little girls shouldn't play with fire," he said a bit harshly.

It was over as quickly as it started, and she was left standing there, mouth agape as he walked down the hall.

Chapter 11

Wraith stood at the door to Pim's studio, watching as she rehearsed the next morning completely unaware of his presence. When he woke up, he thought he had been dreaming, the elusive bird of prey just out of reach, but the music was real. She must have gotten up early to practice. She was mesmerizing, exquisite really. The words fragile and beautiful sprang to mind, as she moved and turned across the floor, her arms as graceful as a swan's wings. So different than the rebellious, hard girl she wanted the world to see. He admired her discipline as she had been at it for the past hour and a half. She finished, turning the music off and wiped her face with a towel.

He cleared his throat. "Odette, the white swan," he said softly.

She looked up at him, taking off her pointe shoes and the white practice tutu she wore. "You know the story."

"A bit. I was dreaming of that blasted owl mask when I woke up. It must have been the music."

Pim laughed. "Rudolf Nureyev re-choreographed it in 1984 for the Paris Opera Ballet, using Freud as his inspiration. To

Stripped

sum it up, Freud said when you dream of a bird or flying, it signifies nothing more than an inner desire for sexual activities." She raised her eyebrows. "Hence, your owl."

He coughed and surprisingly felt his cheeks grow warm. He should never have allowed the kiss to happen. God, she was eleven years younger than he was, and it was against The Watch's policy. "About last night, I, um... I think I drank—"

"For fuck's sake, grow up. It was a kiss. We had been drinking. I'm not looking for a relationship or a ring from you."

"I suppose not." Now he felt like the child. He knew she wanted to get by him, but he blocked the door. "Anyway. You're good. Very good. I thought you would have given yourself the day off."

She shook her head. "There are no days off. One, because there is always someone who is willing to work harder for your spot, and two, my body wouldn't allow it. It takes this long to warm it up, so I can move."

"I picked up breakfast for us. You didn't have anything in the house." He moved so she could get around him.

"You trusted me to stay alone?"

It was his turn to laugh. "I just went to the coffee shop on the corner." He handed her a cup. "I wasn't sure what a dancer ate so I got a little of everything. If I'm going off yesterday, I would say nothing, but it's going to be a long day and you'll need something in you."

She grabbed a hard-boiled egg and a sausage roll. "I eat," she said a bit defensively, sitting down on a barstool.

"What time is the funeral today?"

"One, but I need to stop by my grandfather's place and pick up my eulogy."

This would give him an opportunity to look in Angus' office. Gabriel had texted Wraith this morning saying there were no police records on Andrew McNeil's death. Either there was never a case, or someone had them removed, and he was banking on the latter. "If it's okay, I'm going to shower and get ready," he said.

Pim nodded, getting down from the stool. Wraith stopped her, and bending down, he held her leg. "You're bleeding."

Blood soaked the tape around her toenail. "I had to pull it off this morning. It's the second one, my other one came off yesterday. It's fine."

"It doesn't look fine. Christ, that must have hurt." He gently unwrapped the tape, the last part sticking to the raw skin where the nail used to be. He felt her flinch as he quickly tore the rest of the bandage off. The bleeding started up again.

"I'm used to it. My feet were never anything to look at anyway," she joked, but he could feel the tension in her calf muscle. He knew it hurt her.

"Go clean it up," he said, standing. "How are you going to wear a shoe today?"

"Really, it's nothing. I'll rub some tooth numbing gel on it. I won't feel a thing."

Pim sprayed perfume on her neck and wrists and looked at herself in the mirror. She wore a tight, black, sleeveless dress, reminiscent of Audrey Hepburn, with a string of pearls her grandfather had given her, adding a pair of three-quarter length black gloves to complete the ensemble. Slipping her feet into her black pumps, she checked her hair and tucked a flyaway strand into her low bun. Wraith was waiting for her on the couch. He stood as she came in the room, buttoning his suit jacket. "Sorry I took so long," she said, trying not to look at him. He looked handsome in his black suit and tie and it reignited the small spark of desire from last night. She had never been kissed like that before—restrained to where she couldn't move, rough and controlled. She liked it. It was when he touched her leg to look at her toe, gentle and concerned, that made her uncomfortable. No one in nineteen years had cared if she was in pain. Ballet bred a culture of risk, normalizing pain. She had been taught to both suppress and trivialize it.

"It was worth the wait. You look grand," he said, helping her with her coat before grabbing his own. "You know you're going to freeze."

"Work partners, remember. If I freeze, it's my fault."

They headed downstairs and Wraith drove the short distance to Kingsborough Gardens, pulling up to her grandfather's townhouse. The day was cold and dreary. Dark clouds, heavy with rain, sat low in the sky, disagreeable and threatening. Pim got out of the car, pulling her coat tight around her as they walked up the path to the door. She turned the key in the lock and let them in, punching the code into the alarm. "That's weird."

"What?" Wraith asked, taking his coat off and hanging it up.

"Someone disabled the alarm. I know I set it when I left on Sunday, but it was deactivated."

He looked over her shoulder. "Does someone else have a key?"

"No, I should be the only one besides my grandfather." She headed into his office.

"Are you sure Graham Rankin doesn't have one as his solicitor, or a housekeeper perhaps?"

"I'm sure. I let Graham in the other day. It's why he wanted me here, and the housekeeper was given the week off after everything happened." She picked up her notebook on his desk. "My eulogy's been moved."

"I'm sure there's a logical explanation," he said, scanning the bookshelf. "Do you mind if I look around in here?"

She shook her head. "Go ahead. Graham already looked on Sunday. I'm going upstairs to check the bedrooms." She took the stairs two at a time to the second story. Her grandfather's bedroom was at the end of the hall. Giving it a cursory look from the door, it appeared as if everything was in order. She couldn't bring herself to go in. It was still too emotional, and she needed to remain strong for today. The other bedroom was hers. He had it set up for her after her father died and her mother moved. She popped her head in. The large, four-poster bed was unmade, the pale pink duvet pushed down to the bottom. Someone had slept there. She looked around, opening the closet and drawers. Everything seemed to be in order until she got to the bathroom. The floor of the bathtub was still wet, and a damp towel hung from a hook.

Wraith picked the lock on Angus' desk, flipping through the papers. Most, were to do with his corrupt businesses, deeds to properties, titles, and bank drafts organized in files. He closed them and continued to search. At the back, he found what he was looking for, the police report for Andrew McNeil. He pulled out his phone and took pictures of the papers as he quickly glanced at them. At the back was a stack of photographs. To describe them as violent, wouldn't do them justice; they were brutal and savage. He imagined Pim looking at them as a young girl and shook his head. No one should remember their father this way. He closed the folder and put it back, pulling out another one. This one was labeled Natasha. Inside, was a picture of a young girl. It looked like the same girl from the viewing yesterday. She was wearing a traditional Russian sarafan folk dress and her blonde hair was in two braids. The only other thing in the file was a bank draft for twenty thousand pounds. Wraith stuck the photograph in his pocket and put the rest back, shutting the drawer.

"Someone's definitely been in the house," Pim said, standing at the door. "My bed has been slept in and the bathtub is still wet."

"Show me," he said, following her upstairs.

She opened the door to the room. "It doesn't make sense. If you were going to break in, why would you spend the night? I can't find anything missing."

Wraith ran his hand over the bed. She was right; someone had been here and not just one person, but two. He could see the imprints of their bodies where they lay on the sheets. He looked at his watch. "We need to get going. We can come back after the funeral."

Pim nodded, her brows pulled together in a frown, clearly troubled. Wraith put his hand on her shoulder, guiding her downstairs. He put his coat on and sent Gabriel the pictures and a text, while Pim set the alarm.

Found the file. Andrew McNeil was murdered. He was found with his wallet and car keys. Definite cover up.

Chapter 12

The church was already packed by the time they arrived. It would be standing room only soon. Graham Rankin approached, kissing Pim on the cheek. "How are you holding up, sweetheart?"

"I'm fine. I wasn't expecting it to be this crowded," she said, looking around sadly.

"Your grandfather touched a lot of peoples' lives." He brushed her cheek briefly before helping her with her coat, the diamond and gold rings on his fingers garish.

Wraith scanned the growing crowd. The elite of Glasgow society had turned out, not a great representation of the working-class city, and definitely not emblematic of the lives Angus ruined. How many of them did he have in his pocket through extortion and bribes?

"The front pew is saved for you and the other speakers," Graham said, giving Wraith an unwelcome sideways glance. Clearly, he was not invited to sit there. "We'll walk in when the service starts."

Pim looked up at Wraith. "Sorry," she mouthed.

Stripped

He hushed her. "I'll go get a seat," he said. "I'll find you when it's over."

Graham took her purse from her, adding it to her coat. "I'll put these in the side room."

She clutched her small notebook, taking a deep breath and blowing it out slowly.

Wraith pulled her aside before leaving. "Are you sure you're okay, Primrose?" he asked.

"I'm fine," she said sharply, rubbing at an invisible spot on her arm. "I just want this to be over."

The thug from the viewing yesterday came out of the room with Rankin, giving Wraith a tight nod. He was to be watched again. "I'll be in the back if you need me."

"I won't," she said. Wraith gave her shoulder a squeeze and kissed her on her forehead before walking off. He could hear her behind him, muttering, "Fuck off."

He smiled to himself. Entering the chapel, he found a place against the back wall where he could stand, giving him a good vantage point of the room. The guests talked amongst themselves in small groups, laughing and exchanging pleasantries as if they were at a party instead of a funeral. Even Graham Rankin had a sense of nervous excitement about him, taking on the new self-appointed role of boss now that he was out from under Angus's shadow. The coffin was already up front, along with several large flower arrangements and a portrait of Angus, looking smugly out at the congregation. Somehow, Wraith imagined the man would enjoy a day like this, people paying their respects, thinking him a grand and important man. A packed house and not a true friend in attendance, he surmised. Looking around, he spotted Peter Brindy, apparently recovered, and several of the dancers sitting in a middle pew, along with the SNB board members.

The sounds of a bagpipe filled the church, resonating

through the pews and indicating the start of the service as a piper led the small processional down the aisle. Graham escorted Pim, followed by a few other men and the reverend. Peter reached out for her hand as she passed. He clutched it for a second as he held his other hand over his heart, in a dramatic show of sympathy and affection. *Fucking bastard*. The muscles in Wraith's jaw clenched. The service was short, in and of itself, thankfully. He couldn't imagine a man like Angus having a soul, much less being religious and worthy of God's blessing into the afterlife. When it was Pim's turn to deliver her eulogy, he was impressed with how eloquent she was, remaining stoic and poised, for someone so young. The reverend gave the benediction and the piper began to play, the drone of the pipes splitting the stillness as he led the recessional out. People began to leave, shaking hands and offering their cheap condolences about a man most of them probably either hated or feared. *Bloody circus*. Wraith stayed back, watching. He thought the chapel was empty when he spotted the girl from yesterday. She was by herself today, the young boy nowhere to be seen, and she stood up front praying. He moved closer. She was speaking in Russian and crossed herself, then touched the coffin and said, "Pokoysya s miron, Papa."

Wraith didn't mean to scare her, but when she turned around and saw him, all the color left her face. She looked for a way to escape, spying an exit toward the chancel.

"Natasha, wait," he said. "It's okay. I won't hurt you."

"Net. Net," she said, backing up toward the door. "Please. Leave me alone."

She fled before he could say anything else, but he knew enough Russian to understand what she said. *Rest in peace, Papa.*

Stripped

Pim stood at the bar with Peter. The relaxed chatter of the guests, absolved from the somberness of loss with the conclusion of the service, filled the room as they shared toasts and tributes over drams of whiskey and fried appetizers. Rankin arranged for one of the restaurants her grandfather owned to close to the public for the evening, in order to host a private reception for some of the funeral attendees. Tomorrow, their lives would resume, as if nothing had ever happened. These were not friends, yet they continued to offer her their sympathy as if they cared.

"Who's the guy?" Peter asked casually, handing her a white wine.

She looked over her shoulder at Wraith. He was in the corner on his phone. He saw her watching him and hung up. "He's a friend of the family. He's staying with me right now."

Paul, her dance partner, came up behind her and put his arm around her, kissing her on the side of the head. "God, I miss you, Pim."

She gave him a smile and looked at her wine warily. Her mouth was parched, but she refused to drink anything Peter gave her. "Thanks, I miss you too."

"I heard what Zora did, kicking you out of class." Peter lifted her chin, so she had to look at him. "She didn't have the right to do that. She was just upset because of Irina."

Wraith joined their group. Peter dropped his hand and she was glad to be rid of his touch, now finding it disconcerting. "Sorry if I interrupted." He took the glass from her and set it on the bar.

"No, not at all." She gave him a faint smile. "Wraith, this is Peter Brindy, artistic director of Scottish National Ballet, my dance partner Paul and his fiancé, Richard."

He gave the men a curt nod. "Robert Wraith, it's nice to meet you."

"Does that mean Pim can come back when she wants?" Paul asked, picking back up on the conversation.

"Of course," Peter said. "The sooner, the better."

"Thank God, I can't lift Catriona another day, she doesn't help at all," Paul said, rubbing his shoulder for emphasis. "It's like picking up a Highland coo."

Wraith cleared his throat. Pim nudged him with her elbow to keep quiet. He wouldn't understand that nasty comments were not only accepted, but often characteristic of the ballet world. Thick skin was required. "The solicitors are reading the will in the afternoon, but I can come for the morning."

"Good," Peter said. "I want to run the coda from act three and the pas de deux. You're missing something, Paul."

"It's Catriona's fault. I can't do it without Pim. It's why she's my partner."

Wraith's phone rang. "Excuse me. I have to take this." He made his way back to the corner.

A gentleman in a cheap suit with a paunch belly approached them. "Primrose McNeil?" he inquired.

"Yes," she said.

"I'm Charlie McGuire from The Scottish Sun. I had a question about your grandfather." He pulled a reporter's notebook from his front pocket.

"This is a private party," Peter said. "How did you get in here?"

Paul put his arm around her protectively.

"Can you tell me if the allegations against your grandfather are true. Is he Glasgow's biggest drug lord?"

"Get the hell out of here," Peter yelled.

"What are you talking about?" Pim took a step forward.

"I have a witness who will testify your grandfather was the largest distributor of opioids in western Scotland. Some called him the Godfather."

Pim's heart sunk. They were the same rumors she had

heard before. The day was catching up to her and she was no longer able to keep the smile plastered on her face. "You fucking piece if shite." She pushed the man in the chest hard enough to cause him to take a step back.

"Can I quote you on that?" he asked, putting his pencil behind his ear as he readjusted his tie.

People were starting to turn around and stare and she felt the room closing in around her. She needed air and a place where she could think by herself. "Piss off," she said, and pushing past the reporter, she grabbed her coat from the hostess table and ran out of the restaurant.

Chapter 13

Wraith watched as she fled, hanging up on Gabriel as he made his way over to the gathering crowd. Peter was yelling at a man.

"What happened?" he asked Paul.

"This dobber walked in and started accusing Pim's grandfather of horrible things. Some kind of reporter."

Wraith inserted himself between Peter and the balding man, ripping the notebook from his hand. "What paper?" he asked. McGuire, much shorter in stature than Wraith, backed up. He grabbed the reporter's cheap polyester shirt, bringing his face within inches of his own. "What God damn paper?"

"The S-S-Scottish Sun," he stuttered, little balls of spit gathered in the corners of his mouth.

"Fucking tabloid." Wraith gripped his shirt tighter, twisting it in his fist. "If you so much as print one fucking word about the McNeils, I'll make sure you're on a liquid diet for the rest of your pathetic life. Understand?"

The man raised an unkempt eyebrow and straightened his back. "Free speech," he had the guts to say.

Wraith punched him squarely in the stomach, and he

dropped to the ground, writhing, as he tried to catch his breath. "Someone get this arsehole out of here." Grabbing his coat, he left. Pim couldn't have gotten far; she was wearing four-inch stilettos. It was sprinkling rain and the streets were wet and dark, the headlights of passing cars reflected off the water in long streaks. He looked around, but she was nowhere to be seen. Paul followed him out. "Where would she have gone?" Wraith asked.

Paul looked at him with what might have been respect. "Somewhere she could be alone. She was wearing thin, I could see it in her eyes. You don't dance with someone for years without learning to read them intimately. My guess is she either went home or to Òran Mór."

"Òran Mór, the bar?"

"Aye, but she won't be in the bar or clubs. You'll find her in the auditorium if there's not an event going on."

Wraith drove to her flat first, but found it empty. He left the car and walked the short distance to the pub, using the time to process the past events. Gabriel agreed that Andrew McNeil's murder had been intentional and not a random mugging. The brutality of the attack was probably meant as a message, and the fact that he was at the docks meant it was presumably for business. Import or export was the question. And of what? Drugs in Edinburgh were funneled up from London; even Angus wasn't crazy enough to impinge on that area. It would start an all-out turf war. The other question was Natasha. Gabriel couldn't find any records of her in Scotland but that would be hard with only a first name. He had clearly heard the word *papa*. Was she a relation of some sort? She had to be around the same age as Pim. The fact she kept turning up the past two days suggested some type of connection.

Wraith climbed the stairs to the entrance of the old brick church. It was Tuesday night and the venue sat practically empty, except for the restaurants. Climbing the spiral staircase, he found her in the balcony of the auditorium by herself, sitting at a table. He stopped and watched her, his conscience in juxtaposition with his responsibility to The Watch, the contrasting effects both destructive. Either way, she would get hurt in the end. The more time he spent with her, the guiltier he felt. He was asking for her trust. She was helping him find her grandfather's killer, the very thing he himself was—an assassin. He weighed the principles of responsibility he felt. Where on the spectrum of evil did he lie if he was willing to use Pim as his pawn, if he was willing to kill? How far removed was he from Angus's morality?

She felt his eyes on her as he studied her and glanced up as he sat down at the table. "You shouldn't have run off," he said. "You're still in danger."

She regarded him with narrowed eyes, taking a sip of her drink. "This was the last place I saw my father before he died. He brought me here to see the mural."

Wraith looked up, taking in the celestial ceiling, a mix of ancient mythic symbolism, astrology, and local legend, as it creeped down the walls.

"It's beautiful," he said. "I can imagine one could spend hours here looking at it, trying to interpret it."

"Alasdair Gray became one of my favorite artists. I read *Lanark* five times that year as I tried to come to terms with my father's death. I came here when I could, constantly trying to find the answer."

He reached out, taking her hand in his, their fingers interlocking. "He told me that day, an artist should have broad experiences and a good education, to listen to music, read poetry, literature, visit exhibitions. The more an artist knows, the deeper their spirituality and the better their art." She smiled, shaking her head as she finished her drink. "I'm sorry. I'm rambling."

"No, please continue." His thumb stroked her palm.

"I wanted to be that artist, that dancer. I thought if I could be perfect, then maybe I could make him proud. But no answer came, no matter how hard I tried or searched. There was no answer to the violence he experienced and the one thing I loved, I began to resent. Then hate. There's no perfection in art. That's what Gray finally taught me. What defines you as an artist, is the bravery to be extraordinarily different. Not perfect. But still, I try."

"Can I get you another drink?"

She held up her empty glass. "Sure."

Wraith came back with two whiskeys, setting them down.

"And you, Robert Wraith, what secrets do you have lurking in your past? What made you want to become a private investigator?"

"You can say I didn't chose it. It chose me."

"So, we have that in common." She gave him a smile. "But you're not from Glasgow."

"No."

She held up her hand, stopping him. "Wait, let me guess. My father used to say Glasgow was like the black swan. Gritty, yet mesmerizing." She looked at him then reached out for his hand, missing his touch. "No, you're too good for Glasgow. You are more Edinburgh. Definitely Edinburgh. He used to say she was the white swan, beautiful and refined."

He frowned. "Close. I'm from a small town called Killin, but I went to academy in Edinburgh. Merchiston."

"How very posh of you."

His thumb resumed its gentle perusal. "It wasn't like that. My parents were both killed in a car crash. My grandmother raised me. She didn't have much money. I got a scholarship and she insisted I go." A shadow crossed his eyes.

"I'm sorry," she said simply. She understood better than anyone and knew there was really nothing else she could say.

He gave her hand a squeeze. "Well, Ms. Glasgow, I guess that makes you the black swan then."

"Always." She looked up at the ceiling and wondered, not for the first time, if her father was proud. "We should probably go."

He helped her up and they went downstairs, leaving. The light rain had turned into a downpour. "I knew I should have brought my car," Wraith said, opening an umbrella.

"It's fine." She smiled. He put his arm around her as they walked to her place. They were drenched by the time they made it back. "I'm sure these shoes are ruined," she said at the bottom of the stairwell, wobbling on a broken heel. "They'll never be the same."

He lowered the umbrella and picked her up, carrying her to the third floor. The hallway that led to her flat was pitch black, and she fumbled with her key after he set her down. "I don't remember it being this dark," Wraith said, concerned.

"It's not. The lights must be out." A shadow in the corner moved and took off running the other direction. Wraith shoved her through the door. "Lock yourself in. Don't answer it unless I tell you to," he yelled, taking off after the person.

Pim shut the door and locked it, her hands shaking.

Wraith returned within minutes, knocking. "It's me, Primrose," he said. She looked through the peephole and let him in.

"Did you see who it was?" she asked, shivering.

"No, they disappeared down the stairs. Whoever it was, broke all the light bulbs. They wanted it dark." He checked the windows. "Have you set the alarm."

"Not yet." He limped over to the panel, enabling it. "We need to upgrade you to one with cameras."

She pulled the scotch down from the cabinet, pouring

them each some. "Do you think this person was waiting for me?"

"Yes." He took the glass from her. "You're shaking. You need to go warm up."

She nodded and, taking her drink, went into her room and turned on the shower. The bathroom quickly filled with steam. She slid her dress off and piled her damp hair into a bun on top of her head then got under the hot water, hoping to wash off the memories of the day and now this new threat. When she was finished, she got out and dried off, going into her room. Wraith stood in the doorway holding his drink. He had taken off his tie and rolled up the sleeves on his white dress shirt. "I'm sorry," he said, his eyes not leaving her. "I was just making sure you were okay."

She sat down on the edge of the bed, holding the towel around herself as he turned to leave. "Wait," she said. "Stay."

Chapter 14

He should walk away. He rubbed his face, the stubble from his beard rough against his palm. *Walk away. She's too young.* Yet her thoughts and actions today spoke otherwise. She had what he would call an old soul. In truth, he found her fascinating and the darkness that haunted her mind provoked something in him, challenged him. Green eyes from his past, continued to warn him. *Walk away.* He blinked, trying to clear his mind of their noble innocence. They did not belong to him. They never would.

He found himself sitting on the bed next to her. She let the towel drop. Her body, while extremely thin, was strong, each muscle, long, lean and developed. He set his drink down on the nightstand and laid her back, running his hand down the flat planes of her stomach. Throwing the towel on the floor, he kissed her. She responded instantly, arching underneath him. She brought her hands up and started to unbutton his shirt, but he stopped her, pinning one of her arms above her head.

Her eyes narrowed, intent on his face. "I'm not fucking you with your clothes on."

"Christ, the mouth on you. I should wash it out with soap," he said, slightly taken aback at her bluntness.

She laughed. "Tit for tat. I'm naked." She stared at him boldly, daring him.

He sat her up, so she straddled him as he sat on the edge of the bed. "It's not a pretty sight, princess."

She undid the buttons, sliding the shirt off his shoulders, and froze. Her hand came up, touching his ruined chest softly. "Pretty is an understatement. It's a bloody, fucking mess," she said, pushing him back.

Maybe it was the viciousness of the scars, red and welted, that covered his upper body in an ugly and intrusive way, but the same unguarded lust from last night came over her. He understood her nightmares. He had his own, and it made her want him even more.

"Someone once said they were beautiful."

"Someone was lying." She undid his belt, sliding it from his pants. "They're bloody gruesome, but I like them."

"Of course, you do." He had her flipped over on her back in an instant and a large hand grabbed both her wrists. His fingers dug into her skin, reminding her he was in control. The wetness grew between her legs. "You don't get to touch," he said, placing her hands above her head. He unfastened the button on his pants and pulled his cock out. Already hard, he spread her legs apart and ran it along her cleft. He entered her in one thrust as she cried out, stretching to accommodate him.

While her past was certainly not innocent, it had been over two years since she was with anyone. She brought her hands between them.

"Leave them," he barked, putting them back above her, holding them there. She started to say something, but he silenced her, kissing her coarsely. Her orgasm began to build deep inside as he continued to drive into her with an incessant hunger, and an intoxicating heat unfurled throughout her body.

"Please," she begged.

"Petitions?" he asked in her ear, his breath sending shivers up her spine, bringing her that much closer to the edge. She had never felt so consumed by a man before. "Please what, Primrose?"

She couldn't speak, couldn't think. At the moment, he devoured any rational thought with his control and power. She cried out as her climax shattered within her, and his body tensed with his own release. He looked down, his eyes dark with satisfaction and let go of her wrists as he pulled out of her. They were silent, the only sound, the ragged inhale and exhale of their breathing as they lay on the bed, returning to reality.

His hand covered his face. "Christ, we shouldn't have done that."

She rolled over on her stomach, her head turned so she faced him. "You worry too much. I've already told you I'm not looking for a relationship. It was sex, plain and simple. It doesn't have to be complicated."

"I don't think sex is ever just plain and simple. I'm supposed to be protecting you."

She laughed at this. "After the reading of the will tomorrow, we go our separate ways. That was the deal. If you haven't figured out what you need by then, I don't think I can help you."

"Primrose, the threat against you is real, just like it was for your grandfather, or did you already forget that someone followed us in the car and was waiting outside your flat?"

She reached out tentatively and touched one of the scars on his chest. "Why should I trust you?"

He didn't stop her, though he didn't answer right away. When he did, his voice was far off as if he were missing more than remembering something. "It was an IED blast during the war. I was stationed in Afghanistan. It should have killed me."

"You were a soldier?"

"Aye, SBS. I was just a lad. I couldn't have been much older than you."

If he meant to offend her, she ignored it. "Some of these scars look new."

His jaw tightened. Whatever he was recalling or lost, obviously caused him suffering. "I had shrapnel removed." He turned on his side, looking at her. "You're right; you shouldn't trust me."

"I don't."

It was his turn to ask a question. His finger traced the primrose tattoo down her back. "I wouldn't think a dancer could have a tattoo so visible."

"It's not forbidden. I have to cover it when I perform, which can be difficult, but when I got it, I wasn't really thinking of those things. I wasn't going to dance again."

"*Behind every beautiful thing, there's some kind of pain*. Words to live by."

"For people like us," she said.

He took her hand. "What do you mean, *for people like us*?"

"People who live with guilt and regrets. People who know what it feels like to hurt. We feel guilty about all the little things because we don't want to face the big ones."

"I've killed men. They died in my care because of my decisions. What's your big one?"

She pulled her hand from his, tucking it under her cheek, missing the warmth it offered almost immediately. "I think my grandfather bought me my position in the company. SNB needed money and he was one of their biggest benefactors."

He tucked a piece of hair that came loose from her bun

behind her ear, his touch delicate. "Confessions of the broken," he said and gave her a delusive smile. "Why the primrose, other than it being your name?"

"My father chose my name. Scottish primrose grows in the north, by the coast. It has five heart-shaped petals. I like to think they stand for hope, grace, faith, truth and love."

He laughed outright at this. "Yer aff yer heid," he said in broad Scots. "Bloody bullshite."

She smiled. "Fuck off."

"Now, that's my girl." He kissed her quickly on the lips. "Get some rest, Primrose. You're safe tonight."

She closed her eyes but knew sleep would elude her. *That's my girl.* No one had ever said those words to her, especially not a handsome man she had just slept with.

Chapter 15

Wraith watched from the corner of the studio as Pim rehearsed. He had dropped her off this morning for class and went to the café to do research on his laptop, hitting dead end after dead end. No one stuck out as a possible suspect for the thief assassin, and if it was drug related, he could find no correlation to the person threatening Pim. The CCTV cameras near her flat had all been disabled. Whoever was following her, knew they were being watched. As for the persons who trespassed at Angus' house, there were no cameras facing his door, a convenience Wraith was sure the old man paid for to conceal his iniquitous business dealings, leaving associates free to come and go unnoticed.

"Take it again from the top of the coda," Peter said, running his hand along his ponytail. "Paul, you look bloody constipated. I need more height on your grande jetés or I'm fucking cutting you."

Wraith watched as Paul mouthed across the room to Pim. "You okay?"

She nodded as the music began and Paul took his place for

the start of his variation. Wraith's eyes narrowed. A suspicious red spot had formed on the front of her pointe shoe. She limped to the corner, awaiting her turn, adjusting the black tutu she wore. As Paul finished his section, she entered, walking gracefully to the center of the room and began a sequence of thirty-two fouetté turns, stirring up the entire space, an enchantress of seduction.

An elderly gentleman joined Wraith in the corner by the door. "She's something to watch," he said admiringly, his aged eyes cloudy and opaque. He pulled a handkerchief from his pocket and wiped them. "A dancer like our Rosy comes along once in a lifetime."

Wraith nodded. "Aye, so different from the white swan."

"It takes someone special to pull off both roles. The innocence and perfection of Odette, fragile and fearful, and the thrill and charisma of Odile, dangerous to even herself."

"Again," Peter shouted. "We'll keep doing it until you fucking get it right. You're bloody Prince Siegfried, you're supposed to be impressing her. Fucking impress her."

The spot on Pim's shoe had grown. "Sorry." Paul motioned to her. She shook her head. The music started and they began again.

"She'll be sore tonight. This is some of the most difficult choreography." He held his hand out to Wraith. "Sorry, Niall Leonard, Ballet Master."

"Robert Wraith. I'm a friend of Primrose."

"I heard Rosy had a companion. I've never seen her with anyone in the two years she's been with us. I'm glad you came."

The music cut off abruptly. "Again," Peter yelled.

"I don't think Pim—" Paul started to say.

"She's fucking fine," he said dismissively, waiving his hand at her. "Maybe if you get it right, she won't have to do it again."

Stripped

"I'm fine," she said to Paul, taking her place. The whole tip of her shoe was red at this point.

The accompanist started again at the beginning of the variation. Wraith watched, disgusted with Peter as Pim danced through the pain without ever letting on her toe hurt.

When she was finished, Peter stopped them. "Fucking hell. I'll run the pas de deux with Pim. Paul, you can fucking watch and I'll show you how it's done. You're supposed to be enraptured with her." He turned to the piano player. "Pick it up at the second stanza."

The dancer playing the evil Rothbart finished warming up and joined Peter and Pim in the center of the floor. Wraith had seen enough ballet to know that Peter was touching her unnecessarily, his hand brushing over and lingering on her breasts and thighs. He brought her down from a lift above his head, their faces inches from each other, and ran his hand down her face and neck, a depraved hunger filling his eyes. A sudden flash of anger burned in Wraith, and he was glad when they were finished before he had to recognize it for what it was—jealousy. Peter let go of her, walking away. "You can go. Catriona will run it with Paul," he said callously, not even looking at Pim as he brushed her off.

Pim took the tutu off and pulled on a pair of sweat pants. Grabbing her bag, she went over and spoke to Paul before leaving. Niall stopped her on the way out. "Soak your foot when you get home, Rosy," he said, patting her hand. "You did well today."

"I will." She gave him a weak smile, but Wraith could see the strain in her eyes.

He followed her out. "Stop," he said, catching up to her. "Let me help you."

She shook her head. "Not here. I can't appear weak. I just need to go."

He took her bag from her as she hobbled to his car, getting

in. Fog blanketed the city in oppressive grayness, limiting visibility. "What the hell was all that about?" he asked, sitting down and starting the engine. "What does he have against Paul?" He reached across and checked her seatbelt.

"It wasn't a punishment for Paul. It was a punishment for me," she said, taking the pointe shoe off her good foot and putting on a soft bootie.

"Why you? You looked amazing."

"Probably for the other night. The fact that I didn't wake up in his bed. He'll have taken it as rejection."

"He's lucky he wasn't arrested. You need to say something. He can't treat you like that."

"He can. The ballet world is really insular. He has the authority to ruin my career if he wants. It's intensely competitive and hypercritical; you can't cave to the pressures. You learn to shut up and live with it or get out. Peter is a control freak. I tested that the other night."

"Christ," he said, pulling out onto the road. His low beams barely cut through the heavy mist. "What did Paul say to you at the end?"

"Paul didn't say anything to me. I told him not to worry that Peter was being a cunt. Then I reminded him that he was the star now. This is a big opportunity for him."

"I thought you were the star."

"Nureyev choreographed it with the prince at the heart of the narrative. The black swan is a symbol of his true homosexual desires. I told Paul to think of me as Richard."

"You said star now? Was this not his part from the beginning?" Wraith reduced his speed as they crept over the Kingston Bridge.

"No, when Irina was hurt, her partner Thomas was so upset, he stepped down. Which was fine with me because I hate partnering with him. He dropped me once."

"And who was the lad playing Rothbart?"

"His name's Jerome. Why?"

"I'm just trying to paint a picture of it all," he said. "It's fascinating. Ballet is so beautiful and graceful to watch. It's a whole other world on the inside."

"It's not that bad, and in the end, we all have the same goal," she said a bit defensively.

"And what's that?"

"The stage. When the curtains open, we want to be perfect."

Pim pulled her foot, pointe shoe and all, out of the tub of hot water and Epsom salts. The water, stained pink from the blood from her shoe, seeped into the towel she set it on, spreading out like a modern art painting, abstract and tangible, offering her a brief emancipation from her mind and the pain. "I think it's soaked long enough." They had an hour before they needed to be at her grandfather's place.

Wraith came from the kitchen and knelt down in front of where she sat on the couch.

"I think I can do it myself," she said.

"It will be easier if I help you." He untied the ribbons around her ankle and slid her heel out of the back. "This will be the worst part," he said as he swiftly removed the shoe from her toe. She grimaced, trying to hold back her tears. She didn't want to cry in front of him. He looked up at her. "You okay?"

She nodded, reaching down toward her tights.

"Let me."

"There's a hole on the bottom; you need to flip it over my toes." Her voice was shaking. "Do it fast."

Wraith found the opening and quickly detached the remaining material from her toe, pulling the foot of the tights to her ankle. The raw and inflamed nail bed began to bleed again. He carefully wrapped it in a gauze.

Pim grabbed her foot, squeezing, her knuckles white from the pain. Spots danced in front of her eyes as she took a deep breath.

Wraith moved so he sat beside her and began to rub her shoulders. "That's it, over." He kissed the side of her head. "That's my girl."

She took a deep, ragged breath as the pain in her foot began to diminish. The afternoon loomed large in front of her and her emotions were already sensitive from rehearsal. The intimacy of Wraith tending her became too much. He would be leaving soon, she reminded herself.

"Who are your main suspects?" she asked, hoping to relieve the tension in the room. "Graham Rankin seems to gain a lot from my grandfather's death."

"It wasn't him."

"How can you be so sure?" She opened the bottle of Anbesol and painted a small amount over her nailbed, sucking in her breath until the stinging sensation subsided and the numbing effect began to take hold.

"Rankin's not a leader. He's hoping to ride the coattails of your grandfather for as long as he can, but men won't follow him."

"You seem so sure."

"I am. He's a formidable strategist, but his abrasive nature rubs people the wrong way. He's nothing more than a sidekick and he knows it. He needed your grandfather more than anyone."

"Do you have any other suspects?" She placed a piece of gauze over the nail bed and tore off a length of medical tape, wrapping it around the bandage.

"It's puzzling. Your grandfather's death, pushing him over the rail, almost seems like a crime of passion. The car chase and stalking your flat were calculated and planned out. They don't match."

"Do you think you'll figure it out?" she asked.

"Yes, but you're not out of danger, princess. I want you to stay close to me and do what I tell you to until we catch this person."

His words cut a direct path to her core, and for the first time, she questioned her decision to get involved with him. Everything he said to her and everything she perceived, was momentary. They were just words; there was no meaning or conviction behind them. Tomorrow, he would be gone.

Chapter 16

The clock on her grandfather's wall struck two, and a soft bell chimed twice, counting the hours, loyal and steady like an old friend. Pim used to love the sound as a girl when she spent her holidays here. It reminded her she actually had a home and offered a sense of security after boarding away and being on her own. Now, she sat on the couch in Angus' office awaiting the reading of his will, though there was no refuge the swing of the pendulum could offer this time. Its ring foreshadowed only perfidious last wishes. It was all pomp and circumstance anyway, anyone who was named a beneficiary in his trust had already received a copy of it. Hers had been delivered yesterday. It sat, unopened, on the counter in her flat.

She looked around at the small group gathered, recognizing a few of his business associates. Graham had set up extra chairs, allowing everyone a seat. Peter entered, along with a board member of SNB. He gave her a nod and smile before sitting down. Wraith put his arm around her, rubbing her shoulder as he whispered in her ear, "Why's he here?"

She didn't have time to answer. Graham stood up from

behind the desk. "As most of you know by now, Angus named me as executor-dative of his will. I have sworn an oath before a solicitor, Douglas Morris," he pointed to a slender, middle-aged man in a tweed suit, "of the true valuation of the estate and that the estate will be distributed in accordance with the law and the terms of the will. If anyone would like to see the affidavit, I have it here." He held up a piece of paper. "The total valuation of the estate, including assets, comes to five hundred and thirty-six million pounds after the inheritance tax is paid."

There were a few gasps and Pim felt a headache coming on. It was an obscene amount of money. Her toe throbbed in the black riding boots she wore. "Angus was a great man. He considered himself a philanthropist," Graham continued. "The following organizations will each be receiving a sum of one million pounds: Community of Helping Hands, Glasgow Foodbank, Feed the Children, Riverside Museum, Scottish National Ballet, Scottish Opera, and Òran Mór."

Pim glanced over at the manager of Òran Mór and smiled. Peter, who was sitting in front of the young man, blew her a kiss, thinking she was looking at him.

"Angus has asked that I continue to oversee the running of his businesses. The rest of the estate has been bequeathed to the pride and joy of his life, his granddaughter, Primrose McNeil."

Someone cleared her throat in the back of the room. Everyone turned to look. A young girl stood there with a little boy.

"Dear God, what are you doing here?" Graham said, going over to the girl. "This is a private family gathering."

"I am family," she said in a Russian accent. "He is family." She pushed the boy in front of her, holding him by the shoulders.

Pim stood up. "What are you talking about? Who are you?"

"I am Angus' wife. This is his son."

Graham motioned with his head to a man standing in the back. He blocked the path of the girl, preventing her from coming in any farther and grabbed her arm, escorting her out as she continued to shout, "He has a right to something. He is his son."

Rankin shut the door. He looked over at Pim, his face, having lost its color, now appeared a dull gray. Wraith took her hand and had her sit. "I apologize for the interruption," Graham said. "The estate will be in confirmation for the next six months, and after that, I will make the distribution…" His voice trailed off. "I'm sorry. I'm afraid that's everything. I'll contact you all with any other information. You're free to leave."

Pim sat, numb, unable to process the girl's words. *Wife and son.* The small crowd began to disperse, talking in awkward, hushed whispers. Peter came up to her. "Call me if you need anything, darling," he said, kissing her on the cheek. "You danced well today, my little Étoile."

Wraith stood up, every muscle in his body contracting. He looked like he was going to hit the man. Pim touched the sleeve of his suit jacket. He cleared his throat and went to stand by the door. When everyone had left, he returned and sat beside her. Graham shut the door.

"Who was that girl?" she asked.

"She's no one. Just a girl looking for money." Graham had regained his composure.

"Don't lie to me. She said she was his wife. She said the boy was his son."

"Pim, I'm not lying to you." Graham sat down on the edge of the table, so he faced her, and took her hand. "Some women look for rich men as an easy way to make money. That's all she was doing."

She pulled her hand back. "I need to get out of here." She stood up, grabbing her purse, and headed for the door. "In six-months, all of this will be mine. I'll be in charge of it," she said without turning around. "I'm going to ask you one more time, who is the girl?"

Graham sighed. "A lot of women threw themselves at your grandfather. It was a brief fling. She's desperate."

She kept her back to him. "How old is she?"

"She's your age."

Pim opened the door, slamming it behind her.

Wraith caught up to her in the street. "Get in the car," he said, rolling down his window.

"Leave me alone." She continued to walk, picking up her pace.

"You can't walk home with your toe."

"Don't tell me what I can and can't do." She stopped short, turning to face him. "In fact, our deal is over. I gave you a way in. You had your chance to meet his business partners and figure out whatever it was you needed to figure out. My grandfather's dead. Finding out if he was murdered, isn't going to change the fact."

"Look, you're upset. That was a lot of news for one afternoon. Let me take you home."

"Fuck off, Wraith."

He watched as she lengthened her stride and made her way down a walking path. Unable to drive any farther, he turned the car around at the dead end and drove the short distance to her flat, calling Gabriel on the way.

"Wraith, what can I do for you?" Grabriel asked.

"I need you to check on the girl again, Natasha, only this time run the report as Natasha McNeil. Look for any hospital reports or birth records."

"Okay. I've texted Dougie. He's on it. What's going on?"

"She showed up at the reading of the will, claiming to be Angus' wife and claiming the boy was his son."

"That must have caused a stir."

"To say the least. I have a sinking feeling that Angus was involved in a lot more than drugs."

"Here we go. There are no hospital records, but Dougie found a birth certificate for a boy, born July 10, 2015. His name is Hamish McNeil. The mother is Natasha McNeil but there is no father listed."

"I think this might explain who broke into Angus' place. Thanks, Gabriel. I'll call you back in a bit." He parked the car and got out, waiting for Pim to arrive. The picture of Natasha as a child and the twenty thousand pounds spoke of only one thing—a child bride.

"Primrose," he called out, intercepting her as she limped toward the door leading to her flat.

"I told you, our deal is over." Her eyes were puffy and bloodshot. He could tell she had been crying.

"I heard you. I need to get my stuff."

She nodded shortly, regaining her composure. "Of course," she said, opening the main door to the townhouse and heading up the stairs to her apartment. She held the door for him as he entered.

"I'll just be a second," he said, retrieving his bags from the closet and zipping the last of his belongs into a rucksack.

She stood there, watching him silently.

"Thank you, truly, for your help," he said, reaching out. His finger stroked her cheek. "I'm still worr—"

"Stop." She pushed his hand away. "Let's just go our separate ways. I told you there was no reason to make this complicated."

"You're right." He pressed his lips together. All her walls were up, so he wasn't going to make any headway with her right now. "Well then, I'll get going."

"Good bye, Wraith."

He left without looking back.

Chapter 17

Pim watched from her window as he got in his car and drove off. *Good riddance*, she thought, but three little words sat in the back of her mind. Three little words that she wished to hell he'd never muttered, 'That's my girl.' She didn't need him to watch her life fall apart. She thought about calling her mom but stopped herself. She wouldn't know what to say and her mom would somehow find a way to make this her fault. She sat down on the couch and pulled her phone out. *I need her name and address.* She sent the text to Graham.

Her phone dinged. *Pim, I don't have it. Leave it alone.*

She typed a message back. *You worked for my grandfather. The way I see it, you work for me now. Name and address.*

Natasha Komarov 8 Murano Street flat 213. She's a liar. She's only after your grandfather's money.

Pim threw the phone down, holding her head. She felt the bile rise in her stomach. If she were smart, she would leave it alone and go about her life as if the last three days never happened, but the girl's words rang out in her mind. She ordered an Uber and went downstairs to wait for it. A black

Stripped

Vauxhall pulled up and she got in. Fifteen minutes later, it pulled up to an old brick council house. It was close to Possilpark, an area in Glasgow known for its drug problems and high crime rates. The building was worn down, a reflection of the deprivation and neglect the industrial community encompassed. She took the stairs to the second floor and knocked on the door. The girl answered almost immediately, as if she was expecting Pim, and they stood there, staring at each other without saying anything.

"You should come in," she finally said.

Pim entered, looking around. The furniture was sparse, and what there was of it, was cheaply made and gaudy.

"Please," Natasha said, pointing to the one small couch.

Pim sat. The young boy was nowhere to be seen.

"Can I get you anything?"

"No, uhm, no, I'm fine." She wasn't sure what she was doing here or what this was going to accomplish. Her grandfather was dead. Even if he did have a fling with this girl, it didn't matter now.

"I'm Natasha." The girl sat down next to her.

"I know," Pim said shortly. She didn't mean to take her frustration out on the girl and her hand shook as she rubbed her forehead trying to calm down, suddenly afraid of what she might learn. "How do you know my grandfather?"

"It's complicated," Natasha started to say. She ran her hand through her long blonde hair. "I lived in Russia with my grandparents. My mother moved away after I was born, for a better life. The village I am from is very poor, and there's not a lot of opportunity."

"So you came here hoping to meet a rich man."

"No, it's not like that at all." She cleared her throat. "One night, a man came to our house. He had a letter for my grandparents from my mother. The next thing I knew, I was being taken away. I screamed and cried and tried to get away from the man. I didn't want to leave my grandparents, but they said I must go." She paused and looked at Pim sadly. "I don't remember what happened next exactly. I was drugged, so the memories are blurred, but I know I was put into a metal shipping container with other girls. Some of them were much younger than I was, and they were crying. They wanted to go home. We had no food, no toilet, just a few bottles of water to share between us. We could have been in there a few days or a week, I don't know, but when the container was opened, two men with guns got us out. I was separated from the other girls and taken away by one of the men. He put me into the trunk of a car and I was brought here."

"Dear God." Pim shook her head as tears gathered in her eyes. The story was worse than she had imagined. "How old were you?"

"I had just turned fourteen." Natasha reached over for a box of tissues on a side table, offering one to Pim.

"Thank you," she said quietly.

"A woman came the next day with food and clothes. She helped me bathe and dressed me in a traditional Russian girl's dress. I had one like it back home. She braided my hair and gave me new shoes to put on. I remember thinking I had never been treated so grandly before. I thought I was going to meet my mother. From the few letters she wrote my grandparents, I knew she had become an important woman."

The girl stopped and Pim wasn't sure if she was going to continue. "Did you meet your mother?"

"No," she said. She looked over at Pim, her brown eyes hesitant. "I was taken to the most beautiful home I had ever seen and introduced to a very kind gentleman."

Pim felt the color drain from her face and the realization of what she was about to hear hit her like a ton of bricks. "My grandfather," she said numbly.

Natasha wiped her own tears and nodded. "Angus."

"And your son?"

"He was not born yet." She shook her head. "That day, I was so disappointed when I realized I wasn't going to see my mother, I cried and cried. Angus was so loving and gentle. He showed me to the most beautiful room and said it was mine. It was filled with dolls and books in Russian. I didn't speak very much English then. We had a wonderful dinner with more desserts than I could eat. That night, he came to my room. I didn't know what happened between a man and a woman. I was very sheltered. It hurt. I cried the entire time, but he said it would get better and when it was over, he held me."

Pim was going to be sick. "Can I use your bathroom?" Natasha pointed to a door off the sitting room. She ran to it, and leaning over the toilet, she threw up, over and over again. Her grandfather was a fucking child molester. When she recovered from the initial shock, she rinsed her mouth with water and returned. "I think I should go."

"I understand," Natasha said, standing. "I didn't want to upset your life, Pim. You had nothing to do with the situation. I only came today to talk with Mr. Rankin. He refuses to see me and won't pay the rent. He's threatened to send us back."

"Were you married to him?" She couldn't bring herself to say his name or call him Grandfather.

"No, not legally. I have no papers. I don't exist here, but Angus called me his malen 'kaya zhena. His little wife."

"And this is where you live?" she asked.

"Yes. I would go to the house once a week, as long as you weren't there, and he would sometimes visit me here. I grew to love him. I do love him." She began to cry. "I'm not sure what I'm going to do without him."

"I'm sorry. I can't—" Pim stopped and reached in her purse, pulling out a credit card. "Here." She handed it to Natasha. "Pay your rent. Get what you need. There's a ten-thousand-pound limit on it. I-I need time to think." She left, shutting the door behind herself. She wanted to scream, to cry, to hit something, but she couldn't, not now, not at this moment. She hurried down the stairs to the sidewalk outside and ordered an Uber.

A man approached, his eyes darting back and forth nervously. He scratched at his arms and chest as he asked her for money. Heroin addict. She shook her head. "Bitch," he said, walking off. This place was a slum. All his money, and he kept her in a fucking slum. Her ride pulled up and she got in, heading home. *Bloody fucking hell.*

Wraith watched as Pim got in the Uber, hoping she was headed home. He needed information. Besides, he had a bone to pick with the one person who could help him. The fog from the morning had cleared but the day was still driech. Dark clouds sat heavy in the sky, matching the city's dismal feeling of despair. He parked the car and walked the few blocks down the gray asphalt to the old tenement housing. Evidence of the area's rampant drug problem could be seen everywhere. Opening the main door, he walked into the dank hallway. Small wonders, the lift had been fixed since the last time he was here, but he decided to take the stairs to the ninth floor, feeling it the safer option. He knocked on the door, his leg and lungs burning as he waited for the telltale shuffle. *Thump. Scrape. Thump. Scrape.*

"Who's there?" a voice asked. He knew the bastard was watching him through the peephole.

"Open the fucking door, you bawbag." He listened as several locks were turned and the door swung open.

"Well, if it isn't the prodigal son, resurrected from the dead," the inhabitant declared.

Wraith didn't wait for an invitation but stepped into the tiny, one room flat, pushing past Dougal Murray.

"Well, by all means, come in." He shut the door. "At least I don't have to call you fucking captain anymore."

"Aye, there's that." Wraith looked around. Things hadn't changed since the last time he was here. Take-out cartons littered the kitchen counter, along with empty whiskey bottles and ashtrays full of cigarette butts. The curtains were drawn tightly shut, adding to the gloom. Dougal made his way across the stained and grimy carpet. The thump of his walker was followed by the scrape of his one remaining leg, limp and barely usable. His other leg was no longer there, a casualty from the same IED blast that had ruined Wraith's chest. He plunked down in a worn leather chair before a desk full of expensive computers and state of the art monitors, his only connection to the outside world.

"Have you come to thank me?" He motioned for Wraith to have a seat.

Wraith brushed old, discarded ashes off the chair before sitting down. "Thank you?" he asked sarcastically. "What, for ruining my life?"

"Aye. Ruining your life." The bitterness in the young man's voice couldn't be masked and caused Wraith to give pause for a moment. Dougal had been a lieutenant in his SBS unit of the Royal Navy, a handsome lad with a promising future. That was before the ambush in Afghanistan, before Wraith made the decision to get his men out of an irrigation ditch they were trapped in, before Dougal lost his leg and most of his face. "I didn't ruin your fucking life. I think I saved it," Dougie said.

The irony was not lost on Wraith. If anything, it was offensive in its cruelty. Two lives ruined. Two lives barely saved. It was Dougal who gave him the card with The Watch's number on it, to be used if he found himself in a situation he couldn't get out of alive. He sat back in the chair. "I should have died."

"Aye, one day, you'll realize I did you a favor. One day, you'll thank me." Dougal found a bottle of whiskey on the desk, holding it up.

"I wouldn't go so far as to say that," Wraith said, going to the kitchen. He found two tea mugs. Washing out their previous contents, he brought them back over.

Dougal poured them each a generous dram. "The Watch saved my life. The colonel saved my life," Dougal said, taking a sip of the amber elixir. "I owe him everything."

"And he knows about all this." Wraith motioned with his hand to the track marks lining Dougal's arms.

"That I'm a junkie?" He laughed. "You fucking honorable, righteous, prick. I see those qualities didn't fucking die with Captain Robert McFadden. Of course, he knows. He's the one who saved me from the gutter."

Wraith flinched at the sound of his former name. "Why do you live here then? Why not at The Tower?"

"Look at me. I'm not exactly the good-looking agent the colonel normally chooses. I'm a fucking monster." He drained his cup, setting it down. "This works for me. The colonel checks in on me once a month, makes sure I'm okay, keeps me supplied with the finest whiskey and turns a blind eye to everything else. And I, in return, give him full access into the dark web."

"The colonel normally chooses?" Wraith's eyes narrowed. "He didn't choose me. I called him."

"He was looking for a new agent, so I told him about you. I knew you were in over your head with Al-Saad. It was just a matter of time. How do you think those agents were able to scoop you up so quickly after you called the number?" He poured himself another drink. "What do you want, *Wraith*? I doubt you came here to pick a fight. Your principles wouldn't allow that."

"You don't know anything about my new principles."

"What do you want?"

"I need information on a girl."

"Natasha? I already sent Gabriel everything I could find."

"No, Primrose McNeil." Wraith hoped she had made it home safe.

"Angus' granddaughter. The dancer? I thought you were staying with her."

"Aye. I am. I want to know about her past. Boyfriends, acquaintances, anything you can pull up."

Dougal typed several things into his computer, bringing up different databases on his screens. His fingers moved faster than Wraith's eyes could keep up with. "There's not much from the past two years. A few posts on social media, but they're sporadic. I can't connect her to anyone else's account. I doubt she's been in a relationship ever." He continued to type. "There are a few arrests for underage drinking, but they've been expunged from her record. Grandda's doing, I suppose. This is interesting. She was expelled from the Royal Ballet Academy then brought back on probation. A bit of a wild child, it seems."

"Hmm." Wraith sighed. "Not much there."

"Most young people put everything on social media. She's the opposite. It's like she doesn't want anyone to know her."

Wraith nodded. That was exactly his problem. He stood up, placing his mug in the kitchen sink.

"You haven't taken your oath yet," Dougal said seriously.

"Apparently, I haven't proven myself. Especially now, with the botched assassination."

"I took my oath on the first day." Wraith knew he meant it as an insult, insinuating he wasn't competent.

"What the fuck do you want from me, Dougie?" He

rubbed his hands over his face. "I'm sorry for everything. I'm sorry for getting you caught in the ditch that day. For the ambush, for the fucking IED blast that I couldn't save you from and for the men who died. But I don't want this. I want my old life back."

Dougal swallowed; there was a pained look in his eyes. "You didn't have a life, Robert," he said quietly. "You thought you were in love with a girl you could never have. You were hiding in the fringe, barely hanging on. It's what the war did to all of us who survived. You deserve more. The Watch will give that to you. And until you accept it, you'll never understand."

Wraith turned to leave. The Glock that Dougie kept for playing Russian roulette sat on the side table exactly where it was the last time he was here. He picked it up, checking to see if the trigger safety was in place and slid it into a holster on his chest harness. "I hope so, because killing people for a living is not really my thing."

"You're looking at it all wrong. Open your eyes and see what's in front of you," Dougal said. "And for fuck's sake, get off your damn high horse. You were a good person, and you're still a good person. You always will be."

Wraith closed the door behind him. The truth of what Dougie said cut deep. He was hiding in the fringe; he had been his whole life. He ran down the stairs, taking two at a time, until he made it back to his car. Once inside, he put the gun in his glovebox and started the engine. Then he slammed his fist into the dashboard.

Chapter 18

The thumping of the bass from the music in the club pounded in Pim's head, blocking out the sound of her thoughts. She looked over at the guy at the bar buying her a drink and turned to his friends, smiling. She couldn't stay home. Everywhere she looked in her flat, she saw something that reminded her of her grandfather and the lies. After pouring herself a large drink, she decided to change and go out.

The guy came back and handed her a glass of wine. "Here you go, darling." He put his arm around her, his hand resting on her lower back. "I haven't seen you in here before."

She shrugged. She couldn't even remember his name. "We should dance," she said, setting her drink down. She pulled him onto the dance floor. He put his arms around her, grabbing her bum as they began to move to the music. It was wall to wall people. She threw her hands in the air, forgetting this week ever happened. A hand came down on her shoulder and she turned and looked up, staring into green eyes that held nothing but anger.

"Let's go," Wraith said. "*Now.*"

The guy she was dancing with pulled her back against him. "Back off, mate. She's already taken."

"Get your hands off her."

"Or what?"

"You don't want to find out," Wraith said between clenched teeth, grabbing the man by the front of his shirt.

"Stop," Pim yelled over the din.

Wraith pulled the man closer as his friends came over and stood behind him, bolstered by alcohol and ready for a fight. "Back off," Wraith said. "Or your friend here will wish he was never born."

Pim put her hand up, blocking him. "Stop it."

He let go of the man, taking her by the arm. "Go wait outside."

"You can't tell me what to do."

"*Go. Wait. Outside.*" The strobing lights of the club made his eyes appear black and menacing.

The guy began to back up, changing his mind. "You can fucking have her," he said, leaving with his friends.

Wraith grabbed her hand and removed her from the crowd on the dance floor. "Where's your coat?"

"I don't have one," she yelled. "I'm not going with you."

"Jesus Christ. You came out in just that dress?"

She looked down. She was wearing a silver-sequined slip dress. The back was so low, it showed her tailbone. He took off his suit jacket and put it around her shoulders, leading her out of the club. His car was idling up front. He handed the valet a large bill and put Pim in the passenger seat, fastening the seatbelt tight around her.

"Stop it." She pushed his hand away. He ignored her as he got in the car and drove the few blocks to her flat. "Who the fuck do you think you are?" she asked, enraged.

"Let's get inside." He opened her door, his normally controlled demeanor having returned.

"I was on a date."

"Really? You call that a date? What was his name?"

"Fuck off."

"It looked to me like it was just someone you picked up in a bar," he said, following her up the stairs to her flat.

The door to her apartment was ajar. Wraith grabbed her by the shoulder and stepped in front of her. "Wait here," he said, going in first.

She poked her head in. Her place was ransacked. Cabinet doors were open, dishes broken, tables turned over, the cushions on the couch slashed. She followed Wraith down the hallway. Someone had poured red paint over the floor in her dance studio and written *Bitch* across the mirror.

"I told you to wait outside," Wraith said sharply, meeting her in the hall. "Do you ever listen?"

"Go to Hell."

He picked her up, and before she knew what was happening, he had her turned over his knee as he sat on the large bed. He lifted the hem of her skimpy dress and began to spank her bottom, the lace thong she wore offering no protection. She tried hitting him back, but he grabbed both her wrists and held them against her back in one of his large hands, pinning her in place. Her breath caught in her throat for a brief second as the initial thrill of being at his mercy kindled something in her core and damped the secret place between her legs.

"This is for going to a bar and accepting a drink from a stranger, for thinking this was an acceptable dress to wear out, for letting that man touch you, for all your foul language, and most of all, for not following my directions," he said, his tone business-like.

She struggled as his hand came down relentlessly, the flesh on her rear end burning in fiery rage. Her desire diminished, replaced by indignation. How dare he.

"Let go of me, you fucking bastard," she managed to say. The intensity of his swats increased, forging a red-hot trail along her skin. A lump formed in her throat and tears in her eyes, yet she refused to cry in front of him. He continued with his torment, his hand wielding its punishment, over and over. It wasn't the pain that bothered her; she could handle that. No, it was the feelings it was eliciting. At first erotic, it quickly turned punitive, and now it bordered on complete loss of control. He was forcing her to relinquish everything to him, and it made her feel exposed. She cried out. And as abruptly as he started, he stopped and stood her up.

She glared at him. "Don't you ever fucking touch me again," she said as she raised her hand to hit him. He caught her wrist. Her jaw dropped open, and she took a step back, surprised at what she was about to do. At first, she thought he might spank her again, but instead, he sat her on his lap and began to rub her back, his sudden change in demeanor and gentleness overwhelming and the catalyst to her breaking point. She crumpled into him, crying.

"Let it out, Primrose," he said softly. "You don't always have to be so strong."

She cried until there were no more tears left, for her grief, for everything horrible she had learned about her grandfather, for Natasha and her son, and all the while, Wraith held her and offered her the comfort no one else had ever offered in her life.

"Shh, that's my girl," he whispered. "I've got you."

She wiped her face on her arm. "I'm sorry. I didn't mean to break down."

"You needed to. You can't keep everything bottled up. You're safe with me."

Christ. What had he just done? He could not become emotionally involved with her. The fact they slept together the other night was bad enough. But this. This crossed a line. What he just did was intimate and personal; it required trust. *Damn it.* He was developing feelings, where feelings couldn't be. Not with The Watch. He should have driven off when he had the chance, but instead, he'd followed her to Possilpark and then to the club. Whatever was going on in her head, she was acting recklessly. He saw red when that stranger put his hands on her.

"Who did this?" she asked after a moment, her hand still gripping the front of his shirt.

"I don't know, not yet, but I need to get you out of here."

"We need to call the police."

"No," he said. "No police. I'll have my people come and secure it. They can do the crime scene analysis."

She sat up, looking at him. "*Your people?* I thought you were a private investigator. Now you have people?"

"I am an investigator and, yes, I have people who help me." He slid her off his lap and stood up, texting a message into his phone. "Change your clothes and pack a small bag."

"We can go to my grandfather's house or your place."

Wraith shook his head, taking pictures of the vandalism. "No, I need to get you out of the city. Whoever did this will know where your grandfather's place is, and I'm sure mine by now."

"I can't just leave the city. I have ballet. I have rehearsal tomorrow. I perform on Saturday night."

"Primrose, this isn't up for discussion." He threw her a pair of sweatpants and a sweater. "Change."

A shadow crossed her eyes. Fear maybe, or resolve, either way, she let the ridiculously small dress slip from her shoulders and land in a puddle around her ankles, standing only in her black lacy panties.

Wraith swallowed, and his cock hardened. *Fuck*. He was doomed. He took a deep breath. "Pack a bag," he said, leaving to finish taking photos of the damage to send to Gabriel.

She came out a few minutes later, dressed in sweatpants, a wrap-around sweater, scarf and the soft botties she usually wore to ballet, carrying an overnight bag. "I'm going to Uber to my grandfather's or I'll get a hotel room, but I'm not leaving the city," she said boldly.

He frowned. God, she was stubborn. She didn't even have the sense to be scared of him. In fact, he was sure it probably excited her. She lived her life on the edge, constantly seeking out danger, but in her case, he thought it might be stemming more from guilt or self-punishment. "You'll come with me and do as you're told. I thought we already settled that."

"I'm not leaving. I can't," she said, her voice rising. "And let's be clear, whatever *you* thought happened back there, you're not in charge of me." Her face turned a deep red.

He took her bag from her and grabbed her hand. "You're coming with me."

"I'm not. You'll have to kidnap me."

"Fine, if that's what you want, Primrose," he said, whipping out a pair of handcuffs from his pocket. He brought her wrists behind her and clicked them shut.

"You fucking bastard. I'll scream."

"Go ahead. I'll gag you." He loosened the black silk tie from around his neck.

"You motherfucking—" He didn't give her a chance to finish. Folding the tie in half, he put it in her mouth and knotted it tightly at the back of her head.

"We've already talked about your language." He picked her up, putting her over his shoulder and grabbing her around the thighs, to prevent her from kicking him. Then he walked downstairs, depositing her in the passenger's side of the car. Tears streamed down her cheeks as she struggled to shout behind the gag. He fastened her seatbelt and got in on his side of the car. Reaching over, he opened the glove box and retrieved a prepaid disposable phone. He needed to get her out of the city but had nowhere to go. The Tower was out of the question, and when his former identity Robert McFadden died, he lost all his property, including the house that belonged to his grandmother. He took out his wallet. He couldn't use his credit cards, they would be traceable. He had five hundred pounds in his wallet, but a hotel would involve other people and he couldn't take the chance. He had only one idea. Pim continued to struggle beside him, so he pulled her seatbelt tighter. "Stop it," he said. "You're only making it worse."

The idea was extremely risky. He punched the number into the phone. Green eyes hovered in his mind and his heart clenched. There would be no going back. But there were crystal eyes too now, sitting next to him, and though courageous, he could see the fear deep within them. He'd asked for her trust; he couldn't fail her now.

He typed the message. *I need help.*

A message pinged back. *Who is this?*

The less you know, the better. I need a place to stay that is private. A croft on the property that is not being used.

Ping. *Dear God. Sithiche cottage on the northeastern side of the property is empty.*

He typed back. *No one else can know. It's for a young girl.*

Ping. *No one goes there. I'll make sure there are supplies and food.*

We'll be there by midnight. Thank you. It's best if we don't see each other.

He pulled the SIM card from the phone and crushed it between his fingers.

Chapter 19

They traveled north up the A9. Pim was trying to keep track of where they were going. She glanced over at Wraith, confused with the different emotions that coursed through her. The spanking was disconcerting not only for the fact that he did it, but more so for the way she reacted to it. Her bottom still burned with the imprint of his hand as if its heated reflection claimed her as his. *That's my girl*. She had never broken down in front of someone before, had never cried in front of another, not even when her father died. She learned at a young age to keep her tears to herself; they were never allowed in ballet. To submit in the end and have him hold her and not only want, but need, his comfort, left her raw.

"Have you calmed down?" he asked, looking over his shoulder as he changed lanes.

She nodded, the gag rendering her speechless. "No filthy words or I'll pull over and put it back on you." He reached behind her and untied the knot, taking his tie from her mouth.

She coughed several times. Her hands were still bound

behind her back and her shoulders ached from the uncomfortable position. "I'm going to lose my role. Peter will give it to someone else if I don't show up tomorrow." She could feel drool dripping down her chin.

"Then it will be my fault." He wiped her face with his handkerchief. "I'll have you back on Friday. I'll call him and explain something came up with the will and you had to go to Edinburgh."

"We're not going to Edinburgh."

"No, we're headed north, to the Highlands. Somewhere safe until I can figure out what's going on. Why did you go to Possilpark?" he asked, pulling the car over on the side of the road. He got out and opened her door. Undoing the handcuffs, he rubbed her shoulders and looked at her wrists.

She didn't want to look at him. She should be furious with him, but his touch sparked the same feeling of security as before, offering her a refuge.

He kissed the side of her head. "Don't be too cross with me," he said, getting back in.

She bit her lip, wondering how much to tell him. "I went to see Natasha."

"How did that go?"

In the end, she told him everything she had learned. All the horrible things Natasha had gone through, of her grandfather being a child molester, of the young boy, his son, the ugly web of deceit and lies, ensnaring the innocent and tangling everyone involved into its trap. He didn't say anything, just listened, and reaching over, he took her hand in his, lacing their fingers.

It was a while before he spoke, the highway giving way to winding roads the farther north they traveled. "What happened at the ballet academy? Why were you expelled?" he asked.

She looked over at him, but his face looked as if it had been carved from stone. "How do you know about that?"

"Primrose, it's what I do."

"Why do you care? It was a long time ago."

He still held her hand and gave it a reassuring squeeze. "Curiosity, I guess."

"I told you I hit a point in my life when I didn't want to dance anymore. That summer, I was attending a program in New York. Instead of going to class, I got a fake ID and partied. I was completely self-destructive. They kicked me out of the program and called my grandfather. When I got back to London, my reputation followed me and I was expelled from the academy."

"But you got back in."

"My grandfather made a big donation. I was brought back on probation, but there were repercussions," she said. "I was shunned. For six months, none of my teachers would speak to me and the other students avoided me. I went to class, but I never got a correction, never got picked to demonstrate, was never chosen to be in any choreographer's dances. I was basically an outcast."

"That seems a bit extreme." A pained expression creased his face.

"It was, but I learned from it. I knew my father would have been disappointed in me. That's what hurt the most, the thought that he would have been ashamed. So, I became determined not to give up. I held my head high in class and took everyone else's corrections as my own. Eventually, things settled down."

"Did your love for dance come back?"

"It's all I know. And love can change." She pulled her hand from his. "What I felt when I was younger, was naïve. It's more of an understanding now, a give and take, the constant strive for perfection."

Stripped

He looked at her with a depth of understanding, which surprised her. "Why don't you close your eyes. We still have a way to go."

The winter moon slivered the sky, dark amongst the stars. It was late when they arrived. Wraith pulled the car off the dirt road and drove a short distance to a copse of trees, parking it near a small croft hidden by large scotch pines. "Stay here. Let me check it out," he said, going into the cabin. It was a few minutes before he came back and got her. He grabbed her bag, helping her out. The biting cold of the night cut through her sweater and her breath iced before her like a white shadow. Inside, it was no more than one room with a bed, a kitchen table and two armchairs. A dim yellow light lit up Wraith's face as he started an old oil lamp. He set it on the table beside a box of food and supplies someone had left. Pim shivered.

"Here," Wraith said, leading her over to one of the chairs. He took off his jacket and put it around her. "There's no electricity, but it's safe." He bent down and added wood and peat to the fireplace and soon had a warm blaze going. "Are you hungry?"

She shook her head.

"A drink?" He pulled a bottle of whiskey from the crate, pouring them each a glass.

"What happens now?" she asked, shivering as she took a sip.

He grabbed a blanket off the bed. "Come," he said. Sitting down in the chair next to her, he pulled her onto his lap and covered her with the throw. "Christ, your hands are frozen." He wrapped his arms around her as he held her close, and she was thankful for his warmth. "I need to check some things out tomorrow."

"And me?"

"You'll have to stay here. You'll be safe, and I'll be back

tomorrow night." His hand rubbed her thigh. "I need to figure out who's threatening you, and I can't do that and keep you safe at the same time."

"I don't see why I can't come with you." She set her glass down on a table and laid her head on his chest, unsure what it was about him that made her feel so safe. God knows she had never felt this way with another man before. He loosened the tie on her sweater from around her waist and ran his finger up her spine.

"You can't come to the place I need to go. It's private."

"Why?"

"You just can't, Primrose. I need you to trust me."

She turned so she straddled him. "Show me why I should trust you." She looked him in the eyes, his green gaze not wavering.

"You shouldn't," he said, his voice having gone deep and husky.

"And that is why I do. You tell me the truth."

Her sweater had fallen open. She wore no bra, and his hand traced the small rise of her breasts as he leaned his forehead against hers. "We shouldn't do this."

"I told you, no complications. It's just sex."

"Primrose, it's becoming more than just sex."

She ran her hand over his jaw, the scrape of his beard rough on her palm. Her heart quickened. It had always been just sex for her, she'd never let anyone in, she'd never been in a relationship, never *made love*, and the thought scared her. But this wasn't a relationship, she reminded herself. This was nothing more than a work fling. Once Wraith found out who killed her grandfather and who was stalking her, he would leave. This was just sex, and it was safe. She unbuttoned his dress shirt and ran her hand down his mutilated chest, kissing one of his worst scars.

"Bloody fucking hell," he said. Grasping the back of her

Stripped

head, he brought her in for a kiss. This kiss was not fierce or aggressive like the other night. He took his time, coaxing her to open for him as he gently explored her, his breath warm and smoky from the whisky. He picked her up and carried her to the bed, laying her down. He pulled her pants and thong off in one fluid motion. The bed creaked with his weight as he continued to kiss her down her neck and throat to her breasts, where he lightly flicked his tongue over each nipple. Her back arched and she grabbed his hair, trying to bring his head back to her mouth. He sat up, straddling her, and put each of her arms above her head. "Leave them there."

She stilled at his command, the tone of his voice provoking her to obey. A pleasing warmth took root inside her and she felt the moisture grow between her legs. He returned to her breasts, suckling each tiny bud before he made his way down, kissing her stomach until he got to the juncture of her thighs. He started to spread her legs and she tensed. No one had ever kissed her there. Her hands came down, stopping him. "Wraith, no." Her face flushed with the heat of her embarrassment.

"I told you to leave your hands above your head," he said, standing up and removing his pants. His cock stood straight up, thick and large. The sound of his belt whistled through the room as he pulled it from the waistband of his discarded trousers. The warmth flamed in her with anxious anticipation, extending to her sex, and it began to pulse. He bound her wrists, the leather supple and smooth, forming to her skin like a memory. Then he tightened it, ensuring no escape as he attached the restraint to the headboard until it cut into her. *Fuck*, this was not a man to tease or play with. He was in charge and completely comfortable with that role, and she suddenly felt she might be in over her head.

"Now, where were we?" He straddled her again, resting a

forearm on either side of her head as he looked down at her, his green eyes intense.

"Wraith, please."

"What?" He smiled, his thumb caressing her cheek. "You're actually blushing. Have I finally found something my little rebel hasn't done?"

"I—" she started to say.

"Shh." He brought a finger to her lips. "Now, we're going to start over and take this nice and slow." He kissed her again, his lips feather light against hers as his tongue began to prod hers. "Not everything has to be rough, Primrose." He made his way down her neck and chest, again lingering on her breasts until he came to her apex. "Open your legs for me."

"Wraith—"

"Open for me, or I'll start over." He put a hand on her thigh, and she stiffened. "Do as you're told." Her heart hammered in her chest. She had never been this intimate with anyone or allowed anyone this much control. Her defenses were lowered and he had somehow breached her wall. She let her legs fall open. "Good girl." He rewarded her with a kiss. "That wasn't so hard."

His mouth came between her legs, and he ran his tongue up the length of her cleft, separating her bare lips until he found her nub. A moan escaped her, her whole body now thrumming and on the verge of an orgasm. He focused on her sweet button, softly sucking and blowing on it until her legs began to shake. "That's it," he said. "Come for me." His words were enough to send her world crashing down as her core convulsed, over and over, in mind-numbing pleasure. He raised himself over her, undoing the belt and freeing her hands. "That wasn't so bad now, was it?" he asked, placing his cock at the entrance of her passage.

"No," she said, as the world around her began to piece itself together.

"No, Sir," he whispered in her ear, correcting her. "Say it."

"I'm not calling you Sir."

"Say it, or I'll get my belt, and we'll start over." He grabbed her wrists.

"No, Sir," she murmured as he let go.

"Good girl." He entered her, taking her hand in his as he gently thrust in and out. "Open your eyes, Primrose."

"I can't." She felt like she was coming apart at the seams. If she gave up this last bit of herself, there would be nothing left.

"Open them and look at me." The rhythm of his movements were slow and deliberate, binding them in a hazy aura of expectation, his simple order demanding her to comply. "We'll do this together."

She needed to regain some of her jurisdiction. Too much had been taken from her today. The fear of completely losing herself was more than she could handle. She ran her nails down his back sharply. He inhaled. Caught off guard, she pushed him to the side and got on top, sliding herself up and down his cock. He let out a low moan. "Now, you'll come for me," she said, arching her back as she took him all the way in, to the hilt. She felt his body start to stiffen and he grabbed her around her waist. She rode him hard until her own climax exploded within her, and she felt his release.

"Jesus Christ," he said.

She rolled off him and he held her to his chest. "You vixen. I might have to punish you for that."

"You seemed to enjoy it." She rested her head on his chest.

"Aye, but you disappeared on me," he said, running his fingers through her hair.

"I didn't disappear on you." She didn't understand his insistence on breaking down her walls.

"Shh, it's okay. It's been a tough day." He kissed her. "But you don't always have to be so strong. I can carry some of your burdens."

Tears flooded her eyes and one slipped down her cheek.

"That's my girl," he said tenderly. Her world shattered, opening up her wounds from earlier, and she cried in earnest. He kissed her again. "I've got you."

Chapter 20

"Promise me you won't leave the cottage," Wraith said, coming out of the small bathroom, adjusting his tie.

Pim sat up in the bed. "I still don't see why I can't come with you."

"I told you. I need to gather some information and where I'm going isn't open to the public." He sat down on the edge, next to her. "Where's your phone?"

"In my purse."

He stood up. Finding her purse on the table, he opened it and took out her phone. "What's your passcode?"

She got out of bed, pulling on her underwear and wrapping her sweater around her. "Hey, just because we had sex, doesn't mean you can control me," she said, a bit touchy, trying to grab the phone from him.

He laughed, holding on to it. "If that's what you want to call it, that's fine. Now give me your passcode. I want to put my number in your contacts and make sure no one is tracking it."

She tried one more time to take it from him but managed to stub her sore toe on the leg of the table. "Fucking hell."

Tears sprang to her eyes. She grabbed her foot, hopping around.

Wraith sat her down in a chair and went to his rucksack, coming back with a bottle of pills. He shook two out and handed them to her along with a bottle of water. "This will help with the pain and swelling. Now, what's your passcode?"

"Four, four, four, four."

"For the love of God, Primrose, anyone can hack that," he said, shaking his head with a frown. She watched as he punched in the numbers and entered his contact information, then set her GPS so he could track her on his phone, and turned off the passcode. "Reset your code. I've deleted this one." He grabbed his jacket from the armchair and put it on, picking up his rucksack. "Come here." He motioned to her.

She looked over at him and regret for last night hit her like a ton of bricks. She didn't want to have feelings for him, she didn't want to miss him when he left. "No, I'm good."

He came over to her and stood her up, bringing her into an embrace. "Promise me you won't leave the cottage," he said again. "I need to hear you say the words."

She looked up at him. "I won't leave."

He took her chin in his hand and kissed her. "I'll be back tonight."

She tried pulling away, but he held her tight. "About last night."

"There's nothing to talk about."

"I think there is, princess."

"And I fucking don't."

His hand came down hard on the bare skin of her bottom and he cleared his throat. "Language and respect." The same ache from last night took root deep in her and pleaded with her to obey.

"I won't leave," she said finally.

"Sir." He raised an eyebrow.

Stripped

"Don't push your luck."

He laughed then kissed her one more time, lingering as he caressed her face. "I'll be back tonight."

Pim listened as he drove off, the tires crunching on the leaves and pine needles. She grabbed her sweat pants and went into the bathroom. The outline of his hand stood out red on her bum. Something about it excited her, knowing he'd put it there. *Fuck*. There had to be something wrong with her. The sound of a knock on the door made her jump. She pulled her pants up and went to get it, thinking Wraith must have returned.

"Hello?" a female voice called out.

Pim froze and looked around for a weapon. She tiptoed, trying not to make a sound, and grabbed a piece of wood from a stack by the fireplace, holding it in front of her. The handle on the door turned slowly and a face popped around the entranceway.

"Hello," a woman said, surprised, backing up when she saw Pim. "I'm sorry, I didn't mean to scare you. I was just checking to see if you needed anything. My name's Ailsa."

Pim lowered her makeshift weapon and took a deep breath. The girl had a baby strapped to her chest in a carrier. "Oh my God. I know you. You're the American duchess. I'm so sorry, I thought you were an intruder." She set the piece of wood down. The duchess was beautiful. Dark chestnut hair hung down to her waist and her eyes were as green as the pine trees outside.

Ailsa looked around. "I got a text you would be staying here. I brought some fresh scones." She set a basket down on the table.

"Wraith isn't here."

Ailsa looked up at her, her eyes darkened in shadow. "Wraith," she said it as if it were the first time she'd heard the name.

Pim nodded. "I assumed you two were friends."

Ailsa shook her head. "I've never met Wraith. We had a mutual friend, my personal protection officer, Agent McFadden, and he were friends."

"Were?" Pim questioned, speculating just how Wraith was connected to the Duke and Duchess of Torridon.

"He passed away in the line of duty almost a year ago."

'Men died in my care because of my decisions.' And she wondered, not for the first time, what exactly he really did. "I'm sorry," she said.

The duchess' eyes focused on the bed. The blankets and sheets lay in disarray, Wraith's dress shirt and slacks haphazardly discarded on the ground and his belt still fixed to the headboard. Pim felt the heat of a blush stain her cheeks, and her bottom, where he'd spanked her, throbbed with humiliation. "I-I'm sorry," she stuttered. "I never introduced myself. I'm Pim."

Ailsa smiled, turning a blind eye to the bed. "I know. I saw you dance the other night. It was the most beautiful thing I've ever seen. I'm sorry about your grandfather."

Pim nodded. "Thank you. That's right, I remember seeing you backstage. The whole night is a bit of a blur."

"You were with Wraith?"

She nodded, remembering now how odd it was he'd kissed her then.

"I should get going. It will be time for his nap soon," Ailsa said, patting the baby's back.

"He's precious. What's his name?"

"Robert. We call him Robbie." Ailsa kissed the top of his head. "I'll come back later and drop off dinner."

"Thank you, Duchess."

"It's just Ailsa." She paused at the door, as if she wanted to say something else. "He's happy? Wraith, that is. It would be important to McFadden that he be happy."

Pim's eyes narrowed. "He's complicated."

That made the duchess laugh, for some reason. "I'll see you in a bit."

Pim shut the door behind her. Picking up Wraith's clothes, she tidied up the cottage. Someone knocked on the door again. *What now?* She opened it, expecting to find the duchess. The needle of the syringe hit her neck before she knew what was happening and everything went dark around her.

Chapter 21

"Where is she now?" Alex asked from behind his desk, giving Wraith a soldier-like assessment. The tapping of his finger on the polished wood was a direct indication he was still deciding on Wraith's competence. Rain pelted the window, the occasional ping of sleet increasing as the sky darkened in the late afternoon.

"I have her in a safe house for the moment." Wraith sat tensely under the scrutiny, back straight, shoulders tight, in the colonel's office, along with Gabriel. The older man unsettled him, being neither friend nor foe.

"We've secured her flat," Gabriel said, his deep voice resonating throughout the room. "A team is still sweeping it, though, as of now, they've found no fingerprints." He was well built and handsome, with a strong jaw and piercing blue eyes. He kept his face clean-shaven and his blond hair neatly combed. His whole presence exuded an attitude of trust, that, and the fact that in his former life, he was a priest. But he was Alex's right-hand man, his own personal archangel, and Wraith was still undecided on how much to trust him.

He pulled the photograph of Natasha from his pocket and

Stripped

handed it to Alex. "I found it with a twenty-thousand pound bank draft. She was fourteen when he paid for her."

Alex's eyes narrowed as he studied the picture. "Pedophilia. I knew the motherfucker was involved in something else besides drugs."

"How long ago was that taken?" Gabriel asked.

"She's the same age as Primrose, nineteen, so it would have been five years ago. The same year her son was born." Wraith rubbed his forehead. He needed to check on Pim. He had spent the greater part of the afternoon in here, catching Alex up on everything.

"Angus made no claim to the boy?" The colonel stood and walked over to the fireplace, leaning up against the mantel.

"No, but the girl said he's Angus'."

"That was the same year her father was murdered," Gabriel interjected.

"My thoughts exactly. His murder was brutal. Someone was definitely sending a message and Angus had it covered up." Wraith leaned forward intently. "Plus, he was found near the port in Leith. Anyone wanting to bring in young girls and send them out, could do it in one of those shipping containers if they paid off the right person."

"One girl doesn't make him a trafficker, a disgusting, fucking bastard, yes, but a trafficker, no." Alex shook his head. "I don't know. This girl seems personal to him; there has to be a reason he picked her."

"And Andrew McNeil's murder?" Gabriel asked. "The pictures were horrific."

"Maybe he was picking Natasha up for his father, maybe he saw something he shouldn't have," Alex suggested.

"Or maybe he caught on to what his father was doing and tried to stop it," Wraith interjected, giving the man the benefit of doubt.

Alex turned to Gabriel. "Either way, send Sinclair to Leith, have him check out the port."

"He won't like that." Gabriel glanced at Alex then back at Wraith. "Sin hates to investigate. Assassination only."

"I don't give a fuck what he likes or doesn't like. He'll do as I say." The colonel sat back down, a little harder than necessary.

"It could be, Angus saw a business opportunity and infringed on someone else's turf," Wraith continued to think out loud.

"It's a possibility. We need more information, though. Wraith, you stay with his granddaughter, she seems to trust you now. Gabriel have Storm trail Graham Rankin to see who he's talking to and have him keep his eye on the ballet company. We need to keep all roads open." Alex poured himself a whiskey. "Take Wraith to see Dr. Forbes before he leaves."

"Yes, sir," Gabriel said, standing.

"I'm fine, I don't need to see Forbes," Wraith said. "I'll need to get Primrose a new flat. She can't stay where she is forever. She needs to get back to work."

"You *will* see Forbes." Alex's eyes locked with his, challenging him. "And have her stay at her grandfather's place."

"She's in danger. It's too risky."

"Exactly, let's draw this person out." Something in Alex's eyes shone, equivalent to excitement. He liked the game.

"You're using her as bait," Wraith said, standing up.

"Then you'd better protect her."

Gabriel shut the door, joining Wraith in the hallway.

"I don't need to see Forbes. Honestly, I'm fine." He needed to get back to his room and check his phone.

"It won't take long," the agent said calmly. "And it does no harm to have your injuries looked at."

Gabriel walked with him over to the infirmary in the main

building. Now, Wraith sat in his underwear on the exam table as the wiry doctor listened to his chest while Gabriel stood in the corner.

"Have you been using your inhaler?" the older man asked him, putting his stethoscope away.

"No, it was becoming a crutch. I'm fine without it."

"Your right lung sounds like hell, and it wasn't a crutch, it was helping to keep the inflammation down," Forbes scolded. "I'll give you a nebulizer treatment."

"I'm fine, really."

"Wraith," Gabriel said politely. "Appease the good doctor and have the treatment." He knew it was the angel's way of saying he had no choice in the matter.

Dr. Forbes prepared the treatment, placing a mask over Wraith's mouth and nose, and turned on the nebulizer machine. His lung burned as he breathed in the medicine. He didn't need to be wasting his time with this, he was worried about Pim. It would be well after dark by the time he made it back to the cottage, and he didn't quite trust her to stay put. The lass never had anyone she could depend on, she was used to doing things her own way and was impulsive. He wouldn't put it past her to leave, especially after last night. For the first time, he saw the fear in those pale clear eyes, and the intimacy of last night alone could send her running. It explained her reckless behavior and why she kept everyone at arm's length. *Damn.* He'd let things go too far last night. In the end, he had nothing to offer her. The machine started to sputter, the medicine finished. Wraith removed the mask and got down off the table, getting dressed.

"You have scratch marks on your back," Gabriel commented casually, crossing his legs, his blue eyes appreciative in their appraisal of him.

"Last I checked, I wasn't in a confessional." He buttoned up his dress shirt, tucking it into his pants.

Gabriel smiled. "No, but after eleven months, I hope I've gained some of your trust. And you're right, I retired my collar a long time ago."

"He who sitteth on the right hand—"

"True, I do." He chuckled, the pitch deep and with an edge of self-deprecation. "But not everything goes back to Alex. I'm not his puppet."

"Just the same." Wraith grabbed his jacket. "I need to get back to my room."

"Wraith, the scratches?" Gabriel asked bluntly.

"Let's just say our delicate flower has some thorns.

Gabriel escorted him back to his room. "Text me when you leave. I'll let you know what Sin and Storm find out."

Wraith nodded, shutting the door behind himself. He went straight to his rucksack and pulled out his phone. Two missed calls from Pim. He called her back immediately.

"I'm on my way back, Primrose," he said as soon as she answered. "I'll be there in a couple of hours. Don't leave."

"Wraith?"

He froze. He knew the voice on the end of the connection and it didn't belong to Pim. Dark green eyes danced before his face, only to be replaced instantly by pale seafoam ones. His gut clenched. Pim was in trouble. "Yes," he managed to say.

"She's gone. I came by to drop off food for her tea and the door was ajar. She was gone. She left her phone and all her stuff."

"Were there signs of a struggle?"

"No."

Fuck. "Are there any outgoing calls or texts from today on her phone."

"No, just four missed calls from a Peter Brindy and two from Paul Lewis."

"Look, I've got to go. Destroy the phone."

"Robert, wait."

"I can't, Ailsa."

"She's very young."

"I know she's young, and she needs me right now." He hung up and pulled the GPS tracker up on his phone. The pills he gave her this morning were chipped. He would be able to see her location for a few more hours before the chips stopped working. A map of Scotland appeared on his screen and on it, a tiny blue light flashed right over Edinburgh.

Chapter 22

Someone was petting her. Their strokes, soft and gentle, reminded her of when she was a little girl and her mom would run her fingers through her hair. Though, this was wrong, something bad sat just out of reach, something dark. She tried opening her eyes, but she couldn't. In fact, she couldn't move at all. She didn't want to panic, so she focused on the touch of the small hand that continued to rub her until she fell back into the light. She was safe in the light.

A pounding in her chest woke her up. Something was amiss; she was not where she should be, not in the cottage. Wraith would be mad. She felt hung over and her head hurt like it was going to crack in half. She didn't want to open her eyes, but somewhere in the fog and miasma of her mind, she knew she needed to. The blue and white ticking on the mattress was the first thing she saw. The smell of stale urine and sweat, pungent and musty, wafted through the air. She was going to be sick. She pulled herself to the edge of the mattress and threw up, her throat burning from the taste of bile. The small hand returned, wiping her mouth with an old cloth. She rolled on her back and stared into deep brown eyes.

Stripped

"Zdravstvuyte," a young girl said.

Pim shook her head, not understanding.

"H-h-hello," the girl tried again, a dimple appearing on her cheek when she spoke. Her face was made up with cheap makeup—blue eyeshadow, bright pink blush and red lipstick, reminding Pim of a plastic doll.

"Where am I?" She looked around. Two other girls sat huddled in the corner of the room, staring at her.

The young girl shook her head. Her blonde hair was in two pigtails; she couldn't be older than twelve.

"How long have I been here?"

"You come today." Her English was broken. "You okay?"

She pushed herself up on an elbow, her head screaming in protest. "I don't know." A wet spot stained the crotch of her sweatpants, the feeling dank between her legs. Dear God, she must have wet herself at some point.

The door slammed open, startling all of them. A large man entered, his muscles straining against his tight shirt. "Vstavay," he yelled to one of the girls in the corner.

She started to cry. "Net, pozhaluysta, net."

The man went over and grabbed her by the hair, pulling her up. She was wearing a red negligee. One of the straps was torn and it hung off her thin, pointed shoulder. Tears streamed down her face. "Net, net."

"Molchi." He slapped her across her face and dragged her out of the room.

"Sasha—" the other girl called out. The young girl ran to her, putting her arms around her in an embrace. "Shh," she said. "Shh."

"What's happening?" Pim asked, sitting up all the way. "Where are they taking her?"

"To other room," the young girl answered. A single lightbulb hung on a chain from the ceiling. Pim stared at it, willing herself not to be sick again, saliva pooling in her mouth.

"What other room? What's in the other room?"

"Men."

They could hear screaming coming from down the hall, then silence, followed by the squeaking of a mattress as it moved up and down. Her insides clenched, and nausea filled her empty stomach, rising like a tidal wave. She threw up.

The young girl continued to console her friend, rocking her gently in her arms. "Shh," she whispered.

"What's your name?" Pim asked, regaining her composure.

"Annika. This is Ivanna, and Sasha is sister."

"How long have you been here?"

She held up her hand, counting her fingers silently. "Five days. There eight of us, but the others not come back."

Something akin to hysteria filled her and she stifled the scream that threatened, willing herself to calm down. She needed to think if she were going to survive. This must have been what happened to Natasha. It was some kind of sick sex trafficking ring. She stood up on shaky legs, her body still reeling from whatever she was drugged with, and made her way over to the one window. A dirty sheet hung over it. She pulled it to the side and looked out on a narrow close and another gray tenement, giving her no clue to her location. The sun was hidden behind the buildings of the concrete slum, and it would be night soon.

The door opened again, and the same man entered. His square, shaved head looked in as he threw a plastic grocery bag on the ground. "Odevat'sya," he said, before shutting the door.

Annaika stood and picked up the bag, and pulling out a black satin slip, she handed it to Pim. "Change."

"I'm not putting that on," she said, backing up and sitting down on the mattress.

"Pozhaluysta. Please. They hurt you." Her hand brushed

her cheek and Pim noticed the yellowing of an old bruise, covered by makeup. She had fought back. "Please."

"I can't," she said, setting the slip down.

Ivanna started to cry again, murmuring in Russian. Annika went to her and held her. "Sasha's not back. She should be back by now."

"How old are you?" Pim asked, not wanting to know the answer.

"Me, eleven. Ivanna fourteen. Sasha twelve."

Pim pushed the tears down. *Eleven. Eleven years old.* Annika reminded Pim of herself. She was strong. She had to be to survive this hell. When Pim was sent away to school, she remembered the sound of the girls in the dormitory crying themselves to sleep each night. She never let herself shed a tear, afraid that one of her ballet teachers would be listening and think her weak. Annika was the same, being strong for the other girls so they wouldn't have to be.

Evening turned into night before the man returned. He came straight over to Pim, throwing the discarded negligee at her. "Odevat'sya," he yelled, his acne-scarred face turning red. "Odevat'sya."

Pim stood up. "No." His nose had the flattened appearance of having been broken one too many times, the cartilage damaged beyond repair, squished and soft. He grabbed her by the hair, ripping it out by the roots, and punched her in the stomach. She fell to the ground, unable to catch her breath. Spots formed before her eyes. She struggled to get breath, writhing on the ground until she lost consciousness. When she finally came to her senses, Annika hovered over her, the pain in her stomach sharp.

"Odevat'sya bitch," the man said.

She changed into the slip.

Chapter 23

They covered her head in a cloth sack, so the only things visible were light and dark shadows, making it impossible to tell where they were taking her. However, she recognized the sensation as an elevator went up and concluded at least she hadn't left the building. She was led down what she assumed was a hallway and through a door, to where she was deposited in a chair. The covering was removed, and she found herself sitting at a table. A crystal decanter of wine and two glasses were the only thing on it.

A man entered, wearing a white dinner jacket. He adjusted his black bow tie as he sat down. His features were crisp and clean, deceiving to his advanced age, which was noted in the spots and wrinkles on his hands. With a baldhead, straight nose, tight goatee and cunning hazel eyes, there was an air to him that reminded Pim of her grandfather. He sat down, crossing his legs elegantly, and set an old-fashioned gold lighter on the table, flipping open the lid. Pim clasped her hands under the table, anchoring herself in reality. The man's presence didn't match the squalor of the room or the situation, creating a schism in her mind. She needed to remain present. He pulled out a cigarette case, offering one to Pim. She shook her head. His hand hovering above the lighter, he snapped his fingers, and a flame magically shot to life, and picking it up, he lit his cigarette. "Illusions, they distort our senses, misleading our brains. We think we know something when we really don't. Then, of course, there are delusions. Especially those of grandeur when one has a false belief about one's greatness or skill. Most people make the mistake of calling them illusions of grandeur, but they're delusions." He took a deep pull on the cigarette, the tip lighting up bright orange as he studied her. "Primrose McNeil," he said as he exhaled. His speech was refined, as he exquisitely emphasized her name. Though Pim could still detect the slight Russian accent, he seemed to work hard to hide it.

She didn't answer him.

"Will you have some wine?" He didn't wait for a response but poured them each a glass, the color such a deep red, it verged on black. "Chateau Lafite Rothschild Pauillac 2010, excellent vintage."

She continued to stare at him, her heart beating so fast in her chest, she thought it would start skipping as the dull ache in her stomach intensified.

"I'm afraid I insist you join me in a toast. I promise you it's not drugged." He picked up his glass, waiting for her to do the same. Her hand shook as she raised hers. "Behind every beautiful thing, there's some kind of pain." His eyes narrowed as he spoke. "Slange."

"Slange," she repeated. The words of her tattoo resounded in her mind as she set the glass down. Words that had so much meaning to her she'd had them permanently etched on her back, now perversely being used against her.

He pursed his lips, frowning. "Manners, Primrose. I know you were raised properly. You always take a sip after a toast."

She brought the glass to her lips, the wine rich and dense,

quenching her parched throat. Part of her hoped it *was* drugged, so she could escape from this nightmare.

"Your grandfather and I are..." He paused, grimacing slightly and held up a finger to emphasize his point. "Were. Sorry, we *were* associates. My condolences on your loss." He spoke as though they were acquaintances, forgetting the fact that she was his captive. "My name is Viktor Sokolov."

"Associates in what? Sex trafficking?" she asked sharply.

"Sex trafficking. You offend me. I am no sex trafficker." He lit another cigarette, repeating the same trick with the lighter, and took another long draw, filling his lungs and acting as if he were put out by her accusation.

"Explain those girls to me, in the room where you were holding me against my will. They're children."

"Those girls' parents paid me to take them, to give them a better life. Most of them come from very poor villages. There's no hope for a future, no education."

"They're being molested and raped." She spat the words at him. "What you do is vile."

"They are loved. They will be offered a life they never could have had. I give them a chance. Opportunity. You wouldn't understand the disadvantage and destitution of the villages they come from." He spoke the last sentence with bitterness.

Her stomach heaved, his words repugnant. "Why am I here? What do you want with me?"

He stood up and walked around the table, placing a hand on her shoulder. "Your grandfather took something from me. Something very special." His caressed her neck with the back of his finger, causing goosebumps to erupt on her skin.

"Natasha?"

"No." He sat back down. "He paid for her. And he's given her a great life. One she never would have had."

Fucking bastard. "Then, what?"

Stripped

"He owed me a debt, and now you need to repay that debt." He rang a small bell on the table and a man entered, setting a silver domed tray down on the table before leaving. He lifted the lid, revealing a pair of black pointe shoes. "I believe they are the brand and size you wear, and they have been de-shanked as you like."

How long had he been watching her to know that? "You want me to dance?"

"It's a bit more complicated than that." He ran a well-manicured finger over the tip of one of the shoes and proceeded to recite a stanza from a Lord Tennyson poem, his voice calculated and as thin as a razor's edge.

"The Dying Swan," she said when he finished, dread filling her. The poem was the inspiration for the ballet variation. The dance was based off the whole dramatic arc of the poem, representing only one thing. The end of life.

"That's my girl." He gave her a knowing look, malicious in its intent, leveraging his power. "Clever."

That's my girl. The three words tore at her heart. How the fuck did he know? It was like he'd climbed into her mind. She bit her lip, pushing down thoughts of Wraith. He wasn't coming for her. No one knew where she was. She was going to have to step up and play his game. "I know my art, but The Dying Swan is not from Swan Lake," she countered, hoping to throw him off kilter.

"No, it's not. It's much better and do you know why, Primrose?" He stood up and started to pace, not giving her time to answer. "Because it's not a fairytale. There is no happy ending. It is about the everlasting struggle in life and all that is moral. You owe me a debt, a life for a life. That is your dilemma."

He picked up the shoes and handed them to her. "Do you know the variation?"

She nodded. "Yes."

"That's my girl." His hand caressed her cheek, his hazel

eyes boring into her. "You'll dance it for me. And we'll see if delusions of grandeur fill your head too."

She looked down at the shoes. She needed to buy herself some time to think. "The dying swan was a white swan," she said softly, fingering the black slip she wore.

He stood behind her and bent down, whispering in her ear, "But you're not. You know you're not. You're dark and dangerous, a little slut, haunted by nightmares of Daddy's death, seeking out solace—or is it punishment—in the arms of strangers. Nothing more than a dirty flower trying to be something she's not. You are no white swan, Primrose McNeil." His words were ruthless. "Now put the shoes on."

Pim put them on, tying them around her ankles. A man entered and sat down at a piano in the corner. "Now, you will dance for me, and depending on how well I think you do, one of your little friends in the other room will either live or die."

"You can't do that," she begged. "Leave them out of this." Tears streamed down her face.

"Stop crying," he said calmly, pulling a handkerchief from his pocket and wiping her face like a child. "It's not up to me. It's up to you. A life for a life." He sat down, adjusting the legs of his trousers, and poured himself another glass of wine.

Her blood turned cold at his cruelty, leaving her body stiff. "I need to warm up. I can't just dance."

"You have five minutes, Primrose." He turned to the pianist. "Play Stravinsky's Sacrificial Dance, The Chosen Victim, from the ballet The Rite of Spring. It should be appropriate."

A shiver went up her spine. He was playing with her, drawing out his torture both mentally and physically. The man began to play. The music was made up of short fragments that repeated, the sound unsettling. It was harsh and jarring, producing a quality of dissonance that only added to the tension in the room. She didn't want to do this and wasn't sure

Stripped

what he expected. She rose up on her toes several times, her ankles popping in bitter objection, and felt the nail bed on her big toe split open, the pain immediate. While highly developed technique was necessary for The Dying Swan, it wasn't the purpose of the dance. The only time she had performed it was in her last year at the academy. Her teacher wanted to push her artistically and chose the variation for her, calling on her to draw from her experience with the death of her father. He told her every movement and gesture should signify an action emerging from someone trying to escape death. Her teacher had no idea at the time how horrific her father's death had been or the terrifying images Pim had seen. Every time she danced it, she relived the pain of his loss. She turned to Sokolov, unable to take the raw sound of the piano and the disorganization of the music with its chaotic collage of rhythms any longer. "I'm ready."

"So be it," he said, the emptiness of his eyes filling with an anxious eagerness, greedy and expectant. "Take your place."

She went to the corner of the room, adjusting the strap on the backless slip, and turned so she faced the wall. Bowing her head, she put her feet in fifth position and waited for the music to start. Hypnotic, like a heartbeat, it began, dark and emotive. Pim circled the room on her toes in tiny bourrées as her arms floated and folded like the wings on a swan. It was a cry for beauty in the most fragile of moments. Death was more than the destination, it was the journey of grief that accompanied it, penetrating the soul. Her hands glided through the air, bent down at the wrists and turned, hoping to see one last flight, but it wouldn't be so. Death was coming. Death was near. The pain, both subjective and visceral, was at hand. She fell to her knee, and there, transfixed with agonizing grace, she bowed down as the swan, to die.

Pim lay on the ground, overcome with the emotion of the piece and the toll it took to dance it. The enormity of everything came crashing down on her. She curled into a ball, exposed and wounded, not knowing whose life she spared as tears ran down her face. Sokolov came over and untied the ribbons of the pointe shoes, removing them. He helped her stand, putting his arms around her. He held her from behind as he slid the straps of the slip down, letting it fall and puddle around her ankles. "That's my girl," he crooned, his hands running down her breasts and across her bruised stomach. "You did well. Tomorrow, you will dance it for me again."

"No," she cried softly.

"Yes, you can do it," he said, as he pulled the black thong down until she stood stripped bare, exposed, with no place to hide. "You can take it."

The door opened, and the man whose face looked as if it had been hit with a shovel, came in with Ivanna, a knife to her neck.

"No, God, please, no." Pim struggled, but Sokolov grabbed her around the waist, pinning both her arms down. His other hand held her forehead, pressing the back of her head against his chest so she had to watch. "It will make you a better dancer. Isn't that what we're striving for? What Daddy wanted? Perfection."

"Fuck you."

Ivanna whimpered from behind a gag, tears streaming down her face.

"Watch her eyes," Sokolov whispered in her ear. "See the fear. Focus on the fear she's feeling. She knows death is coming, and it scares her. She's terrified."

The man slit the girl's throat in one clean stroke. Ivanna's eyes opened wide as she reached for her slender neck. A thin red line graced her lily-white skin before blood poured out.

"See her struggle for breath. She's trying to fight off the inevitable, panicking as she begins to suffocate. Watch—" Ivanna collapsed in the man's hands, falling forward, unconscious, and he let her drop to the ground. "Did you see the moment of acceptance?" Sokolov turned her, so she faced him. He shook her until her teeth rattled against each other. "Did you see it?"

"Y-y-yes," Pim sobbed.

He pulled her in close, and she folded into him as he rubbed her back, murmuring sweet endearments. The horror of what she just witnessed beyond all thought and reason, she accepted what comfort he offered. "Shh, that's my girl. Take what you've learned, think about how you can improve for me." She nodded. "I can't hear you," he said.

"Yes."

"Good. Your awakening has started. We'll try again tomorrow, when we wager another life."

"No. Please, no, not again."

He ran his hand down the side of her face and tilted her chin up. "Don't say no to me, darling, and don't ever tell me to fuck off." For a second, she thought he was going to kiss her until he drove his fist into her stomach and she crumpled for the second time that day.

Chapter 24

D<i>amn it</i>. He shouldn't have left her alone. The blue dot remained stationary, indicating that whoever took her at least wasn't on the move and had reached their destination for now. He pressed the button, calling Gabriel.

"Leaving already?" Gabriel asked. "I'll walk you out."

"Not yet. I need the address for these GPS coordinates. Fifty-five degrees north, three degrees west, and I need the phone number for Peter Brindy, the artist director of Scottish National Ballet."

"What's going on?"

"Primrose is missing. She's not at the safe house and doesn't have her phone on her."

"Give me a minute." Wraith waited, his mind wandering to all the possible explanations of where she could be. "The address is in Edinburgh. Four John's Place, near Leith links."

"Christ, that's known as a red-light district. It's a shady part of town." It was where lone, defeated women plied their trade at night, desperate for money, he thought to himself.

Stripped

"Wraith, don't do anything yet. I'll text you the number and head over."

The screen on his phone lit up with Peter's information. He called the bastard.

"Hello," a voice answered.

"Peter Brindy?"

"This is he." *Fucking prick.*

"This is Robert Wraith. I was wondering if you've heard from Primrose today or seen her." Hopefully, the latter.

"No. I've been trying all day. She's about to lose her role in the ballet. She skipped out on rehearsal. The company is headed to Aberdeen for a performance."

"I think she's in trouble."

"Trouble? What kind of trouble?" At least he actually had the decency to sound concerned.

"I don't know. I think it might be connected to her grandfather's accident and the man who was at the premiere wearing the owl mask."

"Dear God. I was going to stop by her place. I'll head there now."

"No, don't. Her place was broken into the other night. She was staying at another location, but she's gone missing. I'm going to look for her, but I wanted to make sure she hadn't contacted you."

"Please keep me informed."

Wraith hung up. He pulled a duffle bag out of his closet, packing it with various guns and weapons, then changed his clothes. The part of Leith he was headed to was seedy and rundown, and he would stand out if he was seen walking around in a designer suit. He pulled on a pair of black tactical pants and a black, long-sleeved compression shirt, throwing a black hooded sweatshirt into the bag. There was a knock on the door and he went to open it.

Gabriel poked his blond head through the doorway,

followed by the colonel. So much for the right hand not knowing what the left hand was doing. Wraith pressed his lips tight together and glanced sharply at Gabriel.

The agent shrugged. "Before you go rogue and run off looking for Angus' granddaughter, we should come up with a plan," Gabriel explained.

"Sit down, Wraith," Alex said, looking displeased.

"We're wasting time." He zipped up the duffle and sat down harder than necessary on a small couch. "I need to go."

Alex raised a cautionary eyebrow. "On the contrary, charging in without a plan is careless. If you're not careful, I won't send you at all," the colonel clarified, his displeasure increasing. "It seems you're running on emotions, not logic, a dangerous choice, considering you're not supposed to develop feelings for clients."

"There are no feelings," he said a bit defensively. "I'm just afraid if we wait too long, whoever has her will take her to a different location."

"How do you know where she is?"

"I gave her two pills to take this morning. They were chipped, but the tracking device will only last for about another hour, so we're running out of time. I didn't trust her to stay put like I told her to; she's strong willed."

"Well, hopefully, that will work in her favor." The colonel continued to study him.

"Sinclair is already in Edinburgh. He'll do an initial recon of the address and formulate a plan. I'll text you the location where you'll meet him, and you'll go in together. He'll be in charge," Gabriel said.

He had never met Sinclair. "It's my case. He doesn't know anything about it. Why is he in charge?" He already knew the answer. They didn't trust him.

"He knows the city and he'll have time to assess the risk," the ex-priest answered diplomatically.

"Wraith, don't mess this up." The colonel walked toward the door. Wraith expected there to be an *or else*, but he left without another word.

"I'll see you to your car," Gabriel said, picking up the bag.

He took it out of the agent's hand. "I've got it." He stormed through the hall and down the wing. Gabriel caught up to him.

"I didn't betray you. This is just bigger than you think. The longer you're here, the more freedoms he'll give you."

"Let me guess, I just need to prove myself," Wraith snapped.

"Just keep me up to date. Let me know when you meet up with Sinclair."

Wraith sped down the A9. *Damn it*. He had lied to the colonel; he did have feelings for Pim and he knew it, no matter how hard he tried to convince himself otherwise. She was smart, and her emotions ran deep, challenging him to think in different ways. It was a mistake to sleep with her, to take her down a path she, too, despite all her self-assurance, was very innocent about. The image of her as she lay beneath him, the blush in her cheeks and her large eyes pale and luminous staring into his, submitting to his commands as she said the words that drove him over the edge, '*yes, Sir,*' squeezed at his already battered heart. Take away her hard edge and bravado, and he had seen glimpses of the girl who hid behind the wall she'd built around herself. She could be hurt, had *been* hurt, and had the scars to prove it. He should never have used her to get inside Angus' inner circle, never convinced her to trust him. It was his fault she had been taken. A girl like her gave her trust to very few people.

The ringing of his phone through the radio, jarred him from his thoughts. He pushed the button on the steering wheel, answering it.

"Robert?" the voice said.

Shite. "You can't call me."

"I just wanted to see if you found the girl," Ailsa said.

"No. Not yet. Look, I need to go. Please don't call me again."

"Wait."

His thumb hovered over the disconnect button. "What?"

"I promise I won't call again, but I need to know if you're happy. Does she make you happy?"

He shook his head, laughing at the irony. "Christ, Ailsa, I'm not in a relationship with Primrose McNeil."

"You're sleeping with her."

"That's personal," he said, his voice rising slightly.

"But you are sleeping with her?" Ailsa insisted.

He felt the thrum of his own pulse increasing. He didn't need to explain his actions to her. "We're having sex if that's what you're asking."

"The Robert I know wouldn't just have sex with someone if he didn't have feelings for her."

His stomach tightened. "Well, the Robert you knew is dead. He doesn't exist anymore."

"I just want you to be happy. She seems very innocent and naïve."

"Look, Duchess, I appreciate your concern, but Robert McFadden is dead. He's gone. My name is Wraith, and I'm not the same man. If I want to fuck Primrose, then I'll fuck her. It's nobody's bloody business."

"I can see I've crossed a line."

He could hear the hurt in her voice, and he instantly regretted it. "I'm sorry I involved you. I should never have brought you into this, it was unfair of me," he said, softening his tone. "And Pim is neither innocent nor naïve, she's actually one of the strongest people I know. I've got to go; we can't talk again. You'll have to destroy your phone."

"I know. And for what it's worth, I'm glad you involved me. It's brought some closure."

"Well, at least there's that."

"Wraith," she said. "You can change a person's name, but you can't change their soul. You'll always be Robert."

He hung up. The conversation rocked him, dredging up emotions he hadn't thought about since the explosion. Ailsa was right; it did bring closure. He knew now that whatever feelings he thought he had for her were in the past. What he had been holding on to for the past year, was nothing more than memories. The longing of wanting to be in love, but not actually love. Dougie was right; he had been living on the fringe. It had been that way since he was a little boy and his parents died. Always on the outside looking in, never a real player in the game of life. But Pim. Pim was tangible, and what he felt when he was around her, as much as he tried to deny it, was tangible too.

He crossed over the Forth Bridge, skirting the city of Queensferry to Leith. The pub he was to meet Sinclair in was near the port. Wraith parked in a back alley at the address Gabriel sent him and crossed the street. Overflowing bins of trash lined the street, spilling out onto the walkway, the reek of rotting food and rancid garbage pungent in the damp night air. The bar itself, appeared no better. The place was dark and dingy inside, Wraith looked around. Drug addicts and scantily clad women made up the clientele, a place where drinkers went to die a soulless death. Sinclair was sitting in the corner. Wraith knew it was him without ever having met. He sat down opposite the agent. "No one provokes me…" he said, giving the sign.

"…with impunity," Sinclair finished with the countersign.

Verification complete, Sinclair began to debrief Wraith, not waiting for introductions. "The building is located across the street. It's owed by a Vance Stevenson. It has four stories and an exit in both the front and back. I have only seen people come and go from the back. A man with a young girl, possibly a daughter, left about two hours ago, and a different man entered not long after. Both men were wearing suits and appeared to have money, not local residents. I have someone tailing the man and girl. I did see a girl peer out one of the lower windows not long before the other girl left with the man."

"What did the girls look like? I lost the signal on Primrose, it's stopped working."

"The girl who left with the man was blonde, and she was wearing a school uniform. The girl in the window was blurred, she possibly had brown hair."

Wraith pulled a photo of Pim up on his phone, showing it to Sinclair.

"It could have been her. I can't say for sure, though."

"What's the plan?"

"We treat this as a search and rescue. We'll go in together. You know her, so your goal is to locate her. William and I will back you."

"William? I thought it was just the two of us."

Sinclair reached under the table, and Wraith noticed for the first time a large sable and white dog. He popped his head up, giving Wraith a discerning look. Wraith held his hand out, so the dog could sniff it, but instead, the dog bared his teeth and growled.

"Be nice, William," Sinclair said. "Stop showing off."

The dog closed his mouth. "Do you have something that belongs to the girl? Clothes, perhaps? William can search by scent."

Wraith shook his head. "No clothes, but I have, uhm, something that was in her mouth and touched her. Will that work?"

Sinclair nodded. "That will do."

"It's in my car."

They walked across the street in silence, to the alley where Wraith had parked. Though there were people out on the street, everyone seemed to be minding their own business, typical in a part of town where latent danger loomed everywhere. Keep your head low and mind your own business. Broken windows, the overflowing trash, graffiti, were all signs of the breakdown of social control. Disorder and crime were inextricably linked in communities ridden with destruction, prostitution, drug dealing, robbery and ultimately serious violence. Hopefully, they wouldn't be noticed. Wraith unlocked his car and pulled the black tie out that had been tied around Pim's mouth, handing it to Sinclair. "Will it work?"

Sinclair's brow cocked in question.

"I had to kidnap her to get her to the safe house," Wraith explained. "She wouldn't come willingly."

"It's a fine line we walk."

"Yes, but at least I know what side I stand on," he said more to himself.

"Really?" Sinclair asked. "Because there's more than one path to the dark side of morality. Welcome to The Watch." He let William sniff the gag. "What weapons do you have on you?"

"A knife and my pistol."

"Okay. Let's go."

Chapter 25

The dog's breath was warm on his hand, his hackles raised in anticipation. Wraith was crouched down, gun pulled, as he guarded Sinclair while he picked the lock on the front door. He could have just kicked it in, but it would announce their arrival to anyone inside and they needed the element of surprise. The door opened, and Sinclair motioned with his head to proceed. Wraith stood and followed the other agent in, along with William. Sinclair paused before opening a door on the right of the hallway and looked around it while Wraith darted to the other side, covering from behind. The room was empty. They went to the next door in the hallway, finding it locked. They wouldn't have time to pick this lock, so Sinclair glanced at Wraith before kicking it.

A group of young girls, five in total, sat huddled in a corner, their faces etched in shock. Wraith put his finger to his lips, warning them to be quiet. Footsteps could be heard overhead. They backed out and continued down the hall. The last door was open. A man stood in the room with a knife to a young girl's throat. "YA ubivayu yeye," he shouted. *I'll kill her*.

Stripped

Sinclair took the shot before the fat fuck even had time to think. He fell to the ground, blood spreading across his forehead, still clutching the young girl as he pulled her down with him. Sinclair rushed to her side.

William stood at the doorway whining, as he looked toward the stairwell. "Follow William. He's got her scent. I'll take care of whoever is above us and stay with the girls."

Wraith followed William up a staircase to the next floor. Footsteps could be heard coming down the hallway. He pressed himself up against the wall and waited until a man ran past. Aiming, he shot him. The man hit the top of the stairs and tumbled down. William continued to whine, and they hurried up two more flights to the fourth floor, leading to a small foyer with an elevator and a door. The elevator was in use, heading down. William scratched at the door, barking. Wraith opened it. Pim lay naked on the ground, curled in a ball on her side. He ran to her, scanning the room at the same time. Another girl lay lifeless, in a pool of blood.

"Primrose," he said, shaking her gently. "Primrose. Dear God, what did they do to you?" Massive bruises covered her stomach.

Her eyes blinked opened then popped wide. "Watch out!" It was too late. A man came up behind him and kicked him on his side. His breath left him, and he saw spots for a moment. He managed to stand as he turned and pulled his gun. The man was prepared and kicked it from his hand as it clattered to the ground. Wraith grabbed his knife from his belt. The man stood ready; he also had a knife in hand. Wraith tightened his stance, holding his blade pointed at the man, his free hand held vertically, to protect his already injured chest and ribs. The man advanced, and Wraith stepped forward at a forty-five degree angle, meeting him. He swung, catching the man in the chest as he cut down with his knife. Wraith felt the blade slice his deltoid. Pim screamed. The man looked away, attention diverted. Wraith took advantage of the distraction and charged him, grabbing him by the shirt while he sliced either side of his throat. He fell to the ground as blood drained from his neck.

Pim sat on her feet, the gun shaking in her hands. Wraith went to her and removed it. "I was going to shoot," she said, her voice shaking. "I was going to kill him."

"Primrose." He held her to him, as the fear of losing her set in. "Hey, I've got you, baby. You're safe."

Sinclair bounded into the room. "Everything okay?" he asked, looking around. William ran to his side.

Wraith removed his sweatshirt, covering Pim with it, hiding her body from Sinclair's view. "She's injured." His breathing was becoming ragged, the pain in his ribcage where he was kicked intensifying.

"So are you," Sinclair said. "You're bleeding."

He touched his arm where the knife cut him. "I'll be fine." Sinclair came over and looked. "It's deep." He tore the ruined sleeve off Wraith's shirt and wrapped it around the wound, tying it tight.

Wraith began to cough. He wiped his hand across his mouth, discovering blood.

"We need to call an ambulance and the police," Pim begged.

"I'll handle it," Sinclair said, tilting Pim's chin up. "He can't go to A&E. I'll stay here with the girls. If I give you an address, can you drive him there? It will take a couple of hours."

She was numb. Everything she had seen and experienced seemed far away. The only thing keeping her present, was Wraith. She pulled his sweatshirt over her head, the rent in the sleeve still wet with blood, and followed Sinclair into the elevator and down as he helped Wraith out the back door to the car. "What will happen to the girls?" she asked.

"I'll get in contact with the proper authorities and make sure they're taken care of," Sinclair assured her.

"There were more. They've been sold to men. The girl who died, her sister was taken." She could feel the panic in her rising as she spoke. She pushed it down, better if she didn't talk about what happened.

"We're already on it. I promise I'll do everything in my power for them." He assisted Wraith into the passenger seat and came around to see Pim settled.

She moved the seat forward and turned on the car. Sinclair leaned in and pressed a button on the console. "Call Gabriel," he said.

Pim recognized the voice that answered. "Wraith?"

"No, it's Sin. Wraith is down, he's in the passenger seat, probably the lung again. The captive has been rescued. She is driving him to you."

"What was the outcome?"

"Three tangos killed. One innocent victim, female child, DOA. Six female children survivors. The place is secured. Waiting for backup."

"Dear God. Children?"

"Yes."

"I've got to go. Send the address to Wraith's car."

"Done."

Sin ended the call and turned to Pim. "Call Gabriel if you need anything or if he takes a turn for the worse."

She nodded. Pulling out of the alley, she headed north.

It was a while before Wraith finally spoke. "You okay?" he asked.

"I'm fine," she lied, concentrating on the road. She floored it when she got to the A9, shifting gears as she sped up the motorway, dodging in and out of traffic.

"Jesus Christ, slow down," Wraith said, holding his chest.

She pressed on the accelerator. The engine revved. "Fuck off."

"Now, that's the girl I know and love," he teased. Sweat covered his forehead, a small bead escaping and running down his cheek.

"You're not just a private investigator." She didn't look at him when she said it; she already knew the answer.

"No."

"Military?" she asked warily.

"No, I told you I'm ex-military." It was becoming a struggle for him to speak and she could hear the effort of it in his voice.

"Government?"

"Primrose, the less you know, the better. Trust me." He closed his eyes, the tiny lines at the corners creased with the strain. She changed lanes without looking, a car swerved getting out of the way, and the person laid on the horn. "Shite. Pull over," he said, sitting up straight and grimacing.

"No, it's fine."

"Pull over now, or else. You're out of control."

She slowed down, stopping on the verge, and slammed her fists into the steering wheel, over and over again. Hot tears she had tried to hold off flooded her eyes. She covered her face with her hands and let them come. Diving into the pain, she no longer tried to fight it. Strong arms came around her.

"Shhh. Let it out, baby. Let it out," Wraith said softly. "You don't have to tell me what happened until you're ready, just let it out." He continued to hold her gently, and eventually, she managed to stop crying. "That's my girl. Why don't you let me drive the rest of the way?"

That's my girl. The words made her stomach turn and she

Stripped

quickly opened the door, retching onto the pavement. Words she used to treasure, now vile. Anger welled up inside her, replacing her fear. Anger at Sokolov and anger at herself for letting him get inside her head. "I'm fine," she said, wiping her mouth on the sleeve of his sweatshirt. "You're injured worse. I promise I'll drive slow."

It was past midnight when she finally pulled off the A9 and started down the winding road that would lead her to the destination. She pulled up to a large, wrought iron gate, where a car was waiting for them, and a man got out.

Pim stopped the car, putting it in park, and rolled down her window. The man came to her side. "He needs help."

"Aye, I'll get him into my car." She recognized the voice. It was the man named Gabriel. She shook Wraith, as he'd fallen asleep. "Wake up. We're here."

Gabriel opened the passenger door and unbuckled the seatbelt. Wraith's eyes squinted open. "Can you walk?" Gabriel asked him. He nodded.

"Thank you for bringing him. I'll take him from here," the handsome man said.

"We can't leave her." Wraith looked over at Pim.

"Wraith, you know I can't allow an outsider onto the property. She can't stay."

Chapter 26

"She's injured. She has no clothes—" Wraith started to say.

"It's fine. I'm fine," Pim said, rolling up her window.

"It's not fine. You're injured. You don't have enough gas to make it back anywhere and you can't get gas wearing just my sweatshirt. For God's sake, you don't even have a phone or identification." Wraith looked over at Gabriel. "I don't even know what's happened to her."

Gabriel shook his head. "Wraith, you don't understand."

"I do understand. We involved her in this; we just can't leave her."

Gabriel clenched his jaw. "Fine. Follow me in my car."

Pim drove through the gates and down a narrow road until they came to a large mansion. She parked Wraith's car next to Gabriel's. He came and helped Wraith out as Pim stayed seated. "Are you coming?"

"No. I'm fine. I think it's best if I go," she said shortly. Whatever this was and whatever they were hiding, she didn't want to be a part of it.

Stripped

"I was wrong. Please come and at least get checked out by our doctor."

"I'll manage on my own."

"Primrose. It's not a suggestion. It's an order, lass," Wraith said between gritted teeth. He leaned against Gabriel for support. "Now I'm about to pass out, so let's hurry."

She followed the two men into the mansion and down a dark hallway. They came to a door on the right. Above it, on a metal plaque, was the word *Infirmary*. Gabriel opened the door and deposited Wraith onto a wheelchair. An elderly man, small in stature with white hair and a strong gravelly voice, walked in, adjusting the sleeves on a lab coat. "I just put you back together, Wraith…" He paused for a moment when he saw Pim and his eyes narrowed, giving Gabriel a questioning look.

"This is Primrose McNeil, Dr. Forbes," Gabriel explained. "She was injured, along with Wraith. She'll need medical attention."

Pim pulled at the hem of the sweatshirt. "I'm fine, really."

"Put her in room two. I'll be in after I take care of Wraith."

Gabriel showed her to the room. "Why don't you change? I'll be back."

She looked around the room. It looked like a standard hospital room, with a bed and various medical equipment. A green gown lay across a chair. She went into the adjoining bathroom and changed. It was huge on her, made for a man, and hung well below her knees. Sitting on the edge of the bed, she waited for someone to come in. Dr. Forbes knocked and entered, followed by Gabriel.

"How's Wraith?" she asked.

"He's getting a chest X-ray. He'll do. It doesn't look like the kick he took to his back broke a rib, so no lung puncture," the doctor said. "Now, why don't you tell me what happened to you, Primrose?"

"It's Pim. No one calls me Primrose." *Except Wraith.* "I'm okay, really. I was punched a few times in my stomach. I'm not sure why they only hit me there."

Gabriel sat down in a chair by the bed, apparently staying for the exam. "They didn't want to ruin your beautiful face, so they hit you where no one would see the bruises."

"Go ahead and lie back so I can take a look."

Pim reclined back on the bed while Dr. Forbes covered her with the sheet. He lifted up her gown, exposing her stomach and two deep purple bruises, which covered her entire abdomen. He didn't say anything but cleared his throat; she didn't miss the downward turn of his brows and the tightening around his mouth.

"Bloody hell." Gabriel leaned forward, exchanging a look of displeasure with the doctor.

"Any pain besides the bruising?"

Pim shook her head. "No."

"This will be uncomfortable." He began to palpate her stomach.

Pim bit her lip. She had a high tolerance for pain, ballet had taught her to mask what she was experiencing. "I'm not feeling anything. We'll get an MRI and I'll keep you here and watch you through the night."

"If you don't think it's bad, I would rather get going. I have someplace to be in the morning." She needed to get in contact with Peter. She needed to let him know what had happened. Tears pricked the back of her eyes.

"You're not going anywhere, lassie, until you get the MRI. Then we'll talk," Dr. Forbes said gently after a short silence. "I need to go check on Wraith. I'll be back in a bit to take you for the MRI."

Gabriel made no move to leave with the doctor and,

instead, pulled his chair closer to her. "It will have been a long week for you."

She nodded, not sure who to trust anymore, so she thought it best if she remained silent. A week ago, she knew none of these people. A week ago, her life had been just about perfect. "Do you have a phone I could borrow? I need to make a phone call."

He removed his from his suit jacket, handing it to her. She looked down at it. She had no idea of Peter's number. She had it stored in her phone but never memorized it. As if reading her mind, Gabriel said softly, "If you need a number, I can get it for you."

Master of information and traffic lights, she thought. "No." She handed the phone back.

"Wraith won't have told you much about our organization." He leaned back and crossed his legs gracefully.

"Nothing. Only that he worked for my grandfather."

"Aye. He wouldn't have been able to. What we do is rather confidential. It can be a bit delicate."

"He only said he was a private investigator."

Gabriel nodded. "Aye, that's a part of it." He looked introspective for a moment and Pim hoped the conversation was over, so she could be alone. "I was a priest before I came."

She looked over at him. "Was? I thought once a priest, always a priest, forever."

"A metaphysical fact. You're right. One's indelible spiritual character can never be erased." Gabriel gave her a half smile. "I asked to leave. It's considered a loss of clerical state. I can no longer exercise the power of orders, but in the Church's eyes, I'm still a priest."

Pim thought she understood. She would always be a dancer, even when she would no longer be able to dance. Even when she gave it up during her rebellious stage, it was a part of her soul. It never left her, maybe not until now. Sokolov had stolen that. "Why?"

"I was a chaplain, serving in the Royal Regiment of Scotland during the Iraq war." He ran his hand through his blond hair. "I saw horrible things and heard the nightmares and confessions of my men. I guess it made me question myself. Question my faith. Question the existence of God himself. So, when I returned, I asked to be released." He leaned forward again. "I know you have no reason to trust me. And dear God, considering what you went through, I completely understand if you don't want to, but the sooner we talk about what happened, the sooner we can catch who did this to you."

"Will the girls be okay?"

"They're being taken care of right now." He reached over and took her hand.

"It's my fault Ivanna is dead. I couldn't give him what he wanted." A tear slipped down her cheek.

"Pim, whatever happened, I guarantee it wasn't your fault."

"It was; he told me I could save her. I should have been perfect. I should have died at the end."

"Who told you this?"

She pulled her hand out of his and wiped her eyes. "Viktor Sokolov. He said he was an associate of my grandfather's and that my grandfather owed him a debt. It was up to me to repay the debt. A life for a life. I could have saved Ivanna."

Dr. Forbes opened the door and stuck his head in. "Ready?"

"How's Wraith?"

"Twenty sutures to his deltoid. Needle aspiration to relieve the pneumothorax. He'll be fine. Bloody cat with nine lives, that one."

"Can I see him?" she asked.

"Well, he's heavily sedated and asleep, but you can peek in."

Gabriel helped her off the bed and followed her to the room next door. Wraith lay on the bed with a bandage on his ruined and scarred chest and one around his arm. She went to his side, running her hand down the side of his face and over the stubble of his beard. His eyes opened slowly, and he smiled. "I must be dreaming."

"I'm just making sure you don't fucking die on me."

"Never. How's my beautiful girl?"

"I'm not yours, and I'll live."

"Come here," he whispered to her. She looked back. Gabriel stood at the door watching. He nodded and stepped back. She leaned in to hear him, but instead of saying anything, he kissed her. "Don't leave me."

"I have to go get a test done."

"I thought you said you were okay?"

"I am, but the doctor is insisting. I'll come back later." She turned to leave.

"Primrose," he said. She didn't move. "I'm falling in love with you." Not looking back, she left the room. Gabriel led her to the room for the MRI. When the procedure was over, they waited in a small room for Dr. Forbes to come back with the results.

He came in, pushing his small, round glasses up on his nose. "I'm surprised, with how tiny you are and the violence of the injuries, you aren't hurt worse, but I'm finding nothing wrong with your internal organs."

"That's means I'm good to go?" she asked.

"I would rather you stay another twenty-four hours. Some injuries are late to show themselves, especially contusions."

"How about if we move her to Wraith's flat? She can at least take a shower and get a good night's sleep."

"I would agree to that. I'll come by in the morning then."

The doctor took her hand. "Promise me, if anything develops overnight, you'll call Gabriel right away."

She nodded, thankful at least to get a shower and some privacy. Gabriel showed her to Wraith's flat on the other side of the mansion. Unlocking the door, he entered and turned on the lights. A stack of women's clothes sat on the bed. "I think you'll find everything you need."

"Thank you," she said awkwardly.

"Call me if you need anything. There's a phone for you on the nightstand. My number's in it." He stopped at the door. "Pim, Wraith can never offer you anything. There's no relationship in your future. If there is something there, you need to end it."

She was thrown off guard and suddenly felt foolish. "I-I-I know. There's nothing there. He was just havering on because of the drugs."

"Okay, lass. Just making sure." He shut the door behind himself.

Pim went to the bathroom and started the tub. She found a bottle of men's body wash in the shower. She poured a dollop in the hot water then took off the hospital gown and sat down in the foamy bubbles. The first tear fell, then the second. She let them come, one by one, as she washed off the foul touch of Sokolov and Wraith's words, '*I'm falling in love with you.*'

Chapter 27

Pim fingered the stack of new clothing. Designer jeans, sweaters, pajamas, underclothes, all in her size, all with the tags on, sat on the bed. She went to one of the dressers, and opening the drawer, she found one of Wraith's t-shirts instead, slipping it over her head. She walked around the room. It was not unlike his place in Glasgow, beautifully furnished but zero personal items. Nothing that spoke to the life he had lived or who he was. She sat down on the bed and picked up the phone, turning it on. The screen lit up, a brand new I-phone. Under contacts, were Gabriel's, Wraith's and Peter Brindy's numbers. *Master of reading minds, apparently.* She looked at the time, two-thirty, too late to call Peter. She would try him in the morning.

Still unsettled and curious with the sterility of the place, she opened the drawer on the nightstand. Inside, she found two books and a small box. Reaching for the box, she removed the lid. Inside, was a Victoria Cross Medal. She flipped the medal over. Inscribed on the back, were the words, *Captain Robert McFadden, Royal Office, killed in the line of duty protecting his country*. Underneath, someone had added an additional inscription, *My Protector*.

She picked up one of the books, *Political Murder, From Tyrannicide to Terrorism*, and put it back, her heart beginning to pound. Not exactly peaceful bedtime reading. The second one, *How to Kill, The Definitive History of the Assassin*, was not much better. Assassin? *I've killed men.* It seemed like a lifetime ago since he'd said it to her, and at the time, she didn't think much of it. What exactly did her grandfather hire him to do? A clipping from a newspaper article fell out. It was a picture of the Duchess of Torridon. The headline read, *Duchess mourns her PPO amidst rumors of a relationship*. Her mind began to jump to various assumptions. What exactly did Wraith do for a living that was so secret? How was he connected to the Duchess and Robert McFadden? Why did he have no signs of a past? But in the end, it focused on only one. Why did Gabriel give her that warning about a relationship? All at once, she wanted to leave. She was not wanted here, that much she was sure of. A prickle of apprehension crept its way up the back of her neck, telling her to get out. She grabbed the phone and called Peter.

"Hello?" his voice, laced with sleep, answered.

"Peter. It's Pim."

"Pim," he said anxiously. "Where are you?"

"I'm not sure exactly. North of Edinburgh, off the A9. I need a place to go."

"I'm in Aberdeen at the Malmaison hotel. Come here, darling. Are you all right?"

She felt herself beginning to crack as tears flooded her eyes. "I'll be fine. I just need a place to go."

"I'll be waiting for you. Call me if you need anything."

"Okay. See you in a bit." She hung up and changed into a pair of jeans and a thick sweater, putting on the boots that were left for her. She looked for a paper and pen, to leave a note for Wraith, but then thought better of it. Best to walk away. She shut the door behind herself, navigating the endless dark hallways in the mansion, getting lost a few times before finding her way to the wing they'd entered through. It was then, she heard the footsteps behind her. She kept going, picking up her pace and exiting through the heavy door as it closed with a thud. She ran to Wraith's car and got in. The keys were still in the ignition where she'd left them, and as she started the engine, a knock on the window made her jump. Gabriel stood outside. She rolled it down part way.

"You won't get far without gas and money."

"I'll figure something out," she said, looking at the indicator. There was a quarter tank left. It was worth the risk.

"We haven't finished our conversation." He'd changed from his suit into pajamas and tightened the cloth belt of his robe around his waist.

"I have nothing to say. I don't remember anything else of importance."

"Not even on Viktor Sokolov? What he looks like? You're the only one who's seen him."

They didn't care about her, they only wanted her for information. In the end, she would gain nothing. She might even be disposable. "He looks old."

"Pim, come back inside. It's the middle of the night. I'm sure you're scared and tired. Let's get some rest, and we'll talk in the morning."

"You were right. The less I know about you and what it is you do, the better. If this week has taught me anything, it's that you never really know someone. Especially the people you love."

"What about Wraith?"

"Your message about Wraith was loud and clear." She put the car into reverse.

"Pim, please don't go."

"Fuck the hell off." She revved the engine, pushing in the

clutch and releasing the brake. The car sped backward. She shifted into first and turned, peeling out as she drove off down the lane. The gate was closed ahead, and she slowed down. She looked in the rearview mirror, but thankfully, no one was following her. When she was close enough to the gate, it began to open, and she went through, her whole body shaking as adrenaline coursed through her blood. It was a while before she pulled over. She rolled down the window and threw the phone out, convinced it was being tracked. The car would be, also, but it was too soon to abandon it. She'd have to wait until she was closer to Aberdeen. *Fuck, fuck, fuck.* She had no idea what she was doing. *Bloody hell*, now she would have Sokolov and Gabriel both looking for her. She glanced around for something to wipe her eyes with. Finding nothing, she opened the glove compartment. Wraith's wallet sat neatly tucked inside, next to a gun. She picked it up. The leather on it was rich and smooth. Inside, was his driving license, several credit cards, and over five hundred pounds. She checked the side slot, pulling out two more driving license cards. One belonging to Robert McInnes, the other to Robert McLeish, but both had Wraith's picture. There were also credit cards issued in the same names. She reached back in the glovebox and carefully moved the gun, finding matching passports to all his aliases. Her heart sank. She had been nothing but a fool, played from the very beginning.

"What the hell do you mean, she's gone?" Wraith asked, getting out of the hospital bed and putting on a pair of trousers.

"Calm down," Gabriel said.

"Do you know what that motherfucker did to her? He'll come after her."

Stripped

"Neither of us know what he did to her, but I have a fair idea, and she's not gone far. She's in Aberdeen with Peter Brindy."

"That bastard's not any better." *Why in bloody hell did she go running to him? She knows better.* Wraith tore the IV from his arm and pulled on his shirt, just as the door burst open.

"I can hear you two all the way down the hall," the colonel yelled. "Jesus Christ, I'm gone for one night, and all hell breaks loose. Both of you are to be in my office in twenty minutes."

Wraith strode down the hall to his flat. He changed into a suit and brushed his teeth. He was nearly leaving when he noticed the drawer to his nightstand was askew. *Damn it.* He frowned, opening it. The books and box were misplaced. He picked up his undershirt on the bed and smelled it. Pim had been in here. No wonder she fled; she must have put two and two together.

By the time he made it to Alex's office, Gabriel was already there talking in hushed whispers. He sat down in one of the armchairs.

"Tell me your version of this shite show," Alex said, sitting down in the chair opposite him. Sinclair would have already informed him of the events, so there was no point leaving anything out. He told him the entirety of it. "She was injured, wearing only my sweatshirt. We couldn't leave her to drive herself to A&E."

Alex glanced at Gabriel. The priest must have at least corroborated that part.

"Aye, I suppose not." The colonel stood up and began to pace. "Where is she? I'll need to talk to her. We've never been in this situation before."

Gabriel cleared his throat, exchanging a look with Wraith. "She's not here. She left in the middle of the night for Aberdeen."

"You let her go?" Alex asked angrily.

"I wasn't in a position to stop her. Trust me, I tried. The lassie has a mind of her own; she nearly ran me over with the car."

Wraith laughed, shaking his head.

Gabriel threw him a dirty look. "She's at the Malmaison hotel. I have Kian on it as we speak."

"And this Viktor Sokolov? Why have we never heard of him?" Alex stopped his back and forth march, leaning against the mantelpiece.

"We've turned up a few possible aliases, Vance Stevenson, Val Smith. The names pop up in some real estate schemes and now, of course, the sex trafficking."

Gabriel's phone started playing *Pachelbel Canon.* "It's Kian." He answered it, going over to a corner.

The colonel turned to Wraith. "Sinclair spoke highly of you and your skills."

Wraith eyes narrowed cynically. "I was just doing my job."

"Aye, but Sinclair speaks highly of no one." Alex sat down and inclined his head. His voice lowered. "I know we've discussed this before, but you need to stop the battle going on inside you. I guarantee those girls thank you for what you did. This Sokolov is a sick bastard. We'll give him the kind of justice he deserves."

Wraith didn't have time to answer before Gabriel came back over. "They're gone. Pim and Peter left the hotel in the middle of the night."

"Bloody hell."

"Scottish National Ballet performs in Aberdeen tonight," Wraith said. "They won't have gone far."

Chapter 28

Pim sat up on the small, olive-green sofa. She felt like she could have slept for twelve more hours. "What time is it?" she asked Peter. She had abandoned the car on the outskirts of Aberdeen. The cash in Wraith's wallet paid for a taxi, and when she got to the hotel, she convinced Peter to move to a different one.

"Eleven. I have to head over to the theatre," he said, looking at his watch. "The company will be arriving. I'll wait for you to get ready and we'll go together, darling."

She had told him everything, from her grandfather's apparent murder to Sokolov and the dead girl, all as he held her. She knew she shouldn't trust him, but the company was the closest thing to family she had right now, and as dysfunctional as it was, in the end, it was the only world she knew. Peter had his faults, but he would always be there for her.

"I don't think I can dance tonight. The thought makes me sick."

"You don't have to decide that now. At least come to the theatre and try class. You can't stay alone."

"I don't have any supplies."

"Paul said not to worry. He's bringing you everything you need."

Showered and dressed in the slightly wrinkled clothes from the night before, she sat next to Peter as they caught a taxi to the venue. The streets were packed with visitors. The solid granite buildings that made up Aberdeen and gave the city the name *Silver City by the Golden Sands*, sat stalwart, protecting the people from the cold North Sea wind. The Aberdeen International Market on Union Street, along with the ballet, were in town, and the city was abuzz with vendors and spectators. The taxi pulled up in front of His Majesty's Theatre. Peter helped Pim out of the car, grabbing his various bags. "Come along."

The theatre was considered a national treasure. Edwardian in its architecture, it was both opulent and awe-inspiring. Pim should be excited to get the chance to perform here. Instead, she felt nothing. The dancers had already arrived, portable barres had been set up on the stage, and most were beginning to warm up for company class. Paul came up and gave her a hug. "I brought you a bag. It's in your dressing room. How are you doing?"

"It's been a long week." She bit her lip; she didn't want to cry.

"I can imagine."

"No, I don't think you can." She took a step back, glancing at the ground, not able to look at his face. "I can't perform tonight. I'm sorry, Paul. You'll have to do it with Catriona." She turned and made her way backstage to the dressing rooms. There was a sign on a door next to the general changing rooms, *Primrose McNeil*. She had never had her own dressing room before, not even in Inverness. The door stood ajar, and she pushed it open, entering. A lighted mirror hung on the wall before a vanity, where her makeup was all laid out. Her costumes hung on hooks from the ceilings, the tutus standing out like open umbrellas. A vase with a dozen white roses sat on a table by a pink velvet armchair. She fingered the card, *To my darling Etoile. The most beautiful swan. Love, Peter.* A knock on the door made her jump.

"Sorry, Rosy," Niall said, peeking his head inside.

She did her best to give him a smile. "Did they send you to make me change my mind?"

"No, I came on my own, to make sure you're okay."

"I'll be all right. I just can't dance right now, or maybe ever."

"Rosy, I've been around the ballet world longer than most. I haven't seen someone with your talent for a long time and not just technically, but artistically too. You're strong. Whatever's happened, use that strength to push through, don't let it break you."

"I'll try, Niall."

"I know you will." He turned to leave and stopped, coming back. "I almost forgot," he said, picking up a flower from a table in the hall. "This came for you."

Pim shut the door, her hands shaking as she set the flower down on the vanity. A single black rose whose danger wielded its dark warning intentionally. She opened the card. *When a thing is perfect, it is eternal. Safe in the past forever. A life for a life. I'll be watching - V.S.* She threw the rose and the card in the trash bin. It was a play on a quote from Alasdair Gray's *Lanark*. Ruthlessly honest, and its truth scared her. Perfection lay in the timelessness of death, sanctified forever. Sokolov had not only breached her mind, it felt like he now owned her soul. And a damaged soul at that. He brought something out in her last night not only terrifying and repugnant, but inspirational and beautiful. He had linked the two of them in a deadly game of transcendence and had found a way to create that which she had always strived for—perfection. But perfection could not only be cruel, it was also offensive. She sat down at the vanity and began to apply her stage makeup. She would dance, but it would come at the cost of her or another's life.

Wraith, Gabriel, and Kian approached the theatre. Wraith had called ahead and confirmed that Pim would be dancing the lead role this evening. Intermission was just ending, and the men went to their agreed upon places. The colonel had insisted on sending three agents, not knowing if Viktor Sokolov would be in attendance. Wraith waited for the house to darken and the music to begin before he made his way stage left, into the wings. Dancers warming up, racks of costumes, along with changing assistants, and stagehands with props, filled the sides of the stage in silent giddiness. The buzz of excited energy reverberated through the air. Pim was onstage, dancing the black swan. She looked different from rehearsal, no longer holding back. She, as the seductress, filled the stage, daring Prince Siegfried to choose her and commanding the audience to love her. Peter stood watching, awe-struck.

"She's bonnie," Wraith said, coming up behind him.

"I've never seen her dance this way. She'll bring the house down." Peter pulled his eyes from the stage, giving Wraith a dirty look. "She almost didn't dance. No thanks to you."

Wraith wondered what exactly Pim had said to Peter. "I would never intentionally hurt her."

"Aye, but you did. You're not welcome here; you'll only upset her. Leave."

"I'm staying. She's in danger."

"Danger brought on by you."

The gun sat heavy against Wraith, holstered against the side of his chest. He would use it if he needed to, but Peter made no move to kick him out, caught up once again with Pim. Act three finished, and she exited the stage. Two women

Stripped

pounced on her, unhooking the bodice of her costume and pulling it down as she stepped out of it. She stood only in her tights as the dressers fumbled with the white swan costume. Peter came over and grabbed it from the hand of a portly woman. He helped Pim step into the satin bodice and rigid tutu, pulling it up her body and fastening the tiny hooks up her back.

Wraith watched as his fingers lingered, softly caressing her bare shoulders as he adjusted the nude elastic straps. His jaw clenched, that was *his* body, the same beautiful body he'd made love to two nights ago, when she had surrendered to him. No one else had the right to touch her so possessively. Peter kissed her cheek as the other woman pinned a white-feathered headdress in her hair. Her clear eyes caught Wraith's for a second before she returned to the stage, and for a moment, he wondered if she even recognized him.

"So alluring," Peter said, his chest thrust out like a puffed up bird, as he came to stand beside Wraith.

"How much longer until this happily ever after is over?" He was feeling a bit set off by Pim's blatant disregard.

Peter laughed. "It's not a happily ever after. How classically redundant that would be. No, this is a sinister tragedy. I don't go in for the fairy princess stuff. That ending of Swan Lake would be wasted on Pim." Wraith watched as she, Paul, and the dancer playing Von Rothbart, the evil owl, began a wicked pas de trois. Pim's eyes grew wide for a moment, akin to shock, and Wraith saw in an instant what she did. It was the same man from the other night who had run through the audience, knocking people over.

"Who's playing Rothbart?" he asked Peter.

"Thomas Laurence, our original Siegfried. I got a note during intermission from Jerome, who normally plays the part, saying he fell ill. Thomas agreed to fill in."

"We need to close the curtain," Wraith said. He glanced

across the stage to the other wing, where Gabriel stood, giving him a quick nod and running his hand across his forehead as a sign.

"Are you fucking mad? This is the best performance SNB has had in years."

"Close the fucking curtain. Pim's in danger." Siegfried and Rothbart continued to battle it out on stage for Odette, dancing in a mad-lover's embrace until Siegfried fell to his death, leaving just Odette and Rothbart, a red stain growing on his chest. Wraith saw the fear in Pim's eyes; it was real. The music grew in a heartbreaking climax. Rothbart put his wings around her, picking her up as mist filled the stage and the background changed, giving the audience the illusion he was flying away with her. His razor-sharp talon was placed strategically on her throat. A small red light appeared on Rothbart's forehead. "Shut the fucking curtain." Wraith charged the stagehand, pulling the gold cord himself as sheets of red velvet came tumbling down. The audience exploded in applause. He rushed out on stage, but Rothbart had fled. Pim lay on the floor, blood dripping from her throat. He picked her up and ran offstage, toward the dressing rooms.

Chapter 29

"Bloody hell," Wraith said, setting Pim down in the back corner of her dressing room. "Are you okay?" He locked the door, shoving a chair under the handle.

Pim stood up, wiping the blood from her neck as she looked around for a cloth. He would have killed her. Thomas would have killed her if Wraith hadn't intervened. He had said as much to her on stage.

"Stay in the corner," he barked, coming over to her and handing her his handkerchief.

"I have to check on Paul."

"Primrose, Paul will be fine. It's going to be pandemonium out there. It's safer if we stay in here. Trust me." He tried to dab at her neck, but she pushed his hand away, holding the cloth to her wound.

"Trust you?" She sat down in the corner, suddenly light-headed. "You want me to fucking trust you. Maybe I should trust Robert McInnes or Robert McLeish?"

He frowned. "They're aliases. In my business, I need them."

"In your business?" She laughed. "And what exactly do you do?"

He ignored the question. Instead, he pulled the discarded rose and note from the bin, and reading the card, he put it in his pocket and found a towel, running it under warm water from a small sink. He came over and knelt down, gently cleaning her cut. "It's not deep."

He was too close, his presence overwhelming. "What about Robert McFadden? Should I trust him?"

"Robert McFadden is dead," he said, drawing back.

"Really? I don't think he's dead to the duchess, nor she to him." There it was, she said it, what hurt her heart the most. More than Sokolov or Peter or the agony and torment of the deadly dances, Wraith's betrayal. She knew she told him it was just sex, but somewhere in the moment, she had surrendered a piece of herself to him. *Stupid girl.*

"Robert McFadden *is* dead and any feelings or thoughts he once had are dead too." There was a bitterness in his tone that turned her blood to ice. "I meant what I said to you before you left. I am falling in love with you."

"She still holds a flame for you."

"And at one point, I thought I still had feelings for her. The first night I kissed you backstage, I thought I was so happy because I got to see her. It was the first time in a long time I felt alive, but I know now it had nothing to do with her. What I was feeling was about you. It was the possibility of experiencing desire again."

"Don't tell that to Gabriel or that crazy, fucked up place you work."

"I don't give a damn about Gabriel." He stood her up, anchored her against the wall and kissed her hard, claiming her as his. "You're mine, Primrose. There's nobody else."

"You can't just take me and say I'm yours."

"I beg to differ," he said. "Does Peter normally help you change costumes during scenes?"

"What in bloody hell are you talking about?"

"Peter changing you in the wings? Touching your body."

"I have dressers who help me change. There's no time to go to the dressing room. If Peter helped, I wasn't aware."

"Did you see me?" he asked.

"No, I was too caught up in the dance. I didn't notice anything." She was too caught up wondering if Sokolov was watching.

Panicked voices could be heard coming down the hallway. "Change. We need to get out of here."

"I need help with the bodice," she said, her heart beating madly in her chest. She turned her back to him as he undid the hooks down her back. His hand brushed over her shoulder. Coming around, he cupped her breast. "You're mine."

She stepped forward and cleared her throat. He was as dangerous as he was seductive, nothing more than a silent executioner. "I know what you do." She removed the costume and slipped on a pair of black nylon dance pants and a pale pink sweater, tying it at her waist.

"Do you?" He listened at the door.

"Who did my grandfather hire you to kill?"

He stood up straight at the frankness of her question. "No one," he said, turning his attention back to the noise in the hallway. Someone knocked on the door. Three knocks, silence, then two more in quick succession.

"I asked you a question?" She could feel the anger in her grow.

"And I said no one." He removed the chair and opened the door, letting a man with short red hair inside. The man gave her a brief nod. She backed up into the corner, realization dawning on her. Her grandfather didn't pay Wraith to kill anyone. She doubted he ever worked for him. Wraith had been there to kill her grandfather.

"What's going on?" he asked the man. He was tall like Wraith and well built.

"The fool playing Rothbart is dead. I found him backstage with his wrists cut. The man playing Siegfried will be fine, it was just a flesh wound. No sign of Sokolov, but that was definitely a laser scope on Rothbart's head." He glanced between Wraith and Pim, handing her a black rose. "This was left at the door."

Wraith tried to take it from her, but she held on to it, reading the card that was attached.

Every time you dance, you shed an old skin. Liberation and pure bliss are near. V.S.

Wraith grabbed it from her hand.

"We need to go. Gabriel will be outside with the car," the man said.

Pim shuddered, the frisson of the words on the card inciting both excitement and fear. She grabbed her bag off the pink chair and reached in for a jacket. Wraith's gun from the car sat heavy on the bottom, her fingers brushing over the cold, hard metal. If she pulled it out now, she would be no better than him.

"Let's go." He held his hand out to her.

She shook her head. "Did you kill my grandfather?" She needed to know.

"No."

"Liar," she spat.

"Primrose, we need to go." Police sirens could be heard in the distance

"I'm not going anywhere with you. Stay the fuck away from me. You go."

He took a step toward her, grabbing her arm, and the rose

dropped to the floor. Why was she such a fool to fall for him? He was a killer, no better than Sokolov.

Wraith sat in the backseat of the car with Pim. Her hands were cuffed in front of her and he had gagged her to get her out of the theatre quietly. He touched the scratches on his neck, their sting attesting to the struggle that had ensued. She hadn't made it easy. "I'll take the gag off if you promise to be quiet."

She glared at him. His phone rang, and he looked at the screen. Peter. He answered it. "Where is she?" Peter asked, panicked. "Is she all right?"

"I have her with me. I'm taking her somewhere safe."

"I want to talk to her."

Wraith looked over at her. She had turned her back on him, but he could tell she was listening. "She can't talk right now."

"She needs to be with her family right now. Where she's loved."

He paused. She *was* loved; he loved her. He couldn't say as much with Gabriel and Kian up front. "Look, Peter. Where do you perform tomorrow?"

"Glasgow. The film festival is going on and with the crowds in for the gala, we were asked to perform."

"I'll have her at the theatre." He hung up. He reached behind her and undid the knot in the cloth. Removing it, he wiped her mouth.

"I'll have kidnapping charges brought against you," she said.

"No, you won't." He rubbed his arm, the wound from the knife attack aching from overuse. "By the way, where's my car?"

"I don't give a fuck where your car is."

Wraith grimaced; she was shutting down. Kian, the bastard, laughed, up front.

"I have documents in there I need to retrieve."

"I'm sure you'll manage without them, and I guarantee your car's gone. I left it on the side of the road with the keys in the ignition."

"Aye, she's right," Gabriel said. "Whoever has it ripped the GPS tracker off it."

Gabriel pulled through the iron gates of The Tower and pulled the car up to the round tower house instead of the mansion.

"It's late. Can't this wait until tomorrow after she's had some sleep?" Wraith asked.

"No. He wants to talk with her tonight." Gabriel parked the car and got out with Kian.

Wraith undid the cuffs on Pim's wrists. "Don't be frightened. I'll stay with you the entire time."

"If you think that's going to make me feel better, you can go screw yourself."

Chapter 30

Pim followed the men into the tall stone house and down a hallway. Wraith kept his hand on her lower back, probably fearful she would flee at the first possibility. She should be used to meeting strange men at this point, but her heart rate increased, the closer they got. She was obviously being taken to their leader. Gabriel held the door open for them as they entered. The room was warm, a fire burned in the fireplace, reflections dancing off the richly polished wood walls. A handsome man in his sixties sat in one of the leather armchairs. He stood as they came inside. "Lads, you're not needed. I'll speak with you in the morning. Gabriel, be sure a room is prepared for her."

"Yes, sir."

Wraith put his hand on her shoulder. "I told Pim I would stay with her."

The man smiled. "I think she'll be fine on her own. And for a child, she managed to outwit all of you. She can handle a conversation with me."

Pim looked over her shoulder at Wraith and glared. "Child?"

"I'll wait for you outside in the foyer."

"That won't be necessary," the colonel said. "I'll make sure she gets to her room."

Wraith gave her shoulder a squeeze before leaving with the other men. She stood there, looking at the man. He was dressed in gray slacks, white shirt and a navy sweater. The sweater brought out the deep blue in his eyes. "Ms. McNeil, let me introduce myself. My name is Alexander McKay." He held out his hand, smiling.

She put her bag down and took it, keeping her grip firm as she shook it. *Child?* She had been called a lot of things but never that. "Primrose McNeil, but you already know that."

"Please, have a seat." He motioned to one of the armchairs by the fire.

"I think I'll stand." She moved closer to the fire; the sweater she wore was thin and the tower house was cold.

His smile tightened. She was sure he was used to people obeying him, but she wouldn't give him the pleasure. He was the enemy, no better than Sokolov. "Would you like a drink? Sherry or brandy, perhaps?"

"Alcohol for a child?"

"I meant no offense, and I think you are an intelligent young lady, not a child. It was a dig at the lads, not you."

"Whiskey's fine." She spied his unfinished glass on the small end table by his chair.

"Of course." He poured her a glass from a crystal decanter and handed it to her, picking up his own. "Slange," he said.

She raised hers. "Slange," she repeated. "The Macallan eighteen years. Ginger, vanilla and hints of cinnamon."

"Clever," Alex said. "You know whiskey."

"I know good whiskey."

"Your performance made the news. An intense and brilliant rendition of the swans, I believe they called it."

She wasn't sure why they were engaging in small talk, but he seemed to be moving cautiously with her. "Are you going to kill me, like you did my grandfather, after I give you the information you want?" she asked, getting to the point of the matter.

"We didn't kill your grandfather."

"But you were going to. Wraith was going to."

"Primrose. Will you please sit for a moment, lass?"

She sat down on the edge of the chair. "It's Pim. No one calls me Primrose."

He scooted his chair closer until their knees were practically touching. His blue eyes searched her face and she saw something close to empathy in their depths. "Pim. I think we find ourselves in uncharted territory." There was something about him that nagged at her. "I'm hoping we can find some common ground."

"I beg to differ, Mr. McKay. Your organization kills people. There is no common ground."

"Aye, it's true we do eliminate some very bad people, but that's just one part of what we do."

She stiffened, clenching her jaw. He sat forward, invading her personal space. She had nowhere to go. "I know you don't want to hear what I have to say, and it will be painful, but you deserve the truth." He looked her in the eyes as he spoke. "Your grandfather was the leader of an organized crime gang called the Tartan Mafia. He ran the entire west coast operation of opioid trafficking, laundering his dirty money through his various businesses, and loaning money to people who could never repay him, so he would control them. He was using children and the mentally disabled to ply his drugs. He has cost thousands of people their lives. We know about Natasha, and now we believe he was also caught up in the sex trafficking of young girls."

She knew what he said was true. This just confirmed what

she wanted so desperately to deny. "Then why wasn't he in prison? We have a justice system."

"He had a lot of people, including government officials and the police, in his pocket. There was no way he would ever have been tried and convicted."

"So, you take it upon yourself to *eliminate* people you deem bad, and play God," she said bitterly.

"No, we do it to help the victims, the innocent ones. I don't pick the targets; our client does."

"And who's your client?"

"Even I don't have that information." He sat back, and she crossed her arms in front of her protectively, looking down. The empathy was back in his eyes. He held himself with quiet authority. This was a man who knew how to lead people and demanded compliance. "Will you tell me about Sokolov?" he asked softly.

Her eyes grew wide as she realized what was nagging at her. Alex reminded her of her father the last time they were together in Òran Mór. He had been involved in her grandfather's business. Was he as evil as her grandfather and Sokolov? She shook her head as disappointment and disillusionment filled her. "No, I'm afraid I can't talk about it."

He grasped her chin, tilting her head up so she had to look at him. "Did he violate you, lass?"

"Not how you're thinking."

"But he did violate you?"

She pushed his hand away. "I think I'm done with this conversation. I'm tired," she said, standing up. "If you could show me to my room."

He stood up next to her. "Of course."

They walked back to the mansion in silence. Alex held out his hand to slow her, pointing up at the sky. Vivid lights in green and purple snaked across the clear night sky, setting it alive with rainbows of light, nature's own spectacular theatrical performance. "She called them the heavenly dancers, merry dancers in the sky," Alex recited the lyrics from a song.

"It's a cheery thought but not very accurate. The lights of the night sky belong to the dead," Pim said.

His head tilted to the side. "Aye, how so?" he asked.

"Some believe it's the souls of those murdered still bleeding."

"You'll be thinking of your Da," he said matter of factly.

She continued to look at the aurora borealis, hoping he couldn't see her face, and shrugged, surprised at his bluntness.

"He had no part in your grandfather's business if that's what you're wondering." She felt him eyeing her with concern. "Or none that we can connect. I'm sorry, I should have told you earlier. Of course, it would be weighing on your mind."

She looked down, the sudden show in the heavens gone as quickly as it started. "I never thought he was," she lied, disappointed in herself for ever having the traitorous thought.

Gabriel was waiting for them in the foyer when they arrived. "I've put her in the west wing."

"Put her with Wraith."

"No," she said. "I'll take my own room."

"We'll take her to Wraith."

"Yes, sir," he said as he led them down the east wing to his flat and knocked on the door.

Wraith wrapped a towel around his waist and answered the door. He had taken a shower and was about to rewrap the wound on his arm. Alex stood there with his hands on Pim's shoulders. Tears filled her eyes. "I want her to stay with you tonight."

"I really would like my own room—"

"Of course, she can stay," Wraith cut her off, leading her in. "Why don't you go take a bath?" he said quietly to her.

She went into the restroom, shutting the door.

"What's going on?" he asked, turning to the other men.

"Here, let me get that for you." Gabriel took the bandage from his hand.

Wraith brushed him off.

"Let him attend you," Alex ordered.

He sat down, biting his tongue so as not to say something he would regret, as Gabriel wrapped the bandage around his arm. "She doesn't want to stay here. She doesn't trust me."

"She does." Alex sat down next to him.

"What did she say to you?"

"Not much, but I told her exactly what her grandfather was involved in. It will have been hard for her to hear."

"And Sokolov?"

"Nothing. She'll need to talk tomorrow." Alex cleared his throat. "I'm taking you off the investigation."

"You can't do that. No one knows the situation like I do. I'm so close to piecing this all together."

Alex held his hand up. "You're on protection only. I don't want you to leave her side until this bastard Sokolov is caught, and I have a feeling it's going to get very dangerous."

Gabriel finished with his arm. "Thanks," Wraith said under his breath.

Alex stood to leave. "Have her in my office by nine tomorrow."

He watched as they shut the door behind themselves. *Damn.* Now what? He went to his drawer and pulled out a starched white handkerchief. Opening the bathroom door, he waved it around. "Truce?"

Hearing no response, he peeked his head in. She sat in the tub, knees pulled up to her chest, holding her face in her hands. The bubbles had dissipated, now just small islands of white foam floating here and there on the water's surface. He went and sat on the edge.

"Was he that rough on you then?" he asked quietly. "Because he can be a right bastard."

She looked up, resting her chin on her knees. "No, on the contrary. He was very kind, which can be worse. He reminded me of my father." Wraith picked up a sponge and started washing the makeup covering her tattoo off her back. "You won't get it with that," she said. "You'll need remover."

He looked over on the counter and saw a package of wipes. Taking one, he cleaned off the remainder. He ran his hand over the muscles that covered her spine and ribs. "I'm sorry."

"Somewhere in the back of my mind, I knew something wasn't right. It was hearing the name, the Tartan Mafia, that made it true. I've been in denial."

"It still hurts, though," he said. She bit her lip. "You don't have to be strong with me, Primrose."

"Yes, I do."

The water had turned cold. He stood her up and wrapped a towel around her. Picking her up, he carried her into the other room and sat down on the couch, with her on his lap. She rested her head against his chest. There were questions he wanted to ask and things he needed to say, but he didn't want to scare her away. "Talk to me. Let me in."

"Wraith—"

"Please, Primrose.

"I don't know how. I'm broken. I've always been broken."

"You're not broken to me. You're strong and smart, maybe a bit willful, but not broken. But you can't do this alone. No one could."

"Would you have taken the shot if someone hadn't gotten to my grandfather first?"

It was an honest question, and it deserved an honest

answer. If he wanted her to open up to him, he needed to do the same. "Yes," he said after several minutes. "I would have taken the shot."

She stiffened in his arms, and he caressed her back, hoping to offer her some reparation. "I told you I was ex-military, SBS. I was a special operative sniper. If I was given an order, I followed it. This was no different. It's not that I don't have emotions. I've just learned to harness them. Acknowledge, process, execute. It's like living life constantly in code red." He kissed her on the head. It was his turn to ask a question. "Tell me what Sokolov did to you?"

She shook her head. "I can't."

"Did he touch you, Primrose? Is that why you can't tell me?"

"No."

"I found you without any clothes on."

"He took them, but that's not what he wanted from me."

"What did he want? Help me understand."

"It's like he's linked us."

"Linked you?"

"He knew things about me. Everything from the way I wear my pointe shoes to the books I've read, the variations I've danced, my relationship with my father. He even knew the phrase you would say to me, *that's my girl*. He took it all and warped it and used it against me."

"Christ." He pulled her in tight to his chest.

"He said I owed him a debt from my grandfather. A life for a life. He made me dance for it. Then he killed one of the girls in front of me and made me watch her die, saying it would make me a better dancer."

"Jesus Christ."

"The thing is I am a better dancer. With him, I'm a better dancer."

"That's not true."

Stripped

"I think it would have been easier if he had just used my body, but he penetrated my mind, seducing my soul into some kind of morbid dance with him."

"No. He doesn't control you, Primrose. I promise you that."

"I hate him, yet I need him. I'm flawed without him."

"No one can control your mind." He stood up with her in his arms. "You need to get some sleep." He set her down on the large, king-sized bed and lay next to her. She rolled over, the towel falling off, and kissed him, running her hand over his chest. "Fuck me until I forget."

"I'll make love to you but not fuck." He flipped her over on her back.

"You know there's no future for us," she said, putting her hands between them and pushing them apart.

"There's right now. We have right now." He felt her stiffen as he traced the curve of her cheekbone. "You're afraid."

He didn't say it as a taunt or an offensive, she could tell by his voice. It was more of a realization. "I'm not afraid. I just don't see the point." She felt as if her insides had been turned out. Raw and exposed. He was a killer, he had told her before, *'I've killed men,'* warned her. She watched as he slit the throat of the man in Sokolov's room when he rescued her. Yet she wanted him, somewhere inside her, she trusted him, this Robert with a hundred names.

He gently moved her hands down to her sides and kissed her. "The point is you need to know what it feels like to let someone in and to feel safe," he whispered as he kissed her again. "Truly safe."

She didn't have a response. His hand, warm and large, cupped her bottom as he eased her on her side and pulled the towel from around his waist. Lifting her leg, he entered her so they faced each other. "What do you want, Primrose?"

She wanted him to hold her down and fuck her. This was too gentle, too intimate. She put her hands above her head, prompting him.

"No, darling. I mean, what do you want in life?"

"What kind of question is that?" Her voice came out thick and husky. He was large and the feel of him inside her began to dominate her senses.

"Tell me what you want."

"I've told you, I want to be perfect."

"No, you don't. That's what you want people to believe." His hand traced the curve of her cheek. "And you don't need to prove yourself to me. I see your value."

"What do you want?" She tried pushing him on his back, so she could be on top, but he was too strong and forced them to remain on their sides.

"Fine. I want to be the main player in my life. I've always been on the sidelines, watching or providing security to other people while they live out their dreams. I want the dream now."

"So, you don't want to protect me anymore?"

"I want to protect you but not because I get paid. I want to protect you and take care of you because you're mine."

"But I'm not yours." She tried forcing him away, but he held her tight, the soft rhythm as he moved in and out of her becoming overpowering.

"You're mine."

A tear slid down her cheek. She didn't want him to say things like that. She belonged to no one.

"There you are," he said, wiping it away. "I knew you were in there."

The words were spoken softly, but they cracked through

her, opening up a barrage of feelings and leaving her defenseless.

"Primrose, look at me."

She opened her eyes, locking in on his, and glimpsed a part of his soul as he claimed the last private bit of herself.

"Shh," he whispered. "I've got you." He held her head to his chest as they rode out the silent waves of ecstasy. When their bodies finally separated, he turned her, wrapping himself around her in a protective shell. "I'll handle Alex tomorrow. You don't have to worry about anything."

Chapter 31

Wraith was gone when Pim woke up. She rummaged through her ballet bag, pulling out a pair of sweats and an off-the-shoulder warmup sweater. The pile of clothes Gabriel had procured the other night sat on a chair in the corner. She wasn't sure what to expect, but she would handle it better in her own clothes. Changed, she pulled her hair back into a bun and slipped her feet into her warm up boots. She needed to call Peter, but she had no phone. No doubt, he would be worried.

She took a last look in the mirror, pushing a stray piece of hair behind her ear, and opened the door to leave. The agent from the other night stood in the hallway. If she remembered right, his name was Sin. His steel gray eyes cold and dark, he looked her up and down. A large sable and white dog sat next to his feet. "Keeping guard, so I don't escape," she said a bit harshly.

"On the contrary, I'm keeping guard for your protection. We don't know much about Viktor Sokolov and as long as he's out there, you're vulnerable." He held his hand out to her. "I don't think we've been formally introduced. Sinclair Stuart."

She gave it a brief shake. "Pim."

"This is William."

"I believe we've met before," she said to the dog.

He gave her a loud woof.

She followed them down the hallway. "Are the girls okay?"

"As good as they can be. The ones in the house are getting reunited with their parents. The authorities are still trying to locate the few who were already sold, but that, unfortunately, can be nearly impossible once they leave the country."

"There was a little one. Annika was her name," she started to ask.

Sinclair stopped and shook his head. "I'm sorry. I couldn't tell you. Once I turned it over to the police, I was out of the picture."

She was reminded, in the moment, exactly who she was dealing with. These men were killers themselves. "What makes a man evil, do you suppose?" She wasn't sure why she asked it and regretted it almost instantly.

Sinclair kept walking, but she noticed he slowed just a bit and stiffened. "In what manner are you speaking?"

"In the manner of taking a life."

"In that case, it would depend."

"Depend? A life is a life."

"What about in war? Euthanasia?" he countered. "Self-defense."

"I'm talking about when you don't have authority."

"What if those in authority aren't doing their jobs and people continue to get hurt?" He stopped outside a door. "Are you asking if Wraith is an evil man?"

"No." She looked down, feeling her face grow warm.

"He's not." He tilted her chin up. "Sokolov is an evil man. What he did to you and those girls is evil. Wraith is not that. Me, on the other hand, watch out for; they call me Sin for a reason." He opened the door, not giving her a chance to respond. She followed him into a dining room. Wraith, Alex and Gabriel stood up when she entered.

"I'm glad you could join us, Ms. McNeil," Alex said, setting down his napkin.

"Pleasantries aside, I didn't think I had a choice."

The corner of the colonel's mouth quirked up. "Please, have a seat." He motioned to the chair next to him. She followed Sinclair over to it as he pulled it out for her. Her eyes briefly caught with Wraith's.

"Can I get you anything?" Sin asked.

William seemed content to settle himself at the foot of her chair.

"I'll get it," Wraith said. He went over to the sideboard and made her a plate. When he returned, he set a mug of black coffee and a poached egg with toast down in front of her.

"Can I borrow your phone?" she asked quietly.

"I've already called Peter. He wants you at the theatre by five. We have plenty of time." His hand brushed her bare shoulder, sending goosebumps down her arm.

"Oh." She wanted to respond, to say he had no right to do that, but the look he gave her kept her quiet. Not here, not now.

"Ms. McNeil—"

"Please, it's Pim. I thought we established that last night."

Alex gave her a nod. "Pim. Wraith filled me in on your encounter with Viktor Sokolov."

She poked the yolk of her egg with her fork, watching the thick yellow center ooze across her plate. A heart—she quickly sliced her knife through it, the paradox mocking her.

Sinclair took the seat next to her, setting his plate of bacon rolls down. She didn't want to look at any of the men, ashamed they now knew what had transpired, ashamed she had let the girl die.

"I was hoping we could work together." Alexander leaned forward as if to emphasize his point.

"I'm not sure how much help I would be." The yolk coagulated on her fork in sticky clumps, turning her already tense stomach in knots. She set it down and picked up her coffee.

"On the contrary, you've seen him. You know his personality."

"What do you want from me?" she asked directly, mustering the courage to look him in the eyes. "I'm not one of you. I'm a ballet dancer. I'm not a fucking detective."

"Sinclair does composite drawings. Sit with him for an hour and see what you can come up with. Then we want you to dance at the gala tonight. Sokolov will be there. You have become his obsession. He wouldn't miss the opportunity."

She laughed, the idea of what he was asking now dawning on her. "I apologize for being a bit slow." She pressed her lips together. "You intend to use me to lure in Sokolov." He would be there, she knew it, and something tensed at the base of her spine she couldn't quite put her finger on. Trepidation? No, that wasn't right, possibly anticipation.

"Not use you. Wraith will be there the entire time to protect you while we take care of Sokolov."

She looked across at Wraith. He had remained silent this entire time. His brows were drawn down in a frown, looking grim.

"This would make me an accomplice. It would make me a part of whatever it is you call this organization."

"And what about those young girls?" Sinclair asked. "He will keep doing what he does to them. Taking them from their families in Russia, promising their parents a better life for them and then selling them into sex trafficking."

"Don't put that on me." She shook her head. "How dare you put that on me. He should be arrested. Put in jail. There are legal ways to handle this."

Sinclair turned his chair to face her. "Do you think a man like Viktor Sokolov would be stupid enough to get arrested? And even if he was, he has enough money, lawyers, and contacts to get him off. Bloody hell, one of his aliases is a foreign ambassador. He would be given diplomatic immunity at this point."

"*Enough*," Wraith shouted. "She'll do the composite, and then we'll go to Glasgow. We're running out of time."

Her head shot around to him, her eyes opening wide. "Or what? What if I say no? Will you kill me?" She regretted the words as soon as she said them, knowing she made him no better than the colonel with his threats. Tears pricked the back of her eyes and she blinked several times, trying to stop them. Wraith's eyes narrowed ever so slightly as he cocked his head to the side, rubbing his chin. "Don't tempt me."

"Wraith's right. We are running out of time," Alex said. "I won't force you to do anything you don't want to, Pim, but we could use your help."

Her eyes were still locked on Wraith. Could she trust him to protect her? The feel of his body as he held her after they'd made love sent a shiver down her spine. Maybe that wasn't the right question. He would protect her. The real question was would she *allow* him to protect her? "Fine," she said. "I'll help."

She spent the next hour sequestered in Alex's office with Sinclair, as he grilled her on Sokolov's appearance and personality. He wanted to know the fine nuances, traits and tics, of the man, anything that influenced the make-up of his person and his character. In the end, they had a close enough resemblance she thought to be useful. Sinclair proved himself to be a fine artist.

"You asked what makes a man evil," he said as he put away his charcoal pencils and wiped the black dust from his fingers.

"I don't think I want to know anymore." She was exhausted from the questions and reliving the experience.

"Perhaps we all have it in us to be evil and we all find ourselves there on some scale."

She thought of her own dark thoughts and her need to dally in the shadows of life. She much preferred dancing the black swan over the white swan. There was truth in what he said. "Then the real question is how do we keep from going there fully? How do we prevent ourselves from becoming Viktor Sokolov?"

He looked at her thoughtfully "By surrounding ourselves with people like Wraith."

Chapter 32

The drive back to Glasgow was silent. It wasn't until they hit the mid-point on the M8 between Edinburgh and Glasgow and The Horn, the great sculpture, standing twenty-four meters high, could be heard blaring out its message to the passing traffic, '*Modern science speaks to us of an extraordinary range of interrelations,*" before it faded away out of earshot that Pim got the courage to speak. "I'm sorry for what I said at breakfast. I know you wouldn't kill me."

Wraith gave her a sideways glance. "Don't think of it. Your nerves were fraught. Alex and Sin can be difficult."

"I'm still sorry."

He reached out and gave her knee a squeeze, leaving his hand to rest there casually. "Stop. I know you didn't mean it."

"I've been wondering who really did kill my grandfather." She looked out the window. Gray clouds sat low on the horizon, mixing with the mist on the fields, blending so there was no beginning or end.

"What do you mean? Sokolov had him killed."

"I'm not sure."

Wraith glanced over his shoulder, switching lanes to pass a

slow-moving lorry, the Land Rover easily over taking the truck. "I thought you weren't a detective."

"I'm not, but it was something Thomas said on stage to me, about being rid of my grandfather's grip."

"He talked to you on stage and you didn't tell me?"

"I don't know. I just remembered it and Sokolov never said he killed my grandfather, he just said my grandfather owed him a debt. A life for a life."

"Aye, a life for a life. Your grandfather must have taken someone from him and Sokolov repaid the debt by killing him."

"No, he implied that my life was the debt, and it was my debt to pay now that he was dead. What if Thomas killed my grandfather?"

"He had the opportunity to kill you and Paul, and he left you both with scratches. I don't think he had it in him. And remember, someone took him out."

"I don't know."

"Jesus Christ. Leave it for the professionals, Primrose."

"But they're just assuming it was Sokolov."

"I said leave it." The tone of his voice told her it was best if she dropped it for now.

"I will, but before we go to the theatre, I need you to do me a favor."

"What?" Wraith pulled off the M8 and onto Great Western.

"I need to see Irina. Offer her my condolences. I owe her that."

He shook his head. "No. Wait a bit. There will be time later this week."

"No, she blames me for her accident. I need to clear my name. I need to see her today."

"Primrose—"

"Please, Wraith. She lives in Kelvinside, on Mingarry. It

won't take long."

"Fine." He pulled off on Queen Margaret Drive, taking them over the River Kelvin and eventually onto Mingarry.

"It's the flat with the red door. I won't be a minute," she said as he parked.

"I'm coming with you." He closed the car door behind him, following her up the path.

She knocked on the door, taking a deep breath to calm her nerves. Zoya Petrov opened the door. "What the hell do you want?"

Pim's heartbeat picked up at seeing the ballet mistress. "I just wanted to speak to Irina for a moment."

"You are the last person she wants to see right now."

Wraith put his hand on the small of her back, a small reassurance. "I know. I realize that but—"

"Let her in," Irina's voice called out from inside.

Zoya held the door open, letting them in. Irina was tucked up under a blanket on the couch, her broken ankle casted and propped on a pillow. Dark circles rimmed her red eyes and a pile of discarded tissues lay on the floor. "Who's this?" she asked.

"My friend—"

"Robert Wraith. I'm Primrose's boyfriend."

Pim glared at him.

"Have a seat." Irina waved her hand around the living room. Pim picked the chair closest to her.

"Irina, I just wanted to say how sorry I am about Thomas."

"Thomas was a fool, but he was my fool…" Irina's voice trailed off at the end.

"I want you to know I had nothing to do with your accident. I've always respected you as a dancer."

"We all had a part to play in it," Irina said.

"You should go. You're upsetting her," Zoya replied, standing at the entranceway. "She needs time to heal."

Pim glanced between the two women. "Irina, Thomas said something strange to me on stage. He said he was glad to be rid of my grandfather's grip."

"Aren't we all." Irina picked up a tissue and wiped her eyes.

"I don't understand," Pim said.

"You wouldn't. You're spoiled and naïve. You only see what you want to see."

Pim bit her lip. The accusation stung, especially now that she saw the truth in it. "Does the name Viktor Sokolov mean anything to you, because when I mentioned it to Thomas, he froze. I know he had heard it before. I could see it in his eyes."

"You really need to go." Zoya said, her voice rising. "I insist she gets some rest."

"Primrose," Robert said, standing.

"Wait. She has a right to know." Irina pushed herself up on the couch, grimacing as she readjusted her leg.

"Know what?" Pim asked. "Tell me."

"You know I'm from Russia. When I was eight, my stepbrother offered to send me to Moscow to study at the ballet. He had escaped the village and was a successful businessman there. I begged my father to let me go, and after many discussions and fights between him and my mother, he finally agreed."

"Irina, don't do this," Zoya interrupted.

She held her hand up. "It's fine. I have nothing to lose now. I studied there until I was fifteen. Until I became pregnant." She paused, taking a deep breath. "I was sent home, disgraced. My parents tried to hide it. They wanted to raise the baby as their own after it was born, save our family from the shame. I went back to Moscow after… well… the ballet wouldn't take me back. The only person I had on my side was my stepbrother. I stayed with him until I was recovered, then he sent me to Edinburgh to finish studying dance. When I completed my studies, I was accepted into SNB, the corps de ballet. It was a start. It was there I met your father. He served on the board in your grandfather's name. We became close, fell in love."

Pim let out a soft gasp. Her father and Irina. She wasn't sure she wanted to hear any more.

"Shall I continue?" Irina asked with a softness in her voice that hinted of sympathy.

Pim nodded.

"No one knew. We kept it hidden, out of respect for your mother, until one day Angus found out. He was furious and flew into a rage, threatening to have me fired. You see, Angus had approached me many times, flirted with me and had made several propositions toward me, all of which I had either avoided or turned down. He had become obsessed."

"Christ." Pim rubbed her hands over her face. Wraith moved to stand behind her, putting a hand on her shoulder.

"There's more," Irina continued. "Angus sent your father to Edinburgh to work. It was to keep us separated. A week later, your father was killed, and I was named principal dancer. I have no proof, but I know it was all Angus' doing. He held it over me. He knew I couldn't go home, that I was no longer welcome there. He threatened me, and when I still wouldn't oblige him, he did the unthinkable. He found out about my child and bought her, like some piece of meat from the market."

"Natasha," the name escaped Pim's lips as the realization of Irina's story hit her like a ton of bricks.

"Natasha," Irina said surprised. "You know about her?"

"Only for a few days. She came to the reading of the will. But I didn't know she was yours."

"I have not met her, but Angus used her against me. He

ruined her, sending me pictures of her in bed, posing for him. My sweet doch'. I gave him what he wanted. For years, once a week, I met him and played the whore to him. He rewarded me by letting me keep my position in SNB. He bought me expensive gifts, gave me pain pills to keep me dancing, and all the while he was using my daughter. It stopped when you joined the company. I should have been thankful for you, but he threw me aside like an old dog. I knew it was just a matter of time before the company would let me go. I saw your talent. I knew I couldn't compete, especially when you became a soloist and I no longer had his supply of drugs to keep the pain at bay. I was desperate. I tried making up to Angus, but he refused me, so I reached out to my stepbrother."

"Viktor Sokolov," Pim said.

Irina nodded. "Your grandfather and he are two of a kind. Cruel men."

"And Thomas, how did he play into all this?"

"My dear Thomas. So loyal. He thought he was doing me a kindness. He wanted to be out of your grandfather's control more than I ever did. He wanted us to leave Scotland and start a new life together in America. He was the one who put the grease on the floor, so I would slip. I had gone to Angus the day before, begging him for another chance, for more pills, but he said my time was over. Apparently, he approached Thomas and threatened him to get me to quit or he would see me ruined forever. Thomas was afraid. He knew I wouldn't leave Scotland because of Natasha. He thought if I went out on an injury, it would be better. He didn't know how bad I would be hurt. He was riddled with guilt. He went to the theatre the night of the performance in Inverness to kill your grandfather. He was the one dressed as Rothbart, but he said someone beat him to it."

"Viktor," Wraith said.

"I'm sure it was." Irina looked up at him.

"She's told you everything. You should go now," Zora said.

Pim looked at Irina and gave her a pained smile. "She's right. We should go." Wraith gave her his hand, helping her up. She turned to Irina. "For what it's worth, I am sorry. I know I can't undo what's happened, but I am truly sorry. I had no idea."

Irina stared directly at her, however, whatever sympathy she had shown before was gone. There was no warmth in her eyes. "Really," she said coldly. "I think we choose to see what we want to, but somewhere deep down, we always know the truth. Your turn will come one day when you are no longer the star, and you will be left with absolutely nothing."

Chapter 33

"Are you all right?" Wraith asked Pim when they got back in the car.

"I'm fine," she said. She sat rigid, looking out the window, her arms crossed over her chest.

"It was a stupid question; of course, you're not." He turned onto Great Western. "No one would be after learning all that."

"Stop assuming things about me," she said, glaring at him. "I said I'm fine. I need to go by my flat, so I can pick up clothes for tonight."

"Very well." He reached over for her hand.

"And don't tell people we're a couple. We're not. You're not my boyfriend." She pulled out of his grasp. "I know nothing about you. Just like I knew nothing about my grandfather or father. Yet you expect me to trust you blindly."

"What do you want to know, Primrose?" He rubbed his forehead.

"I want to know who Robert McFadden is?"

He took a deep breath. "I told you, McFadden is dead."

"Yes, you've said that before. But he's not, is he? You're not dead. I want to know that I can trust you."

Wraith parked the car, turning off the engine. "No, you're right. I'm not dead, but that part of me is and I'm glad." He turned to her with his eyebrows raised. "I spent eleven months trying to come to terms with it. Mourning a man I'm not sure I even liked. Holding on to a past where I never truly understood who I was. It took me *dying* to figure out what I wanted in life. To become the man I'm supposed to be." Pim started to say something, but he stopped her. "And then I met you. Christ, I thought you were the exact opposite of me. So full of life, so full of passion. Edgy and reckless. Being with you, is like trying to hold a flame. And even if I get burned, it will be worth the risk. You make me feel alive. I can't force you to trust me, but I can assure you I am not your grandfather."

"I'm not so hot right now."

"Aye, you're a bit of a mess." He smiled then leaned over and whispered in her ear, "But you're my mess."

A knock on the door startled them both. "Fucking hell, what does she want?" Pim said. A woman stood outside the car waving at them while she talked on her phone.

"Do you know her?"

"It's my mother." She undid her seatbelt. "Can this day get any fucking worse?"

Wraith opened his door and got out, fastening the button on his suit coat. He walked around to get Pim's door. Her eyes were closed, and she appeared to be counting. He looked up and smiled at the woman.

"Is she going to get out?" the woman asked, having hung up her phone.

"Give her a second," Wraith said.

After a minute, Pim opened the door and he gave her his hand, helping her out.

"Darling," the woman said.

"Mother. What are you doing here?"

"Why, we're here to see you perform."

"We're?" Pim asked.

"Yes, darling, Craig and me. We got your message with the tickets to the closing gala and the flight arrangements. We didn't think we could manage it with such short notice, but with it being the Film Festival and all, Craig thought it would be great for networking."

"I never sent you any tickets," Pim said, reaching into the car for her ballet bag. Wraith went to take it from her, but she held onto it tight. "I've got it."

"Well, I assumed you sent them. I figured money was no problem for you now, with your grandfather's trust, and the flights were first class."

"You won't come out and support me during Grandda's funeral, but you'll fly out for a film festival, so Craig can network." She walked toward the entrance of her building. "Fucking shite. That's what this is."

"Pim, you're being rude. I told you I didn't want anything to do with Angus' funeral," she said, following her.

Pim turned on her. "Well, maybe I needed you. For once, maybe you could have put me first."

Wraith followed them both. Taking the key from Pim's shaking hand, he opened the door to the stairwell. "Maybe we should take this inside," he said to both of them.

"No, it's fine. She's leaving." Pim stormed up the stairs, leaving him alone with her mother.

"Christ, she's always been such a difficult girl," she said to Wraith, extending her hand. "I'm sorry, we haven't been introduced. Aileen Martin."

"Robert Wraith."

"Well, Robert, tell her I'll see her at the gala and I hope she'll be a bit more grateful by then."

Pim set down her bag. Someone had cleaned her flat; the red paint was gone, the ruined couches had been removed and the living room stood bare. Wraith came up behind her, putting his arms around her. "She's gone."

"Thomas or Viktor?" she asked, looking around.

"Thomas. From how you've described Sokolov, this doesn't seem like his style." He was right. This was base, it lacked class and sophistication. She pulled out of Wraith's embrace. "I need to borrow your phone. Christ, everything's been taken from me. I don't even have a phone."

Wraith pulled one from his coat pocket. "Compliments of Gabriel," he said, handing it to her. She took it, looking at it suspiciously. "Don't worry, it's not bugged."

"I need to call Peter."

Wraith took the phone back, and bringing up Peter's number on the screen, he called it, putting it on speaker. Pim gave him a dirty look as he laid it on the counter. "I need to know what's going on. You'll play by my rules, or I'll take it away."

Her eyes grew wide. *Rules?*

"Hello," Peter's voice said.

"Peter, it's Pim."

"Thank God. Where are you, darling? And please say Glasgow."

"I'm at my flat, picking up a few things for tonight."

"Okay, darling, head over to the Old Fruitmarket as soon as possible."

"I thought we were performing at the Glasgow Film Theatre?"

"There's been a change of plans. You're performing at the after party. The venue is better and they're giving you the prime-time spot. It will be just you and Paul. I want you to do the black swan coda and pas de deux. I've reworked the choreography for the end."

"Peter, did you send my mother tickets to the gala?"

"No. I don't even know your mother. I thought she was in Canada. Why?"

"Someone sent her tickets."

"They're hard to come by. We were only given three extras. The board was given tickets, though. Maybe one of them sent theirs to your mother as a courtesy to your grandfather. He did leave the company a very generous endowment."

"Maybe," she said, rolling her eyes at Wraith.

"Bring a black leotard. I'm changing the costumes."

"Okay. I'll be there as soon as I can." She hung up.

"What's he up to?" Wraith asked.

"*What rules?* What did you mean when you said I'll play by your rules." She stood up.

"I think it's pretty self-explanatory. I'm in charge and you'll follow my rules."

"Says who?"

"Me. If I'm to protect you."

"I don't think so." She grabbed her bag and walked down the hall to her bedroom, opening the closet.

"Oh, I think so." He pushed her up against the wall, blocking her in with his body as he pinned her arms above her head. "I won't see you hurt tonight."

She swallowed, looking up at him. "Trust me, it would be hard to hurt me now."

He shook his head. "Sokolov will be there. This isn't a joke."

Sokolov. The tension at the base of her spine began to uncoil, moving up her vertebrae. Anticipation turning into contemplation. Would he come? Would she find the shackling freedom in her dance tonight that she did the last time, that bound her to this man in some form of sick liberty?

"Primrose," Wraith repeated. "Did you hear me, lass? This isn't a joke."

She nodded.

He ran his hand down her face, cupping her chin. "I'm serious."

"I know."

He kissed her hard and deep, stealing her breath for a moment before letting her go.

She tried to compose herself, torn between the thin thread of trust that tied her to the man in front of her and the temptation of perfection she had so long sought and which Sokolov offered. She cleared her throat, mindful of the ache that had formed in her core and her body's response to Wraith's authority. "Uhm, I should pack," she said, rummaging through a drawer for a pair of tights and a leotard.

"Don't leave my side tonight. Except when you're on stage. I'll expect you to stay within eyeshot."

"Of course." She chose a long black dress from her closet for the afterparty, putting it in a garment bag and adding a pair of high heels. Then she shoved the rest of her belongings into her dance bag. The gun sat at the bottom.

"We'll go by my place so I can change, then I'll take you to the theatre," Wraith said.

Pim stared at him, the burden of tonight's decisions reaching a critical point. She looked up and gave him a weak smile, zipping up the bag. Her old way of life wouldn't work anymore; she had entered her own code red.

Chapter 34

The afterparty for the gala was to be held at the Old Fruitmarket, off Candleriggs in the Merchant City district, in the east end. They entered into the refurbished and modern City Halls, Glasgow's exciting music complex, renowned for its amazing acoustics and home to the BBC Scottish Symphony Orchestra and Scottish Chamber Orchestra. Another set of doors took them into the Fruitmarket. It was impressive, to say the least, a lofty vaulted auditorium with cast iron columns and a balcony, all made from the old stalls of fruit and vegetable vendors. Reminiscent of a far-gone era, it retained a number of its period features and signs, enhancing the ambiance. Staff were busy setting up round tables, elegantly adorned with white tablecloths and place settings. Pim made her way over to the stage, followed closely by Wraith.

Peter, Niall, and Paul were already there, blocking out the choreography.

"Darling," Peter said, coming over and hugging her. "God, it's good to see you. Are you all right?"

"I'm fine." She looked over at Paul, giving him a feeble smile. "It's all been rather traumatic."

"Aye, our poor Thomas. To take his own life." Peter shook his head.

"Suicide?" Pim questioned.

"Aye, I talked with the police this afternoon. They said it is being ruled a suicide, especially given the events with Irina. It all must have been too much," he said. "To think he really could have hurt you and Paul."

Pim glanced at Wraith. It wasn't suicide. He shook his head ever so slightly, asking for her silence. "What's he doing here?" Peter asked.

"I'm here for her protection," Wraith answered for himself.

"Thomas is dead. There's no reason for it now, hopefully."

"I'll be the judge of that."

"I don't have a ticket for you."

"I have my own ticket. You're not the only person with connections in this city."

"Look, between Irina's accident, Angus' death, and now this tragic event, the company doesn't need any more bad publicity. We were lucky last night that most of the audience was unaware of all the drama, thanks to Pim's stellar performance. Let's just focus on tonight," Peter said, ignoring Wraith. "Pim, you and Paul warm up while Niall and I finish with staging, then we'll go over the new choreography."

She nodded. Wraith looked at her. "I'm going to scope out the venue. I won't be far, within eye distance."

She turned to Paul. "Are you okay?"

"Aye. Just a flesh wound. Scared the bloody hell out of me, though."

"I know."

They moved over to the side of the stage and began with a variety of exercises and stretches, to loosen up their bodies and make their muscles pliable. When they were done, they joined Peter and Niall. Wraith had finished his initial inspection of the place and sat in a chair off to the side.

A young man walked up with a bouquet of a dozen red roses. "Primrose McNeil?" he asked.

"That's me." Her heart began to race. *Sokolov*. Wraith intercepted the delivery, taking the flowers from the boy and handing him a tip. He opened the card and looked at it before giving them to her. The card was signed *From Mother and Craig*. She all but threw them back at Wraith, her expectation turning into frustration.

"Not what you wanted?" Wraith asked.

"I don't want anything from her," she said, trying to hide her apparent disappointment from everyone. "Throw them away."

"If you're quite finished, may we begin? We have a lot to cover," Peter said.

"I'm sorry." Pim joined Paul on stage.

"I want to change up the feel of the piece. Make it darker, edgier. We'll do the coda and pas de deux as is, but I want to cut to the end of the ballet and have Siegfried fall in love with the black swan, choose Odile instead. The audience should be able to feel the tension. I want to leave them feeling uneasy and restive, to bring them to a point where they have to face their own dark desires, their own taboos."

They worked on the new choreography for the next hour and a half. It was evocative and, oddly, at times tender, but mostly raw and suggestive. They might as well have been making love on stage as the black swan led the prince down a path of corruption, to where he himself faced his own demons, giving in to them at the end.

"Let's run it from the beginning. Paul, you look like you're fucking afraid of her. You're supposed to want her, desire her;

stop fucking around," Peter said, then he came over to her. "You're missing something, Pim. You need to loosen up; you're trying too hard. Stop thinking and let what's inside you come out." He removed the bobby pins from her bun, taking her hair out, so it fell down her back. "From the top."

Her eyes caught Wraith's and she could see the jealousy in them.

They ran it three more times, and each time she felt off. Something was not clicking, no matter how hard she tried. Every time someone entered the venue, her attention was drawn toward the door, wondering if it was a delivery for her, which it never was, only increasing her anxiety. The presenter for the afterparty, John MacNab, an up and coming actor, needed to use the stage to practice his monologue. Their time was up.

"We go on at half nine. We have use of the Recital Room to warm up and mark the piece, so be there by eight. Your dressing rooms are off the main promenade in the City Halls," Peter informed them.

"You said you changed the costumes." Pim wiped her face with a towel.

"Aye. I want you in a black leotard, no tights. Don't cover up your tattoo, and I want your hair out. You can pull the front back if you need to, full makeup. There should be pointe shoes in your dressing room." Peter looked to Niall for confirmation. The older man nodded. "Paul, I want you in jeans, no shirt." Peter looked at his watch. "You're free to get something to eat, just be ready to go by eight."

Pim picked up her dance bag. It was already seven. It didn't leave them a lot of time.

"You need to eat something," Wraith said, approaching. He reached for her bag, but she put it up on her shoulder before he could take it, handing him the garment bag instead.

"He's right," Paul said.

Stripped

"I hate eating before I dance. Maybe just a green juice. I'm sure we'll be served dinner after."

"I'll go see what I can find." Paul gave her shoulder a squeeze. "It'll be fine, Pim. The choreography is good."

Wraith followed her down the main hall of the promenade, the deep red carpets thick and plush, to her room. It was small, redolent of the original architecture and sat empty except for the vanity and an armchair. No flowers or bouquets awaited her. She placed her bag under the vanity and sat down. Wraith hung the garment bag on a hook. "What's wrong?" he asked. "You look upset."

She bit her lip. "I'm fine."

"Don't lie to me, Primrose." He crouched down in front of her, tilting her chin up. "There's something wrong. It's written all over your face."

"I guess I thought Sokolov would reach out to me."

"Why?" His brow wrinkled. "It almost sounds as if you're disappointed." He stood up, his hand covering his mouth while he thought. "You want him to contact you."

"No," she said quickly. "I just want this to be over."

"Primrose, you're not connected to him. If you think you need him to be a good dancer, you're wrong."

"You don't understand," she said.

"Oh, I do understand, and this ends now."

She shook her head. He understood nothing. "I'm fine. I promise. I need to get ready." She moved to the vanity, pulling out her makeup from her bag underneath. Wraith came over and put his hands on her shoulders. She looked at him through the reflection of the mirror, her field of perception distorted with thoughts and ideas of perfection.

"I *will* protect you, Primrose."

She nodded, but it was shallow and depthless, lacking the clear visibility her heart now knew. How could he protect her from the very thing she craved? How could he suppress the formation of waves in the glassy water that threatened to rip her soul apart yet offered her the most contemplative view? She had glimpsed her inner most self and, through it, had become closer to her own body, emotions, thoughts and spirit. Sokolov had opened her eyes, giving her absolute understanding, and now she wanted more.

Chapter 35

"Did you find them?" Wraith asked, adjusting the bow tie on his tuxedo."

"No, I'll grab a pair from my bag. I have extras." She never found the aforementioned pointe shoes Niall was to have left for her. Taking out a different pair, she zipped her bag and quickly changed into her leotard.

Wraith cleared his throat. "You look different."

"Like the bad girl people think I am?" The leotard was long-sleeved and came just around her neck. The entire expanse of the back was cut out from her shoulders to her tailbone, exposing her tattoo. She had blackened her eyes, creating a sultry, smoky look and teased her hair, pulling the front back into a barrette.

"No, and you're not a bad girl, no matter how much you want the world to think it." His head tilted to the side, contemplating. "You're more like a temptress."

She laughed then stopped, as she watched him fasten the leather harness around his shoulder and chest and slide his gun into its holster before putting on his jacket. Her throat went dry. "You look handsome," she managed to get out, her voice taking on a raspy quality.

"Come here," he said, holding out his hand.

She went to him, and he pulled her into an embrace. "Stay with me tonight," he said softly.

She knew he talked of her mind, not their proximity. It tugged at her heart. If only he knew what he was asking. "I'll try."

He kissed her, soft at first, then harder, demanding her submission. "You're mine."

She pulled back, narrowing her eyes. "I'm not yours," she said teasingly. Her heart broke inside. She could only belong to one man right now.

The Recital Room was smaller than the Old Fruitmarket, with bright white walls and a white, arched ceiling. The matching arched windows stood out black in sharp contrast, darkened with the night. The polished wooden floor was slick, so Pim practiced in her warmup booties. It wasn't until they were about to go on, that she sat on the floor, putting on her pointe shoes.

"Those aren't the ones we brought you," Peter said. "I wanted black."

"I couldn't find any in my room."

"I know I put them in there," Niall said. He turned to Paul. "They weren't in your room by mistake?"

"No. It was empty when I got in there."

"I'll go check at the front desk," Niall said.

Wraith called her over. "I'm going to go find my place. I'll be close to the stage. Gabriel, Kian, and Sin are already out there." He kissed her forehead. "I don't want you to worry."

"I'm fine," she tried reassuring him as he looked back one more time before leaving.

Niall came back. "They were up front. One of the workers

didn't know the room was being used and turned them in." He handed Pim the box. "Marta already sewed the elastic and ribbons on them.

She opened the box, her heart quickening. A pair of black satin pointe shoes sat on the tissue just like the pair Sokolov had for her. She put them on. Something was at one of the toes, and taking the shoe back off, she reached into the vamp, pulling out a small envelope. *Remember these* was written on the outside. She opened it, her heart now pounding, careful not to tear the card inside. It was a miniature picture of one of Alasdair Gray's artworks, entitled *Mother and Daughter*. She'd seen the original at Sotheby's in London, when a Lot of Scottish Pictures went up for auction in 2009. It was the year she started at the Royal Academy and her father took her to see it. The painting, lot number one hundred and forty, was done in acrylic, pen, and ink and depicted a mother and daughter sitting side by side on chairs. They could be the same person. It was the small nuances that separated them into their apparent categories. The daughter sat on a modern chair, eyes upturned with a smile on her face, full of expectation and youth. The mother's chair was old-fashioned, eyes downturned, and she slouched, frowning, with her hands clasped together, forlorn and despondent. Pim flipped the card over. *Show Mummy Dearest what you can do… it's up to you- VS.* It was Sokolov who had sent her mother the tickets. He was here. He came, and her anxiety, which had built up over the afternoon, seemed to dissipate. She placed the notecard in the box and closed the lid. She went up on point and it seemed by just wearing the shoes, her soul gravitated closer to Sokolov.

Paul grabbed her hand. "We're up, Pim," he said. She followed him down a hallway to a side door that led in to the Old Fruitmarket. Small fairy lights sparkled in the dark venue, lighting up the arena like the night sky. People filled every table, seated cabaret style in grand elegance, and those left standing filled the balconies. She looked out across the audience, her eyes drawn to one table in particular toward the back, where she spotted not only her mother and Craig but also Natasha and her son Hamish. She didn't have time to think before the MC called them up on stage. "We'll kick off tonight's festivities with a performance from Scottish National Ballet and Glasgow's very own prima ballerina, Primrose McNeil, and her partner, Paul Lewis, as they perform a stripped down and modern variation from the ballet Swan Lake."

An electric current ran up her spine, unleashing its power like a clarion call as they took the stage and the orchestra began to play. With each step and move, she became the black swan, tearing Prince Siegfried apart bit by bit, bewitching him with her wicked dance, until he yearned only for her. Niall's comments from rehearsal that afternoon echoed through her mind, guiding her toward the completeness she so desired. *Don't rush. You create your own time in the world. You rule this world.* She became one with the music, big and emotional. There was no longer a stage, no longer an audience, it was just her and Paul as she whipped through the air, arms spiraling like wings, agitating the room in a psychological frenzy. He picked her up over his head, her back arching, letting him move her, create her, as she slowly took control of him. Her hooks set, she used a moment of stillness, counterbalanced against each other in perfect tension, her back against his chest as he ran his hands down her body, to exploit the silence and reel him in. The music exploded in fierce passion, complex and real. He was hers; she had won. They ended in an embrace as intense as the variation started. She looked out at the audience for Sokolov as she slowly returned to reality. He had become her emotional identity. Would he be proud? The audience

Stripped

erupted in applause, standing as they shouted, "Bravo, bravo," over and over.

She and Paul stepped forward, as she curtsied and he took a bow. He stepped back, holding his hand out, so the audience could recognize her alone. She stepped forward again and lowered herself into a grand reverence, acknowledging the audience's applause as the cheering intensified. John McNab, the host, came on stage and handed her a bouquet of two dozen red roses. She pulled one from the arrangement, giving it to Paul. Then they both looked toward the orchestra, recognizing the conductor and musicians before leaving the stage.

Members of the press rushed forward. She could see Gabriel in the distance, making a beeline for her.

"How does it feel to be called Glasgow's Prima Ballerina?" one reporter shouted out.

The sleazy reporter from the funeral pushed himself to the front. "Do you think your grandfather was murdered?"

"Fuck off," Paul said, putting his arm around Pim and leading her out of the room and down the hall that led to their dressing rooms. He stopped outside hers, hugging her. "Jesus Christ, Pim. You were amazing. Fucking brilliant."

"We were amazing. We're partners."

"Aye, but that was something special." He kissed her on the forehead. "I think Richard's going to be jealous."

She laughed. "I'll see you back inside for the party." She shut the door to her room and locked it, leaning back against it. She let the moment sink in and take root. A black rose lay on the vanity. Wraith would be here any minute; he wouldn't leave her alone for long. She pulled the notecard from the flower and put it in her black, beaded purse. Then she threw the rose in her dance bag, covering it with her discarded clothes. Her hand brushed over the gun. She took it out, the feel of it heavy and solid. A knock on the door caused her to jump.

"Pim, it's me," Wraith said, jiggling the handle. "Open up."

She shoved the gun in her purse and closed the latch.

"Just a sec." She turned the lock and opened the door, letting Wraith inside.

"Sorry I couldn't get to you right away. The press was blocking every exit. Gabriel saw Paul get you out." He picked her up and spun her around. "You were absolutely marvelous," he said, setting her down. "Sorry I don't have any flowers. I promise tomorrow, to shower you in them…" He stopped, looking at her. "Are you all right?"

She plastered a smile on her face. "Of course, I am."

"Are you sure? This isn't about Sokolov again? No one has seen him. Even Alex came to watch for him and the colonel rarely leaves The Tower."

"No," she said, shaking her head. "No, there's always a moment when you get off stage and the reality that it is over hits you. You wonder if you could have done better."

"Bloody hell. You were perfect."

"We always seem to be our own worst critics." She sat down and removed her pointe shoes, sliding her leotard off. He helped her stand, running his hand down her back and over the swell of her bottom, the hunger in his eyes evident.

"God help me, but I want you," he said.

The dance had left her aroused too. However, the darkness she sought to quench it, lived somewhere deep in her psyche. That didn't mean she didn't feel the carnal desires of the flesh, though. Her sex began to throb from his touch.

He took his jacket off, throwing it over the arm of the chair, and pushed her over the vanity so her chest lay on top of it. "My little vixen." His hand caressed the back of her thighs, coming between her legs to stroke her cleft. "You'll have left the entire audience aroused and in need." She felt herself grow wet. Undoing his belt and taking the zipper down on his pants, he pulled his cock out. He entered her in a rush, filling her with his presence as he thrust into her, over and over. She clutched at the table, feeling herself come apart at the seams as her climax built. He stopped, pulled out, and turned her over, picking her up as he pressed her against the wall. She wrapped her legs around him, their faces just inches apart, and kissed him, afraid she was going to say something she wasn't ready to say.

He pulled back, looking her in the eyes. Slowly, he placed her hand over her head and covered it with his own, holding it there as they continued to stare at each other, suspended in the moment.

"Wraith," she started to say, then stopped and started over. "Wraith. I love you." She needed him to know. She wasn't sure what tonight would bring or what Sokolov's note said. But she at least needed him to know the simple truth.

"I love you too." He kissed her, entering back into her, their union complete. A tear snaked down her cheek; such happiness couldn't live long. Tragedy was sure to follow; it always did. He wiped it away with his thumb.

"Shh," he whispered. "I've got you." What started as frenzied lust, ended with the gentle waves of bliss. He set her down. Reaching under the vanity, he opened her bag and looked in. Her heart stopped. He would find the rose. He would know she'd kept something from him. A smile erupted on his face as he pulled out an old ragged stuffed bunny, along with a towel. "Never did I think Primrose McNeil still played with stuffed animals."

She grabbed it from his hand as he gently cleaned her up, the intimate act making her feel vulnerable and extremely guilty at her own betrayal of him. "I don't play with it. At least not anymore. It's a good luck charm now."

She took the towel from his hand and put both items back

in her bag, closing it up. A consistent thumping could be heard coming from the room next door.

"Look what you've started," Wraith said, kissing her. "You're going to be responsible for most of the debauchery in the city tonight."

Chapter 36

Wraith watched as she spun around in front of him. "Do I look okay?" she asked, trying to look over her shoulder to see the back of the dress in the mirror.

"You look beautiful."

The dress was scandalous. Made of black satin, it was cut with a deep-plunging neckline which went well below her breasts, held up by thin straps. It was backless and the slit up the leg went almost to her hip. On anyone else, it might be inappropriate, but with her body and considering she was now the belle of the ball, it was breathtaking.

He kissed her on the neck. "Please stay close to me tonight."

She gave him a smile, reapplying her red lipstick. "But with all these fans, I'm not sure—"

"Watch it, lass." He gave her a swift smack to her bottom and her eyes opened wide. Bouquets of flowers had been arriving at her dressing room door in droves. The room already smelled like a flower shop from the ones delivered by Peter, Niall, Paul, the SNB board, Graham Rankin and

Gabriel. Even Alex sent a vase of yellow primroses. Wraith was just thankful Viktor Sokolov had kept quiet and not made an appearance tonight.

"I'm ready," she said, grabbing her purse.

"I don't want to give you up to your crowd of admirers." He gave her one last kiss, his mouth brushing her ear. "You've made me the happiest man tonight."

He took her arm, tucking it into the crook of his elbow, and led her out of the sanctity of the room and into the lion's den.

Pim looked around at the crowd. Wraith had found Gabriel and Alex almost immediately. "Watch her while I get her something to eat and drink."

"You were amazing, Pim," Gabriel said. "When you said you were a ballet dancer, I had no idea."

"I'm sorry Sokolov never showed. I'm afraid it's been a waste of your time." She continued to scan the crowd. Peter was in a corner, surrounded by reporters, enjoying every minute.

"On the contrary," Alex said. "He was here. There's no way his ego would be denied this opportunity.

"What makes you say that?"

"Sinclair thought he spotted something. He's checking it out. But don't worry," Alex said, rubbing her shoulder. "You're safe."

"Excuse me, I need to use the toilet." She stepped back.

"I'll go with you." Gabriel followed her out the door into the hallway.

"It's really not necessary."

He stopped across the hall from the ladies' room. "I'll wait right here. It's not a problem."

Pim opened the door. The bathroom was empty, and she was thankful to have a minute alone. She opened her purse and pulled out the card. *If you want mercy, cry uncle- VS.* Dear God, what did he mean? To cry uncle, was to admit defeat. She had only heard the term used a few times when someone was demanding an opponent to submit. Was he asking her to submit? Hadn't she been doing that all along, every time she danced? She could hear female laughter outside the door. She needed more time to think. There was another door on the opposite side of the room. Opening it, she saw that it led out to the promenade. Guests mingled in the open area, laughing and talking in small groups. She made her way to the front entrance, leaving. The air was cold, the night clear and crisp. She sat down on a bench, thinking. Viktor often spoke in riddles. She looked up and saw there was a commotion at the front doors. "Please help me," a blonde girl was saying to the doorman.

"Natasha?" Pim called out, standing up. "Is everything okay?"

"Hamish has run off. I've searched inside. I don't think he came outside, but I wanted to make sure."

"He's missing?" Pim asked, a dull ache forming in her stomach.

"He's curious. I told him to stay in his seat, but when I got back, he was gone. He's probably hiding."

Cry uncle. Bloody hell. She thought of the connections in her tangled family tree. Hamish was her grandfather's son. That made him her uncle. Sokolov had Hamish. She didn't want to panic Natasha. Where the fuck would he have taken him?

"I need to get back inside and look," the girl said. "Thank you for the invitation. You were beautiful tonight. Your grandfather would have been proud."

She nodded, her mind going in different directions.

Sokolov must have sent Natasha the ticket so he could take the boy.

The nearest subway station entrance was over ten minutes away. With it being the last night of the festival, the streets were packed with out-of-town visitors, and taxis were plentiful. Pim easily flagged down a black cab, getting in. "Òran Mór off of Byres road," she said to the young man driving. He started the meter. "I'm in a hurry."

"Aye, the roads are busy tonight. I'll do my best."

Pim looked over her shoulder. It wouldn't be long before Wraith realized she was missing. She wasn't sure Sokolov would even be at the arts venue. It was a guess at best, but if he was trying to lure her somewhere, there were only a few spots that came to mind.

It took twice as long as it normally would to get to the west end, given the extra traffic. The driver pulled up in front of the bar. She handed the young man her credit card, and he ran it through the reader.

"Thank you," she said, barely shutting the door as she ran up the steps to the building. Its iconic pyramid spire stood valiant in the night sky, alight with a tilted blue halo. The effect was supposed to represent *striving for grace*. Pim often wondered what grace the artist actually meant to convey— charm, mercy, prayer, beauty, perhaps all of them. Tonight, she hoped she had guessed right and it was mercy. The bars and restaurants were packed elbow to elbow with festivalgoers. Live music blared from the clubs and the dance floors were at full capacity. She rushed toward her beloved auditorium, hoping it was empty. No such luck. The entrance was cordoned off and a bouncer stood guard, holding a clipboard. She read the placard. *Green Shore Production Company.* It was worth a shot.

She smiled as she walked up to the man. He was more muscle than anything else, one of those guys who spent every waking moment in the gym. "Hello," she said in what she hoped was a sexy voice. "I was hoping I could get in."

"Name?" He held up the board, waving it.

Apparently not. "Primrose McNeil."

"Primrose. You don't hear that often," he said, scanning the names on the list. "Aye, here you are."

"I'm on the list?"

"You sound surprised." He undid the latch on the rope and held it open. "Looks right boring in there. If you tire of it, you can always come back here and talk to me."

"I doubt it." She entered the room, her apprehension growing. The guard was right; compared to all the other rooms, this one was dead. Tables had been set up, and small groups of people sat eating quietly. A band played at the end of the auditorium as a few couples waltzed across the floor. A man approached her. "You're expected up in the balcony." His American accent was sharp and nasal. She looked back at the bouncer and he gave her a wink.

She slowly started up the spiral staircase that led to the gallery. When she got to the top, Viktor Sokolov was seated on a bench which ran along the curve of the stained-glass windows. He stood when he saw her. "Not only talented, but clever and resourceful."

"Where is he?" The staircase exited in the center of the room and she kept the blue cylindrical casing between them.

"Not here. I wouldn't bring a child out on a night like this. But I assure you he's safe, for now." He adjusted his royal blue velvet tuxedo jacket. "Come and sit. Champagne is in order, I believe."

"Tell me where he is?"

"Tsk, tsk." He clicked his tongue. "I thought I taught you last time that I don't play that way." He sat down, patting the space beside him.

"Or what?"

He stood up quickly, crossing the floor in three strides, and yanked her toward him so they stood inches from each other. His hand ran across the flat plane of her stomach. "It's still tender, I presume," he said into her ear, the heat of his breath on her skin revolting. "You hid it well tonight, the pain, but then you're used to hiding your pain. Next time, you'll wish that's the only thing I'd done to you." She followed him to the cushioned window seats and sat. A man appeared with a bottle of champagne and two crystal flutes, setting the tray down next to Viktor and leaving.

"Green Shore Productions?" she asked. He picked this venue, knowing she would come to it. Knowing she would find the association with *mercy*. What was his connection to the company?

"I'm a silent partner. A very generous partner." His eyes traveled down her body, appreciative in their slow perusal. "In fact, you should be congratulating me. We won an award tonight, for best investigative documentary on our piece about sex trafficking."

"Jesus Christ. There will be men looking for me," she said, hoping it sounded brazen and hid the emptiness she felt. No one would know where to find her. She'd left the phone in her dance bag. There was no way to trace her location.

"If you mean that group of amateurs, I'm aware of them." He picked up the champagne, holding it at a slight angle, and grabbed the cork firmly while turning the bottle until it popped with a soft exhale. "The angels sigh," he said appreciatively as he poured them each a glass. "I'm not scared."

"You should be. They shut down your sick operation."

"A minor inconvenience for the moment. And I have many operations." He handed her a glass.

"Still."

"Still? Yet, here you sit, and where are they?" He held his glass up. "What shall we toast to?" He looked around, searching for an idea. "Work as if you are living in the early days of a better nation. The very words of your sainted Alasdair Gray. Slange."

They were embossed in gold on a wooden beam above them, mocking her with their false inspiration, a plea for people to come together for a better future. "Slange." She took a sip of the champagne, cold and crisp, the bubbles nipping at the back of her throat. "Where's Hamish?" she tried again.

"You're always in such a hurry. We haven't even talked about your performance tonight." He sat back, crossing his legs elegantly, and looked at her over his glass before downing the contents.

"There's nothing to talk about."

"Nothing to talk about? That's rich. I help you achieve a pinnacle, a defining moment in your career, and you have nothing to say." He poured himself another glass.

"You've done nothing but kill people and cause misery." She looked at him with disgust. Not only for him, but for herself, for thinking she needed him.

"You knew the cost. Did you think tonight would be any different? Did you think there wouldn't be a price to pay?" He reached out and cupped her chin, giving it a squeeze.

"I've done everything you've asked. I've surrendered to you."

"A life for a life."

"What does that even mean? My grandfather is dead, Ivanna is dead, Thomas is dead. How many more people need to die until this debt is repaid?"

"One," he said. His voice was devoid of any emotion and as cold as ice. "One more."

A chill went down her spine. "Me."

"You could have saved any of them."

"But I gave you what you wanted."

He raised an eyebrow. "You gave me what *you* thought I wanted, and in return, I indulged you."

"You deceived me." She prayed he could not hear the hurt from his betrayal in her voice.

"I deceived no one." He gave her a short laugh. "A life for a life. Two different levels of meaning for two different audiences. One for me, and one for you."

"That's madness."

"I like to think of it as artistic cleverness, artist duplicity. Just like your fucking Alasdair Gray. You should have recognized it immediately. We've been playing this game from the beginning." He stood up, keeping his back to her. "I can give as easily as I take away. You assumed I was looking for perfection, when all I wanted was for you to throw yourself on the sword. It's why I asked you to dance The Dying Swan. You were supposed to die. But you changed the rules in an instant, by dancing it so exquisitely. You did not suffer from delusions of grandeur as I presumed, and I suddenly wanted more."

"What is this debt?"

He turned back to her, watching her close. "I told you before, your grandfather took someone very special from me."

"Irina."

"You've talked to her, I see."

"She told me you were her stepbrother, nothing more."

"She was so precious to me. The most beautiful little girl, and I gave her everything." His eyes looked far off as if he were reliving the past, his mouth quirked in a smile. "I wanted her to stay that sweet, innocent girl forever."

"But she got pregnant," Pim said. "She betrayed you."

"The child was mine." There was a vengeful gleam in his eyes.

Natasha. She felt her stomach turn in disgust.

"When she came back to Moscow after having the baby, she was never the same. My sweet girl was gone. I sent her to

Edinburgh, hoping that if she started dancing again, she would come back to me. I took her on lavish trips during her holidays, bought her anything she could imagine, but she was never the same. When she signed with Scottish National Ballet, things began to change. She seemed happy again. I moved to Edinburgh and visited her on the weekends in Glasgow. I had my little girl back. But then I found out she was seeing your father. She told me she was in love with him and that I couldn't see her anymore." He threw his hand in the air in disgust. "I went to her flat and she refused to let me in. But your grandfather, oddly enough, took care of that problem for me.

"You're both sick."

"You don't understand, love," he spat. "I wanted to punish Irina for her betrayal, so I sold your grandfather Natasha, our child. I couldn't care less about the brat. All I ever wanted was my sweet Irina. I wanted her to suffer, to have her see the sins of her disloyalty. Little did I know, Angus would betray me by sleeping with Irina too. He turned her old. She is no better than a common whore and drug addict, used up and trashy."

"So Irina is the debt I owe. Killing my grandfather wasn't enough."

"I didn't kill your grandfather. That stupid boy Irina danced with did. Then he got scared and pushed him over the edge."

"Thomas said differently," she said, remembering what Irina had told her.

"He's a liar and a coward. Of course, he would never admit to it."

"Then why were you at the theatre that night?"

"I was there to take something from Angus more precious than his own life." His hazel eyes held a spark of satisfaction.

"You were there to kill me."

"Good girl," he crooned. "That's right, but your grandfather's death got in the way."

"Where's Hamish?" she asked. "Where have you taken him?"

"I'll take you to him. Then we'll decide who lives or dies." He took her hand, leading her down the winding staircase. The party had picked up as more guests arrived, but no one seemed to notice them. She looked to the entrance for the bouncer, but he was gone. They left through a private door that led out back, to a car park. A black Land Rover with its windows darkened was waiting for them. She got in the back seat next to Sokolov.

Pim clutched her handbag, the weight of the gun a talisman. There was no doubt in her mind. If it came to it, she knew she would use it this time.

Chapter 37

"She's gone," Gabriel said to Wraith. "There was a second door in the bathroom. She must have used it to leave."

Wraith pulled his phone out, checking her GPS location. "She's in her dressing room." He headed down the hallway with Gabriel close on his heels and knocked on the door. No answer. "Primrose, open up," he said, trying the handle. The door opened. The room was empty. Wraith looked around for her phone, then spied her dance bag under the vanity. "She hasn't gone far. Her stuff is still here."

He opened the bag, rifling through it, and pulled out the black rose, his unease rising. "Fuck. Sokolov reached out to her." He searched for a notecard in her bag but came up empty handed.

"How do you know?"

"He sent her a black rose after her performance yesterday, only there was a note attached."

Gabriel was already on the phone to the colonel, explaining the situation. "Sin and Kian are sweeping the premises," he said, hanging up. "Alex is on his way here. We'll find her."

Wraith wracked his brain. Why would she leave without telling him? Her lack of trust in him stung and cast seeds of doubt into what she'd said. *'I love you.'* Did she just say it to throw him off track. There was a knock at the door and he snapped upright as Gabriel answered it. Alex entered. "What do we know?"

"Nothing, except for she's gone and Sokolov reached out to her," Gabriel said.

"Wraith?" Alex asked.

Wraith shook his head, pulling himself from his thoughts. "I don't know. I was with her the entire time except for prior to her going on stage and right after. Both times, Paul was with her."

"Was there a change in her demeanor at any time?"

"There was, right after the performance. She seemed concerned but said she always gets like that after she comes off stage."

"That could have been the moment of contact. The flower could have been waiting for her."

"That would confirm Sokolov was here in attendance and the person Sin saw must have been him." Gabriel pulled his phone out. "The question now is where did they go?"

"Call Dougie and have him run a check on Viktor Sokolov, using any of his aliases and the film festival. See if there's a connection. He had to get his tickets to the gala from someone or someplace." Alex rubbed his chin. "Wraith, can you think of anyplace they would have gone?"

His initial worry was beginning to turn to anger. "She's convinced they are linked. That she needs him to dance well. He uses her vulnerabilities against her. So wherever he's taken her, it will be a place that has meaning to her."

"Dougie found a connection," Gabriel said, his phone to

his ear. "There's a Vance Stevens, in partnership with Green Shore Production. They won an award at the festival. Vance Stevens was one of the aliases we connected to Sokolov."

"Was Green Shore Production in attendance at the gala?" Alex asked.

"No, they're hosting their own party."

"Where?" Wraith tried to control his tone, not wanting Alex to see his emotions get the better of him.

"Òran Mór."

"Bloody hell," he said. "Let's go."

"Gabriel, call Sin and Kian and tell them to meet you at the car. You'll go together. Wraith and I will take my car."

"Yes, Colonel."

They ran into Paul and his fiancée in the hallway. "Is Pim in her room?"

"No. I'm looking for her," Wraith said.

"If you find her, tell her we are headed to a different party and I'll talk to her tomorrow."

Wraith nodded.

"And give her these. She left them in the room we warmed up in." Paul handed him a pair of sweatpants and her warm up booties.

"Thanks." Wraith unzipped her dance bag over his shoulder, putting them away when he noticed the notecard in one of the shoes. He picked it up. It was from Sokolov, with an Alasdair Gray print on the back. *Mother and Daughter*. Well, that explained who sent her mother the tickets. How long had she been hiding this information from him?

Sin and Kian were waiting for them in the car park. Dark clouds hid the moon, threatening rain. Wraith's lung seized in the cold night air, allowing no air in or out and he pounded his chest with his fist in frustration until he could breathe again. Alex stared over at him. Wraith held up his hands. "I'm fine," he said, getting into the passenger's seat of Alex's black Porsche.

"Use your goddamn inhaler," Alex said through gritted teeth, starting the car. "Fucking martyr, you'll do her no good if you injure yourself again."

"I said I'm fine." The engine purred to life and they followed the Mercedes the other men were in, away from the east end.

The drive was excruciatingly long, with several traffic accidents involving out of town visitors, turning the wrong way into oncoming traffic, littering the roads. At least thirty minutes passed before Wraith could finally make out the outline of Òran Mór in the distance.

"Have you been here before?" Alex asked.

"Aye. If they're here, they'll be in the auditorium in the balcony."

"Why do you say that?"

"Like I said, he likes to play with her emotions." Wraith scanned the surroundings, looking for any clues. As they turned into the car park, a black Land Rover with darkened windows was pulling out. Something in Wraith's chest tightened. "Turn the car around," he yelled, looking back.

"What the hell?"

"She's in that car. Turn around and follow it."

"How do you know?" Alex questioned, but he did as Wraith asked, making a U-turn and following the SUV on to the street.

"I just do." Doubt filled him. The feeling had been so strong for a second, but now it was fading.

"Call Gabriel," Alex said, pressing the phone button on his steering wheel.

"Where did you go?" Gabriel's voice said through the speaker.

"We're following a black Land Rover, number plate SK69 DTM. Have Dougie check it out."

"Yes, sir. Do you want us to follow you?"

"Dougie can track us on GPS. You check out Òran Mór and see if they have been there. If they've already left, then pick up our location." Alex hung up.

"You'd better be right," Alex said.

"I am." But he wasn't sure. The farther the car got away from them, the more he was afraid he was leading them on a wild goose chase.

Pim glanced back quickly at the sports car as it turned into the car park. *Wraith*. She knew he was in the car. He had come after her. The beating of her heart quickened. She didn't want to draw attention to the Porsche now following them, so she stared straight ahead. Fat drops of rain began to fall, splattering the windows and blurring the view as they inched along Great Western.

"Where are we going?" she asked as they stopped at another red light, resisting the urge to turn around and see if Wraith had caught up.

"It's a surprise. I'm taking you somewhere that speaks to my muse," he said. "I've had enough of your Alasdair Gray. He's fallen rather flat for me."

They came up to another red light. Sokolov made a fist, red creeping up his neck. "Get off this god damn street," he yelled at his driver. "We've gotten every fucking red light." His usual clipped English accent he tried so hard to use was giving way to his Russian.

"We're almost at the highway, sir," the driver replied.

Viktor was right, they had been stopped at every red light,

and it sparked a small ray of hope in Pim. *Gabriel, master of red lights*. He wouldn't have that luxury for long.

They were only on the highway for a short amount of time before the driver exited on Trongate and drove into the heart of the city center. Buildings lined the road, their Victorian architecture stunning as pedestrians and cars navigated the grid system of streets. They pulled up in front of a five-story red brick building. They got out of the car and Sokolov grabbed her arm. "Don't think of trying to run," he whispered in her ear. "Or Hamish will die."

Two large glass windows flanked the front door. Above the first window, spelled out in lights, was *Trongate 103*, and above the second, painted in bright yellow, was the saying *A Centre for Arts and Creativity*. The door was locked. Sokolov inserted a key, opening it. The place was dark and looked deserted. He locked it behind himself and led her up a curved staircase, to the first floor and into what could only be called a performance gallery.

Pim blinked several times, hoping her eyes would adjust to the darkness. She could make out the shadows of large objects and structures around her. Sokolov walked her to the center of the room. Her shin hit a wooden object, as he sat her down on what felt like a bench. The air was heavy with expectancy. Something was going to happen; she could feel it in her bones. And then, as quiet a murmur, she heard it, the soft muffle of a child's cry. Her head turned, trying to locate where it had come from. "Hamish?" she cried out.

A hand came down on the back of her neck, squeezing either side painfully. "Don't ruin the surprise," Viktor hissed. "What you are about to witness is a mechanical ballet that spins the tragic story of the human spirit as it struggles against the ruthless circle of life and death. A story you know so well."

He pressed a button on a remote and the room filled with fog. She strained to hear the child's cry again, and whatever was about to happen waited silently. The room sat in stillness. It started with the electronic soundwaves of Shostakovich's Symphony no.5 hybridized by techno pop, creating a haunting, chaotic sound. Dim lights in red cast eerie shadows on the walls as the objects surrounding them began to move. Machines whirred into action. Pim's eyes opened wide. It was a clockwork of contraptions and automatons. Hundreds of carved figures, frightening birds, grotesque humans and terrifying creatures made up from pieces of scrap metal and wood, lurched to life, as the larger pieces they inhabited awoke from their demented hibernation. The lights began to strobe, flashing to the sound of the music and radiating off the machines, infringing with her thoughts. Countless tiny monsters turned cranks or rode gears, making up a maze of different creations, some standing over eight feet tall and each representing their own theme, spinning and clattering in its own predestined universe. She was rendered speechless, and it created the type of inconsistency of emotions that were not only jarring but nonsymmetrical, not unlike the white swan and black swan. It left her in a dreamlike state, where panic sat just below the surface, as she tried to reason with her own complexity of existence.

"It's beautiful. Isn't it?" Sokolov said.

It was enough to pull her to her senses. The music drowned out other sounds. If Hamish was in the room, she would never hear him. "Jesus Christ, what is this?" She stood up and walked around one of the machines. A spinning disc of artists sat on a spire, while underneath, a tiny skeleton rotated a wheel. And below that, in an enclosed area, a hideous metal creature turned another wheel with its left hand while operating a sewing machine that, in the end, pierced its right hand.

Sokolov came up behind her, brushing her hair off her

shoulder. "Wheels of Life. The connection between inner workings and outward displays."

"I get the symbolism, but what is *all* of this?" She stood still, his touch unsettling. The flickering of the lights matched her rapidly increasing pulse, keeping beat together like a metronome.

"Sharmanka." He kissed her neck. "The genius of a fellow countryman."

She clutched her handbag tight, the feel of the gun a reassurance. "Sharmanka?" She kept her back to him, as she listened for any sound resembling a cry.

"Russian for hurdy-gurdy. A medieval hand cranked instrument reminiscent to your bagpipes because of the drone. The apparatuses are named after it." His arms went around her as he spoke into her ear, his fingers brushing the swell of her breast through her dress. Her nipples hardened in response. "Don't be afraid."

"I'm not afraid."

"Don't lie to me. It's always been fear that motivates you." He pulled the strap off her shoulder, caressing her skin. "It's why you perform so well for me."

Her body flushed with heat. "You're wrong. Fear does not control me. I stopped being afraid a long time ago." The pictures of her father's dead body ran through her mind. "I stopped letting fear rule my life the day my father died."

"Ah, yes, fear of disappointing Daddy and now, fear of disappointing me. You can tell yourself all the lies you want, but it was fear that made you dance so well tonight." His hand ran down her hip and thigh, and finding the slit in the dress, he slid his hand down her panties.

"No, it's you who's wrong." She stepped away from him. "I decide my own fate."

He grabbed her hair. Wrapping his hand around it, he pulled her head back. "I've given you everything, you ungrateful little bitch. I've shown you how to achieve a level of artistry that only the most talented would dream of." He let go, pushing her away.

"Artistry?" she turned on him. "Look around. You've broken into this place and taken someone else's art, subverting it with your debased and perverted mind. You don't know what art is."

That earned her a slap across the face. She stood there as heat radiated through her cheek, the cacophony of the scene suddenly paralyzing. A tear made its way down her face, dripping onto her chest.

He was quick to compose himself. As he straightened his jacket, he adjusted the sleeves at each of his wrists and gently reached out, wiping her face. "That's my girl," he said, embracing her. He looked into her eyes then, ever so gently, put his mouth to hers as he kissed her. "Come. This isn't even the best part." He put his arm around her waist, guiding her through the metal labyrinth of human pain and suffering, disorientating and confusing as each one was acted out by their mechanical performers. He stopped by a large contraption in the corner covered in a white sheet, yet to come alive. "I made this one myself. I call it Death Dance." He pulled the cover off.

Pim covered her scream with her hand. Hamish sat blindfolded and gagged in a cage, whimpering behind the cloth restraint. Sokolov pressed the remote and the machine screeched and rumbled. A wooden figure wearing a plague mask turned a crank, making the cage slowly spin. There were four other mechanical creatures, all wearing the same long-nosed, beak-like mask. Three surrounded the cage, awaiting their time to rotate a gear. The last one sat atop the cage with a sword pointed down through a hole. "Now, we decide."

"Stop. Let him go. You have me, just let him go."

"Wrong." He pressed another button and the second creature came to life, turning its handle. The cage began to spin faster. "No. It's one or the other. One of you must die."

She pulled the gun from her purse, pointing it at Sokolov. "Stop it. Stop the machine, or I'll shoot. You can kill me, but you must let him go first."

Sokolov laughed. "I can't stop it; only you can. This is your death dance. This is your swan song." The shattering of glass could be heard below. He pressed the remote again, and the third figure's wheel began to turn, the cage spinning faster.

"I swear to God, I'll shoot you."

Footsteps could be heard climbing the stairs.

"If you were going to, you already would have." The fourth creature came to life, turning its handle and wheel, the speed at which the cage spun hitting full tilt. Only one figure remained. The one with the sword. "You don't have it in you.'

"Bloody hell," Wraith's voice called out. "What the fuck is this place?"

Sokolov held a finger to his lips, silencing her. His thumb hovered over the remote as he smiled slowly. She counted to three in her mind as she watched it come down on the button. *One, two, three.* All hell broke loose. There was a flash of light and a thick cloud of fog erupted in the room. She turned the gun toward the machine, aiming for the creature on top, and fired.

"Primrose," she heard Wraith yell as the kick back from the gun knocked her down.

The next thing she remembered, she was looking up into Wraith's eyes. "Hamish," she said, sitting up, panicked. "He's in the cage." She looked over. The top of the cage was missing and the creature hung from the side, his head missing, sword still in hand. Alex was helping the young boy out, removing his blindfold and gag. "Is he okay?"

"Aye. He'll do," Alex said, picking up the boy like a small

package. "It's all right, laddie. We'll get you home to your mum."

Pim looked at Wraith. "Where's Sokolov?"

"Gone," he said, a bit coolly. "He disappeared before our eyes."

Master of illusions. More footsteps echoed on the stairs, and Gabriel and Sin appeared. Sin hit a switch, turning on the lights, while Gabriel found a box on the wall at the back that controlled the machines. He flicked the main nob, silencing the contraptions to their dormant state. Silence filled the room.

"Let's get out of here, lads," Alex said. "Before the authorities show up."

Wraith helped her up but made no move to comfort her, keeping his distance. He picked the gun up off the ground, depositing it in an empty holster on his chest. She followed the men downstairs and out of the back of the building, into a close.

"I'll ride with Gabriel. We'll take Hamish," Wraith said, taking the boy from Alex. Pim watched as he piled into the Mercedes with the other men.

"You can ride with me, Pim," Alex said, holding the door of the Porsche open for her. She sat down, adjusting her seatbelt as the colonel got in behind the wheel. "He'll have had a fright."

Pim wasn't sure who he was talking about. The noise from upstairs still reverberated through her mind. She looked at him blankly.

"Wraith, you'll have given him a scare." He reached over and gave her hand a squeeze. "You gave us all a scare, but he was bloody well frightened, knowing what Sokolov did to you before."

"I'm sorry he got away."

"Your and the boy's safety is what matters. We'll get Sokolov."

The ride to City Halls was short. When Alex pulled up in front of the building, the party was winding down and people stood outside, waiting for their cars to pull up from valet. Pim spotted Natasha talking to two security officers.

Wraith got out of the car with Hamish and waited for Pim and Alex. The young boy ran up to his mother. "Mummy," he cried.

"Natasha, can we talk inside?"

The blonde girl looked over at the officers. "Thank you for your help. It seems we found him." She followed them all into the dressing room.

"Where did you find him?" Natasha asked anxiously.

Pim explained the situation as best she could without giving away too much information. "I'm sorry, Natasha. It was one of my grandfather's associates."

"What do we do now?" the young mother asked. "What if he comes back for Hamish?"

"We don't think that will happen," Alex said. "But I will make sure you have around the clock protection until we catch him."

"We need to go to the police."

"We can't," Pim tried to explain. "For now, we have to keep this quiet. These men will protect you."

Natasha nodded.

"I was wondering if you would like to stay in my flat? It's in a better neighborhood," Pim asked. "That is until you can choose one for yourself."

"I couldn't do that." The girl looked down as if she had something to ask but wasn't sure how.

"Natasha, tell me what you want."

"Can Hamish and I go back to Angus' place?"

"You would want to go back there?"

"I know you don't understand, but I loved him. We have good memories there. Hamish likes it there."

"If that's what you want. I'm setting up a trust for Hamish. He deserves half of the estate." She took Natasha's hand. "I know it can't make up for what my grandfather did to you. But please let me help."

The girl nodded.

"One of my men will drive you to Angus'. We'll make sure your things are transferred over as soon as possible," Alex said.

"I'll take her," Wraith said.

Pim looked over at him, but he refused to meet her eye.

"No, you'll take Pim back to your place." Alex picked the small boy up off the chair where he had fallen asleep. "Kian will accompany Natasha."

"Fine," Wraith said shortly. He held his hand out for Pim to go first. "After you."

Chapter 38

Wraith pulled the seatbelt tight across her lap. She started to say something, but he stopped her. "Not a word." His fear had turned to anger as his adrenaline rush subsided, and he didn't want to say something he would regret.

He pulled the Land Rover out into traffic and started the long ride home. The thought of going to the sterile apartment on the west end was suffocating. In fact, he wanted as far away from Glasgow as he could get, far away from that motherfucker Viktor Sokolov. The thoughts and images that had run through his mind for the past two hours, he never wanted to have again. He undid the bow tie around his neck and opened the top button on his shirt.

Pim sat looking out the window. He wasn't ready to talk to her. Her lack of concern and complete disregard for her safety was forefront in his mind. He wondered how they were to move forward. Trust had been broken.

It was the middle of the night by the time he pulled up to the mansion. He opened Pim's door to help her out.

Stripped

"Wraith," she said, rubbing her eyes. "Can we please talk—"

"Not here." He shook his head. "Inside."

Gabriel parked next to him, and turning off his car's headlights, he got out. "We thought you were going to your flat in Glasgow until you got on the M8."

"I needed to get as far away from that city and its foul stench as I could."

"I understand." He started to walk off, but Wraith stopped him.

"Gabriel, I wanted to thank you for your support tonight."

"Of course," the angel said.

"For the first time, this all made sense. I felt like I belonged. I felt the brotherhood."

Gabriel smiled. "We've all been there, you know, in the beginning. None of us chose this for ourselves. You question everything, and then one day you can't image your life any other way. It becomes an honor to be a part of eventually."

"Dougie said I would understand one day. I just never imagined that I would." He shrugged. "Even Alex showed up."

"And that's a rarity. He likes you, I think you remind him of himself when he was young." Gabriel laughed. "But don't get a big head because he'll be back to being a bastard tomorrow."

"I wouldn't expect anything else."

Gabriel's voice turned serious. "He'll want to talk to both of you tomorrow." He glanced over at Pim.

"Aye, give me the morning at least. I have some things to work out."

Gabriel nodded, opening the door. Wraith waited for Pim to go ahead of him before following her down the hallway.

She sat on Wraith's bed, waiting for him to say something.

"Do you want to shower?" he asked.

"I'm fine. I'll wait until morning." She picked at an imaginary spot of the duvet.

"I'm going to then," he said, hanging his tuxedo jacket up.

"Wraith, can we talk?"

"Not right now." He shook his head. "In the morning."

"Am I one of those things you need to work out?" She felt the prick of tears at the back of her eyes. She knew he was upset, but she didn't expect this coldness.

"Yes."

It was one word, but it cut like a knife. "I'm sorry," she said, the tears coming in earnest. She wanted to leave, to run. She didn't want to cry in front of him. It was the shunning all over again, like when her ballet teachers wouldn't talk to her or recognize her. She had brought that on herself, and now she had brought this on too. "I should go." She wiped her tears with the back of her hand.

"You're not leaving at this time of night."

"Why do you care? You can barely look at me, let alone touch me or comfort me."

"Comfort you?" He walked over and crouched down in front of her. "Buggar-all." He put his hand at the back of her head until their foreheads touched. "I want nothing more than to put my arms around you and hold you." His voice was so quiet, she could barely hear him. "You're ripping my heart out." He stood back up and went to the window, looking out. "I've never said those words before. I love you. And I've never had them said to me. It was the first time."

"I've never, either," she said. "I meant it."

"Did you? Or did you say it to throw me off track, so I wouldn't find out about Sokolov?" She could hear the pain in his voice.

"Of course not. I meant it."

"But you already knew about the rose Sokolov sent and you didn't tell me. You had already seen the notecard of the Alasdair Gray painting from him." He leaned up against the dresser.

"Yes."

"Why did you hide it?" he demanded.

"I didn't hide it." She looked down, unable to meet his gaze.

"You did. You hid it in your dance bag, then you let me make love to you minutes later." He smirked, "Or should I say, you let me *fuck* you. I'm sure it was just sex for you." He threw his hands up. "And you chose that moment to tell me you love me."

"I didn't know what would happen with Sokolov. I wanted you to know. I needed you to know," she tried to explain.

"So, you knew you would see him?" His shoulders slumped, and she couldn't miss the hurt in his voice.

"No, not at that moment. I hadn't read the last note yet."

"There was another note?"

She nodded. "It was in my purse."

"With the gun?"

"Yes."

"You had five professional men to protect you and handle the situation, yet you ran off by yourself." His jaw clenched.

"It wasn't like that, Wraith. I swear to you."

"You know what hurts the most. You said you loved me, but you didn't trust me."

"But I did trust you. I trusted you to find me," she said softly. "You know, Wraith, everything I've done in my life, I've done alone. I've been on my own since I was ten. Sent away to school, to figure things out by myself. I lost my father, my one true support, and the rest of the people in my life didn't turn out to be who I thought they were. So, if I'm struggling with letting you in, maybe I have my reasons. But I did trust you today. I trusted that when I ran off to find Sokolov, you would find me, and you did."

"Why did you go to him?" The anger was gone from his voice, replaced with what sounded like resignation.

"He had Hamish. Two other people had already died because of me. I couldn't let him too."

He sat down beside her, his own cheeks wet with tears. "Is that the only reason?"

She was quiet for a moment. "I wanted his approval. I wanted him to tell me I had done well. But as soon as I saw him, I knew I was wrong. He's mad and he wanted to draw me into the same madness. The only thing I could think of was you and of you finding me."

He put his arm around her, pulling her close to him, and she felt safe for the first time that night. "I am sorry," she said.

"Aye, come here." He lay back, bringing her with him so her head rested on his chest. "I've got you." They were both wounded and raw, their hearts splayed open. His hand gently caressed her cheek.

"How did you find me?" she asked after a while.

"Dougie was able to connect Sokolov to Green Shore Productions and the after party at Òran Mór," he said. "When we got there, the SUV was pulling out of the car park and I knew you were in it. I could feel you. It was the strangest thing."

"I knew you were following us. I could feel you too." She had been a fool to push this man away. "Wraith, how do we move forward?"

He took her hand in his, interlocking their fingers. He was quiet for a while, thinking. "Marry me."

She shook her head. "I thought you couldn't be in a relationship because of your job. Gabriel said as much to me."

"I'll handle it."

"I never planned on marrying anyone. Ever." She didn't

Stripped

want to lose him, but marriage was a bit sudden. "There's no rush."

"I know what I want, and I actually know what you need," he countered.

"You don't know what I need."

"In this case, princess, I think I do."

"I'll think about it."

Pim rolled over, covering her head with the duvet, as Wraith shook her awake.

"Get up," he said, pulling the cover down. She squinted at him through puffy eyes. He was already dressed.

"What time is it?"

"It's early, but I want to show you something. Get dressed." He handed her a pair of jeans and a sweater.

She got out of bed and changed, pulling on her boots. He helped her with her coat and she took his hand, following him outside. It was dark, the air still and cold. The world had not yet woken up. He led them down to the river, to an outcropping of rocks that formed a path across the gently flowing water, and let go of her hand. "I'll go first," he said, as he nimbly jumped from rock to rock, forging the trail. She followed, careful not to slip.

The sky was beginning to change behind them. Dawn was on its way. They hiked up a hill out of the tree line and into the heather. Finding a large boulder, they sat down. The secret of the day was beginning to open as the sun rose in the horizon.

"I woke up in The Tower after being in a coma," Wraith said softly, so as not to disturb the serenity of the moment. "Robert McFadden was dead. I had become Robert Wraith. I used to come here when I was recovering, to try to come to terms with it all."

She reached out and took his hand. Incredible rays of color, pink and purple, filled the sky, slashed by moody clouds. The wind whistled around them, blowing their hair.

"The hardest part was the utter loneliness. No one knew me. I had no past to guide me or future to look forward to. No one I could trust." He looked at her, raising a brow. "I didn't know myself anymore. I didn't want to know this new man, Robert Wraith."

She listened as the colors came to life in deep reds, rich browns and vivid greens.

"But when I came and sat here, none of it mattered. To look out on this beauty, offered me a new freedom. The chance, for a brief moment every day, to dream."

"And what did you dream of?" she asked.

"For someone to love and someone to trust."

She looked down. She broke that trust yesterday, broke the confidence they shared. "I'm sorry, Wraith."

"Aye, I know you are, and that's not why I brought you out here." He put his arm around her. "I brought you here because I want the dream. I need to know that you trust me."

"I do trust you."

"Saying it and knowing it deep in your heart, are two different things."

"I—" she started to speak, but he stopped her.

"I need you to tell me what Sokolov did to you. What he said to you. Everything."

She stiffened.

"I need you to open up to me, Primrose. I need to know what he did before we go see Alex. I need to hear it first."

"I'm trying to be open. I swear to you I'm trying," she said. "I'm not sure how."

"I know, baby. But I need you to trust me to get you there."

She knew what he was asking, knew what he expected her to let him do, but the thought of giving up control scared her. She bent over, burying her face in her hands. "I don't want to."

He rubbed her shoulder. "You're the strongest person I know, Primrose. I promise I won't hurt you. I just need to get you to a spot where you can be vulnerable with me. It's between the two of us. No one else."

She nodded. Her stomach was in knots. The thought of sharing what Sokolov did, what she let him do, was revolting. Wraith would leave when he found out. "I don't want to do it here."

He sat her up and kissed the side of her head. "No. Let's go back to the room.

They walked in silence. The sun was now shining brightly, making the situation seem worse. At least in the dark, she could hide her shame.

Wraith opened the door, letting them in. "Go and change. There's a robe in the bathroom."

She took her clothes off, slipping on his robe, the silk fabric cool on her flushed skin. Her pulse raced. A part of her wanted this, to have him bring her to a spot where he alone held her heart in his hand. It was the aftermath that scared her. Would he leave that same heart bruised and shattered in the end? She opened the door. He was sitting on the edge of the couch and motioned with his finger for her to come. An all-knowing ache began to form in her stomach.

"Come here, baby." He patted his lap.

She hesitated.

"Don't shut down on me now. I need you to trust me," he said. "Your walls are up. I need you to get to a place where you can be vulnerable with me." He stood up. "Come here."

She went to him and he brought her to his chest, holding her. "It's going to be okay."

"I'm scared," she said.

"I know you are." He sat back down. "I won't force you, though."

She nodded. He removed the belt on the robe, sliding it off her shoulders. She was stripped, her whole being about to be exposed. He ran his hand down her cheek and nodded back at her. She took a deep breath and lay down across his lap. His arm came down on her back, anchoring her in place. His other hand gently began to rub her back. "I don't want you to be scared." His tone was soft. "I need to know that you trust me, Primrose. This is about trust."

She did trust him, more than she had ever trusted anyone in her life, and it scared her because it had happened so fast. She knew she had hurt him yesterday. "I do trust you," she finally said.

"I'll begin." His hand came down on her bare bottom, the sting instant, and she tensed waiting for the next one. Ten more followed as the burn in her cheeks spread. He knew what he was doing. He paused, rubbing her tender skin. "You're not alone anymore, Primrose. You don't have to do it alone anymore." His words caused a tear to fall as she braced herself. His hand came down again, causing her to gasp as she tried to catch her breath. Another ten were delivered efficiently. She was beginning to waver.

He paused. "I know you're in there, baby. Come back to me. He doesn't have a hold on you." He carried out the last set quickly. She grabbed his thigh to prevent herself from crying out. Her bottom was on fire and she could no longer hold back her tears. "Stop!" she shouted.

Wraith picked her up and settled her on his lap, his arms coming around her. "Shh, I've got you."

She wasn't crying because of the pain. He had done exactly what he said he was going to do and tore down her walls, leaving her to feel exposed and defenseless. She grabbed his shirt, leaning against his chest.

"I've got you, baby. You're safe in my arms," he said. "I'm not going anywhere."

Her tears began to subside as she listened to his heart, the sound of the beat a gentle reassurance that this man loved her and would protect her. "I need you to tell me what Sokolov did to you, Primrose. I know it will be hard."

She nodded.

"Feel my arms around you. I'm here with you. I'll hold you the entire time."

She told him everything. What Sokolov said, how he touched her and kissed her, how she didn't fight back. How he got in her mind then turned on her, betraying her. She knew her words would hurt Wraith. The images she was putting in his mind would become his own nightmares, but through it all, he never let go. When she finished, he kissed her on top of her head. "That's my girl. I won't let him take that from us. You are *my* girl."

She thought the phrase would upset her, that it would bring back the vile memories of Sokolov and how he stole that from her, but they didn't. She was Wraith's girl. She belonged to him and that was all that mattered.

"Aye. We'd best get you dressed. Alex will be expecting us."

Chapter 39

Alex and Gabriel were waiting for them when they entered the office. Alex stood up from behind his desk, motioning to two chairs set up in front of it. Wraith gave the colonel a brief nod. Apparently, this was not to be a casual meeting on the couch. Alex meant business. He gave Pim's hand a squeeze, hoping to calm her nerves before pulling her chair out for her and seeing her seated. He sat down, keeping his hand on her back. She would be feeling tender, not only physically, but emotionally, and he was responsible for that, making him extremely protective of her. The thought of Sokolov touching her turned his stomach, but he was glad he already knew so he could mask his face when she retold it to Alex.

"Shall we begin?" Alex asked. Gabriel stood off to the side. "It goes without saying, Miss McNeil, that you put my whole organization at risk with your actions last night."

"I've already handled that situation," Wraith said. "I don't think Primrose will be taking things into her own hands again." He looked over at her as her face turned a deep red.

"I am sorry," she said.

Stripped

"Very well, since Wraith's taken care of it." Alex looked between the two of them. "We still have the problem of Sokolov. I'll need to know everything."

Wraith took her hand as Pim retold her story.

"Jesus Christ," Gabriel said, crossing himself. "He's a monster."

"Aye," Wraith said.

"With Sokolov on the loose, we find ourselves in unprecedented territory." Alex sat back in his chair.

"I agree, and actually, before we go there, I have something to say." Wraith sat up straight.

"Go ahead."

"I would like to marry Primrose. I know it goes against The Watch, but we brought her into this, and now we must protect her. As long as Sokolov is out there, she's at risk."

"I won't lie, I thought of the same idea last night," Alex agreed. "Marriage would handle a few of our problems and she's still our only link to Sokolov."

Pim started to protest, but Wraith stopped her, giving her shoulder a squeeze. "I'll take full responsibility for her protection, and in return, as my wife and through my oath, she will give her allegiance of silence to The Watch."

"I'm not killing anyone."

Alex laughed. "One, that's not the only thing we do. And two, no one would expect you to. We would ask only for your silence. As you have learned, our organization only works because of trust and loyalty."

She looked at Wraith. "I said I would think about marriage. I haven't agreed yet."

Wraith ignored her. "Gabriel, would you perform the ceremony?"

"I can't," the priest said. "When I gave up the priesthood, I lost the ability to perform holy orders."

"I can," Alex said. "I'm an authorized celebrant. The

sooner, the better. I'll gather the men. Wraith, you'll take your oath tonight, and then you two will be married."

Pim stood up. "I haven't agreed to anything. You can't make decisions for me."

It was Gabriel who went to her. Wraith stood back, listening. "Pim, I know you love Wraith. I've known it from the first time I met you. Give this a chance."

"Why? You were the person who warned me it would never work."

"That was before I saw a way. It was when I thought it was impossible. Marry Wraith. Become a part of our family."

She looked at all three men. "I'll agree, but I have one request."

Alex stood in the Great Hall of the Tower House. Hundreds of candles illuminated the dark room, casting shadows on the ceremony and gracing it with an air of mystery. The smell of incense, deep and woody, purified the hallowed space, evoking a feeling of rightness. He looked around at his men as they stood before him, kilted in their dark blue and green tartan, ready to avow their allegiance. Agents of truth, shattering illusions and exposing often painful and shocking realities. There were twelve of them in total, counting himself and Gabriel. Always twelve, no more, no less. Raising his hands, the nine who were present took a knee. "Come forward, Wraith."

The young man stood and stepped forward, kneeling again. Alex saw himself in the lad. Idealistic and duty-bound, he'd fought the process longer than most. Only now, was he ready to pledge his allegiance.

"Entry into The Watch demands absolute obedience. Are you ready to take your oath?"

"Yes, sir."

Alex nodded, laying a hand on Wraith's head. "What do you pledge?"

"I, Robert Wraith, swear by Almighty God, that I will be faithful and bear true allegiance to The Watch, offering my obedience and loyalty. I have left the man I was behind, through absolution and redemption, and become the man I am today. I am bound by duty to honestly and faithfully defend and serve the truth. United in brotherhood. The Watchers, Royal Black."

Alex offered the lad his hand and he kissed the Black Watch seal on the gold signet ring, consummating the oath.

"In signifying the death of self," Alex said, "we find ourselves united in brotherhood." Wraith lay prostrate on the ground, face down. Alex continued. "Let us all renew our vows together, banded as a family."

The men drew their dirks, making their oaths inviolable, and repeated the words with the utmost solemnity. Alex walked the room, placing his hand on each of their heads. When they finished, Wraith returned to kneeling, and they encircled him. Alex went over to a table and picked up a dirk, presenting it to Wraith. "You enter into an unbroken lineage. Through service, humility, and devotion, these gestures are no longer symbolic but powerful and transformative. Robert Wraith, welcome to The Watch."

The other agents cheered, chanting at the same time, "The Watchers, Royal Black," as they congratulated the young man. They each took turns patting him on the back and shaking his hand. Alex quieted the men down.

"Lads, we find ourselves in a new era. And as the world evolves, so must we. You have all been briefed on our latest threat, Viktor Sokolov. He has become our number one priority. He is still out there, threatening the very existence of morality. Tonight, we welcome Primrose McNeil. I don't want any of you getting ideas that this is the new normal. Relationships of any kind are not allowed. They muddy the waters. But protecting the innocent is one of our tenets, and we must live up to our oaths. Gabriel."

Gabriel came from the back of the room, wearing a white priest's robe, escorting the lassie. Alex gave her credit. She was just as courageous, if not more, than any of the men in the room. He knew from the moment he met her that she was a force to be reckoned with. She looked beautiful, dressed in a long, white satin gown with slender straps and a Black Watch tartan sash across her shoulder. When they got to the front of the hall, Gabriel kissed her cheek. "He's a good man," Alex overheard him tell her. She gave a small smile as Wraith took her hand.

He got straight to the point, as neither of them wanted a long ceremony, not thinking it appropriate given the circumstances. The vows were said, the rings exchanged, and he declared them husband and wife.

"Marriage is a union between two people, establishing rights and obligations between them. Those obligations include protection, loyalty, honesty and love. Through your vows of marriage, you honor each other's oaths." Alex put his hand on Pim's shoulder. "At her request, instead of deferring to Wraith's oath of allegiance to The Watch, Primrose has asked to take her own oath, not as an agent, but as an ally, offering her fealty."

Alex placed a small pillow on the ground and Pim knelt. He placed his hand on her head as Wraith placed one on her shoulder.

"I, Primrose Mcn…" she paused, starting over, "I, Primrose Wraith, swear by Almighty God that I will be faithful and bear true allegiance to The Watch, offering my obedience and

Stripped

loyalty. I will protect The Watch through my silence, honoring the sanctity of trust. Bound by duty through marriage, united in brotherhood. The Watchers, Royal Black."

"The Watchers, Royal Black," the men echoed behind her. Wraith helped her stand, and pulling her into an embrace, he kissed her.

Alex cleared his throat. "Aye, enough of that. Save it for later." He watched as the men congratulated her. He stepped away and joined Gabriel in the back of the hall.

The priest adjusted the tartan stole around his neck. "I don't know why you make me wear this," he said.

"It's good for the lads. It gives them reassurance."

"Reassurance from an ex-priest who's damned to Hell."

"You're not damned," Alex said. A few of the men hung back, keeping their distance from the new couple. "Do you think they'll accept her?"

"They'll accept her because you accept her. Change can be hard," Gabriel said.

"But in this case, necessary." Alex thought of the black rose sitting on his desk. "Do we have any preliminaries yet?"

"Dougie's working on it now. As far as we can tell, it came from a flower shop in Edinburgh."

"I'm glad she and Wraith will be out of the country for a few months with the ballet company, touring."

"Aye, it gives us some time."

Alex fingered the notecard in his pocket.

'Now's the day, and now's the hour. See the front of battle lour. V.S.' The words were written by Robert Burns, in the form of a speech given by Robert the Bruce before the battle of Bannockburn. The smell of jet-fuel filled Alex's nose, sharp and oily, the sound of bullets hitting the twisted metal of the crashed helicopter as the memory of being constrained and helpless crossed his mind. Sokolov had just drawn the line in

the sand. Once the point was crossed, the consequences would be permanently decided and irreversible. He knew the card was meant for him, not the lass, this time. War had been declared.

The End

Finley Brown

Finley Brown's love for Scotland comes from her mother, who was born and raised in the small town of Saltcoats, Scotland. In her free time Finley enjoys cooking, wine, and working out. She works as a holistic health coach and studied at The Institute for Integrative Nutrition. She lives in Texas with her husband, three children and her two British Shorthair cats.

You can contact her at: authorfinleybrown@gmail.com

Don't miss these exciting titles by Finley Brown and Blushing Books!

The Watch Series
Stripped

The Glen Torridon Series
The Laird's Command
The Laird's Contract
The Laird's Chamber
The Laird's Christmas - Novella

Scottish Submission Series
His Sweet Curse
His Little Spy
His Star Princess

Anthologies
12 Naughty Days of Christmas 2020

Blushing Books Newsletter

Please join the Blushing Books newsletter
to receive updates & special promotional offers.
You can also join by using your mobile phone:
Just text BLUSHING to 22828.

Every month, one new sign up via text messaging will receive
a $25.00 Amazon gift card, so sign up today!

Blushing Books

Blushing Books is the oldest eBook publisher on the web. We've been running websites that publish steamy romance and erotica since 1999, and we have been selling eBooks since 2003. We have free and promotional offerings that change weekly, so please do visit us at http://www.blushingbooks.com/free.

Made in the USA
Coppell, TX
11 August 2021